KATE CHOPIN

A Night
in
Acadie

The American Short Story Series

VOLUME 8.

GARRETT PRESS

Library of Congress Catalog Card No. 68-55668

This volume was reprinted from the 1897 edition
published by Way & Williams
First Garrett Press Edition published 1968

The American Short Story Series
Volume 8
©1968

GARRETT PRESS, INC.
Publishers
250 West 54th Street, New York, N.Y. 10019

Contents

A Night in Acadie

A Night in Acadie

THERE was nothing to do on the plantation so Telèsphore, having a few dollars
in his pocket, thought he would go
down and spend Sunday in the vicinity of
Marksville.

There was really nothing more to do in the
vicinity of Marksville than in the neighborhood of his own small farm; but Elvina would
not be down there, nor Amaranthe, nor any
of Ma'me Valtour's daughters to harass him
with doubt, to torture him with indecision, to
turn his very soul into a weather-cock for love's
fair winds to play with.

Telèsphore at twenty-eight had long felt the
need of a wife. His home without one was
like an empty temple in which there is no altar,
no offering. So keenly did he realize the necessity that a dozen times at least during the
past year he had been on the point of propos-
ing marriage to almost as many different young

women of the neighborhood. Therein lay the
difficulty, the trouble which Telèsphore experienced in making up his mind. Elvina's eyes
were beautiful and had often tempted him to
the verge of a declaration. But her skin was
over swarthy for a wife; and her movements
were slow and heavy; he doubted she had Indian blood, and we all know what Indian blood
is for treachery. Amaranthe presented in her
person none of these obstacles to matrimony.
If her eyes were not so handsome as Elvina's,
her skin was fine, and being slender to a fault,
she moved swiftly about her household affairs,
or when she walked the country lanes in going
to church or to the store. Telèsphore had once
reached the point of believing that Amaranthe
would make him an excellent wife. He had
even started out one day with the intention of
declaring himself, when, as the god of chance
would have it, Ma'me Valtour espied him passing in the road and enticed him to enter and
partake of coffee and "baignés." He would
have been a man of stone to have resisted, or
to have remained insensible to the charms and
accomplishments of the Valtour girls. Finally
there was Ganache's widow, seductive rather

than handsome, with a good bit of property in her own right. While Telèsphore was considering his chances of happiness or even success with Ganache's widow, she married a younger man.

From these embarrassing conditions, Telèsphore sometimes felt himself forced to escape; to change his environment for a day or two and thereby gain a few new insights by shifting his point of view.

It was Saturday morning that he decided to spend Sunday in the vicinity of Marksville, and the same afternoon found him waiting at the country station for the south-bound train.

He was a robust young fellow with good, strong features and a somewhat determined expression—despite his vacillations in the choice of a wife. He was dressed rather carefully in navy-blue "store clothes" that fitted well because anything would have fitted Telèsphore. He had been freshly shaved and trimmed and carried an umbrella. He wore—a little tilted over one eye—a straw hat in preference to the conventional gray felt; for no other reason than that his uncle Telèsphore would have worn a felt, and a battered one at that. His whole conduct of life had been planned on lines in direct contradistinction to those of his uncle Telèsphore, whom he was thought in early youth to greatly resemble. The elder Telèsphore could not read nor write, therefore the younger had made it the object of his existence to acquire these accomplishments. The uncle pursued the avocations of hunting, fishing and moss-picking; employments which the nephew held in detestation. And as for carrying an umbrella, "Nonc" Telèsphore would have walked the length of the parish in a deluge before he would have so much as thought of one. In short, Telèsphore, by advisedly shaping his course in direct opposition to that of his uncle, managed to lead a rather orderly, industrious, and respectable existence.

It was a little warm for April but the car was not uncomfortably crowded and Telèsphore was fortunate enough to secure the last available window-seat on the shady side. He was not too familiar with railway travel, his expeditions being usually made on horse-back or in a buggy, and the short trip promised to interest him.

There was no one present whom he knew well enough to speak to: the district attorney, whom he knew by sight, a French priest from Natchitoches and a few faces that were familiar only because they were native.

But he did not greatly care to speak to anyone. There was a fair stand of cotton and corn in the fields and Telèsphore gathered satisfaction in silent contemplation of the crops, comparing them with his own.

It was toward the close of his journey that a young girl boarded the train. There had been girls getting on and off at intervals and it was perhaps because of the bustle attending her arrival that this one attracted Telèsphore's attention.

She called good-bye to her father from the platform and waved good-bye to him through the dusty, sun-lit window pane after entering, for she was compelled to seat herself on the sunny side. She seemed inwardly excited and preoccupied save for the attention which she lavished upon a large parcel that she carried religiously and laid reverentially down upon the seat before her.

She was neither tall nor short, nor stout nor slender; nor was she beautiful, nor was she plain. She wore a figured lawn, cut a little low in the back, that exposed a round, soft nuque with a few little clinging circlets of soft, brown hair. Her hat was of white straw, cocked up on the side with a bunch of pansies, and she wore gray lisle-thread gloves. The girl seemed very warm and kept mopping her face. She vainly sought her fan, then she fanned herself with her handkerchief, and finally made an attempt to open the window. She might as well have tried to move the banks of Red river.

Telèsphore had been unconsciously watching her the whole time and perceiving her straight he arose and went to her assistance. But the window could not be opened. When he had grown red in the face and wasted an amount of energy that would have driven the plow for a day, he offered her his seat on the shady side. She demurred —there would be no room for the bundle. He suggested that the bundle be left where it was and agreed to assist her in keeping an eye upon it. She accepted Telèsphore's place at the shady window and he seated himself beside her.

He wondered if she would speak to him. He feared she might have mistaken him for a Western drummer, in which event he knew that she would not; for the women of the country caution their daughters against speaking to strangers on the trains. But the girl was not one to mistake an Acadian farmer for a Western traveling man. She was not born in Avoyelles parish for nothing.

"I wouldn' want anything to happen to it," she said.

"It's all right w'ere it is," he assured her, following the direction of her glance, that was fastened upon the bundle.

"The las' time I came over to Foché's ball I got caught in the rain on my way up to my cousin's house, an' my dress! J' vous réponds! it was a sight. Li'le mo', I would miss the ball. As it was, the dress looked like I'd wo' it weeks without doin'-up."

"No fear of rain to-day," he reassured her, glancing out at the sky, "but you can have my umbrella if it does rain; you jus' as well take it as not."

"Oh, no! I wrap' the dress roun' in toile-cirée this time. You goin' to Foché's ball?

Didn' I meet you once yonda on Bayou Der-
banne? Looks like I know yo' face. You
mus' come f'om Natchitoches pa'ish."

"My cousins, the Fédeau family, live yonda.
Me, I live on my own place in Rapides since
'92."

He wondered if she would follow up her inquiry relative to Foché's ball. If she did, he
was ready with an answer, for he had decided
to go to the ball. But her thoughts evidently
wandered from the subject and were occupied with matters that did not concern him,
for she turned away and gazed silently out of
the window.

It was not a village; it was not even a hamlet
at which they descended. The station was set
down upon the edge of a cotton field. Near
at hand was the post office and store; there
was a section house; there were a few cabins
at wide intervals, and one in the distance
the girl informed him was the home of her
cousin, Jules Trodon. There lay a good bit
of road before them and she did not hesitate to
accept Telèsphore's offer to bear her bundle
on the way.

She carried herself boldly and stepped out freely and easily, like a negress. There was an absence of reserve in her manner; yet there was no lack of womanliness. She had the air of a young person accustomed to decide for herself and for those about her.

"You said yo' name was Fédeau?" she asked, looking squarely at Telèsphore. Her eyes were penetrating—not sharply penetrating, but earnest and dark, and a little searching. He noticed that they were handsome eyes; not so large as Elvina's, but finer in their expression. They started to walk down the track before turning into the lane leading to Trodon's house. The sun was sinking and the air was fresh and invigorating by contrast with the stifling atmosphere of the train.

"You said yo' name was Fédeau?" she asked.

"No," he returned. "My name is Telèsphore Baquette."

"An' my name; it's Zaïda Trodon. It looks like you ought to know me; I don' know w'y."

"It looks that way to me, somehow," he replied. They were satisfied to recognize this

feeling—almost conviction—of pre-acquaint-
ance, without trying to penetrate its cause.

By the time they reached Trodon's house
he knew that she lived over on Bayou de Glaize
with her parents and a number of younger
brothers and sisters. It was rather dull where
they lived and she often came to lend a hand
when her cousin's wife got tangled in domestic
complications; or, as she was doing now, when
Foché's Saturday ball promised to be unusu-
ally important and brilliant. There would be
people there even from Marksville, she
thought; there were often gentlemen from
Alexandria. Telèsphore was as unreserved as
she, and they appeared like old acquaintances
when they reached Trodon's gate.

Trodon's wife was standing on the gallery
with a baby in her arms, watching for Zaïda;
and four little bare-footed children were sitting
in a row on the step, also waiting; but ter-
rified and struck motionless and dumb at sight
of a stranger. He opened the gate for the girl
but stayed outside himself. Zaïda presented
him formally to her cousin's wife, who insisted
upon his entering.

"Ah, b'en, pour ça! you got to come in. It's any sense you goin' to walk yonda to Foché's! Ti Jules, run call yo' pa." As if Ti Jules could have run or walked even, or moved a muscle!

But Telèsphore was firm. He drew forth his silver watch and looked at it in a business-like fashion. He always carried a watch; his uncle Telèsphore always told the time by the sun, or by instinct, like an animal. He was quite determined to walk on to Foché's, a couple of miles away, where he expected to secure supper and a lodging, as well as the pleasing distraction of the ball.

"Well, I reckon I see you all to-night," he uttered in cheerful anticipation as he moved away.

"You'll see Zaïda; yes, an' Jules," called out Trodon's wife good-humoredly. "Me, I got no time to fool with balls, J' vous réponds! with all them chil'ren."

"He's good-lookin'; yes," she exclaimed, when Telèsphore was out of ear-shot. "An' dressed! it's like a prince. I didn' know you knew any Baquettes, you, Zaïda."

"It's strange you don' know 'em yo' se'f, cousine." Well, there had been no question from Ma'me Trodon, so why should there be an answer from Zaïda?

Telèsphore wondered as he walked why he had not accepted the invitation to enter. He was not regretting it; he was simply wondering what could have induced him to decline. For it surely would have been agreeable to sit there on the gallery waiting while Zaïda prepared herself for the dance; to have partaken of supper with the family and afterward accompanied them to Foché's. The whole situation was so novel, and had presented itself so unexpectedly that Telèsphore wished in reality to become acquainted with it, accustomed to it. He wanted to view it from this side and that in comparison with other, familiar situations. The girl had impressed him—affected him in some way; but in some new, unusual way, not as the others always had. He could not recall details of her personality as he could recall such details of Amaranthe or the Valtours, of any of them. When Telèsphore tried to think of her he could not think at all. He seemed to have absorbed her in some way and his brain was not so

occupied with her as his senses were.] At that
moment he was looking forward to the ball;
there was no doubt about that. Afterwards, he
did not know what he would look forward to;
he did not care; afterward made no difference.
If he had expected the crash of doom to come
after the dance at Foché's, he would only
have smiled in his thankfulness that it was not
to come before.

There was the same scene every Saturday at
Foché's! A scene to have aroused the guardi-
ans of the peace in a locality where such com-
modities abound. And all on account of the
mammoth pot of gumbo that bubbled, bubbled, bubbled out in the open air. Foché in
shirt-sleeves, fat, red and enraged, swore
and reviled, and stormed at old black Douté
for her extravagance. He called her every
kind of a name of every kind of animal that
suggested itself to his lurid imagination. And
every fresh invective that he fired at her she
hurled it back at him while into the pot went
the chickens and the pans-full of minced ham,
and the fists-full of onion and sage and piment
rouge and piment vert. If he wanted her to

cook for pigs he had only to say so.   She
knew how to cook for pigs and she knew
how to cook for people of les Avoyelles.

The gumbo smelled good, and Telèsphore
would have liked a taste of it.   Douté was
dragging from the fire a stick of wood that
Foché had officiously thrust beneath the sim-
mering pot, and she muttered as she hurled it
smouldering to one side:

"Vaux mieux y s'méle ces affairs, lui; si
non!"   But she was all courtesy as she dipped
a steaming plate for Telèsphore; though she
assured him it would not be fit for a Christian
or a gentleman to taste till midnight.

Telèsphore having brushed, "spruced" and
refreshed himself, strolled about, taking a view
of the surroundings.   The house, big, bulky
and weather-beaten, consisted chiefly of gal-
leries in every stage of decrepitude and dilapi-
dation.   There were a few chinaberry trees
and a spreading live oak in the yard.   Along
the edge of the fence, a good distance away,
was a line of gnarled and distorted mulberry
trees; and it was there, out in the road, that
the people who came to the ball tied their
ponies, their wagons and carts.

Dusk was beginning to fall and Telèsphore, looking out across the prairie, could see them coming from all directions. The little Creole ponies galloping in a line looked like hobby horses in the faint distance; the mule-carts were like toy wagons. Zaïda might be among those people approaching, flying, crawling ahead of the darkness that was creeping out of the far wood. He hoped so, but he did not believe so; she would hardly have had time to dress.

Foché was noisily lighting lamps, with the assistance of an inoffensive mulatto boy whom he intended in the morning to butcher, to cut into sections, to pack and salt down in a barrel, like the Colfax woman did to her old husband—a fitting destiny for so stupid a pig as the mulatto boy. The negro musicians had arrived: two fiddlers and an accordion player, and they were drinking whiskey from a black quart bottle which was passed socially from one to the other. The musicians were really never at their best till the quart bottle had been consumed.

The girls who came in wagons and on ponies from a distance wore, for the most part, calico dresses and sun-bonnets. Their finery they brought along in pillow-slips or pinned up in sheets and towels. With these they at once retired to an upper room; later to appear be-ribboned and be-furbelowed; their faces masked with starch powder, but never a touch of rouge.

Most of the guests had assembled when Zaïda arrived—"dashed up" would better express her coming—in an open, two-seated buckboard, with her cousin Jules driving. He reined the pony suddenly and viciously before the time-eaten front steps, in order to produce an impression upon those who were gathered around. Most of the men had halted their vehicles outside and permitted their women folk to walk up from the mulberry trees.

But the real, the stunning effect was produced when Zaïda stepped upon the gallery and threw aside her light shawl in the full glare of half a dozen kerosene lamps. She was white from head to foot—literally, for her slippers even were white. No one would have believed, let alone suspected that they were a pair of old black ones which she had covered with pieces of her first communion sash. There is no describing her dress, it was fluffy, like a fresh powder-puff, and stood out. No wonder she had handled it so reverentially! Her white fan was covered with spangles that she herself had sewed all over it; and in her belt and in her brown hair were thrust small sprays of orange blossom.

Two men leaning against the railing uttered long whistles expressive equally of wonder and admiration.

"Tiens! t'es pareille comme ain mariée, Zaïda;" cried out a lady with a baby in her arms. Some young women tittered and Zaïda fanned herself. The women's voices were almost without exception shrill and piercing; the men's, soft and low-pitched.

The girl turned to Telèsphore, as to an old and valued friend:

"Tiens! c'est vous?" He had hesitated at first to approach, but at this friendly sign of recognition he drew eagerly forward and held out his hand. The men looked at him suspiciously, inwardly resenting his stylish appearance, which they considered instrusive, offensive and demoralizing.

How Zaïda's eyes sparkled now! What very pretty teeth Zaïda had when she laughed, and what a mouth! Her lips were a revelation, a promise; something to carry away and remember in the night and grow hungry thinking of next day. Strictly speaking, they may not have been quite all that; but in any event, that is the way Telèsphore thought about them. He began to take account of her appearance: her nose, her eyes, her hair. And when she left him to go in and dance her first dance with cousin Jules, he leaned up against a post and thought of them: nose, eyes, hair, ears, lips and round, soft throat.

Later it was like Bedlam.

The musicians had warmed up and were scraping away indoors and calling the figures. Feet were pounding through the dance; dust was flying. The women's voices were piped high and mingled discordantly, like the confused, shrill clatter of waking birds, while the men laughed boisterously. But if some one had only thought of gagging Foché, there would have been less noise. His good humor permeated everywhere, like an atmosphere. He was louder than all the noise; he was more visible than the dust. He called the young mulatto (destined for the knife) "my boy" and sent him flying hither and thither. He beamed upon Douté as he tasted the gumbo and congratulated her: "C'est toi qui s'y connais, ma fille! 'cré tonnerre!"

Telèsphore danced with Zaïda and then he leaned out against the post; then he danced with Zaïda, and then he leaned against the post. The mothers of the other girls decided that he had the manners of a pig.

It was time to dance again with Zaïda and he went in search of her. He was carrying her shawl, which she had given him to hold.

"W'at time it is?" she asked him when he had found and secured her. They were under one of the kerosene lamps on the front gallery and he drew forth his silver watch. She seemed to be still laboring under some suppressed excitement that he had noticed before.

"It's fo'teen minutes pas' twelve," he told her exactly.

"I wish you'd fine out w'ere Jules is. Go look yonda in the card-room if he's there, an' come tell me." Jules had danced with all the prettiest girls. She knew it was his custom

after accomplishing this agreeable feat, to retire to the card-room.

"You'll wait yere till I come back?" he
asked.

"I'll wait yere; you go on." She waited but
drew back a little into the shadow. Telèsphore
lost no time.

"Yes, he's yonda playin' cards with Foché
an' some others I don' know," he reported
when he had discovered her in the shadow.
There had been a spasm of alarm when he did
not at once see her where he had left her under
the lamp.

"Does he look—look like he's fixed yonda
fo' good?"

"He's got his coat off. Looks like he's fixed
pretty comf'table fo' the nex' hour or two."

"Gi' me my shawl."

"You cole?" offering to put it around her.

"No, I ain't cole." She drew the shawl about
her shoulders and turned as if to leave him.
But a sudden generous impulse seemed to
move her, and she added:

"Come along yonda with me."

They descended the few rickety steps that
led down to the yard. He followed rather than

accompanied her across the beaten and tramp-
led sward. Those who saw them thought they
had gone out to take the air. The beams of
light that slanted out from the house were fitful and uncertain, deepening the shadows. The
embers under the empty gumbo-pot glared red
in the darkness. There was a sound of quiet
voices coming from under the trees.

Zaïda, closely accompanied by Telèsphore,
went out where the vehicles and horses were
fastened to the fence. She stepped carefully and held up her skirts as if dreading the
least speck of dew or of dust.

"Unhitch Jules' ho'se an' buggy there an'
turn 'em 'roun' this way, please." He did as
instructed, first backing the pony, then leading it out to where she stood in the half-made
road.

"You goin' home?" he asked her, "betta let
me water the pony."

"Neva mine." She mounted and seating
herself grasped the reins. "No, I aint goin'
home," she added. He, too, was holding the
reins gathered in one hand across the pony's
back.

"W'ere you goin'?" he demanded.

"Neva you mine w'ere I'm goin'."

"You ain't goin' anyw'ere this time o' night by yo'se'f?"

"W'at you reckon I'm 'fraid of?" she laughed. "Turn loose that ho'se," at the same time urging the animal forward. The little brute started away with a bound and Telèsphore, also with a bound, sprang into the buckboard and seated himself beside Zaïda.

"You ain't goin' anyw'ere this time o' night by yo'se'f." It was not a question now, but an assertion, and there was no denying it. There was even no disputing it, and Zaïda recognizing the fact drove on in silence.

There is no animal that moves so swiftly across a 'Cadian prairie as the little Creole pony. This one did not run nor trot; he seemed to reach out in galloping bounds. The buckboard creaked, bounced, jolted and swayed. Zaïda clutched at her shawl while Telèsphore drew his straw hat further down over his right eye and offered to drive. But he did not know the road and she would not let him. They had soon reached the woods.

If there is any animal that can creep more slowly through a wooded road than the little Creole pony, that animal has not yet been discovered in Acadie. This particular animal seemed to be appalled by the darkness of the forest and filled with dejection. His head drooped and he lifted his feet as if each hoof were weighted with a thousand pounds of lead. Any one unacquainted with the peculiarities of the breed would sometimes have fancied that he was standing still. But Zaïda and Telèsphore knew better. Zaïda uttered a deep sigh as she slackened her hold on the reins and Telèsphore, lifting his hat, let it swing from the back of his head.

"How you don' ask me w'ere I'm goin'?" she said finally. These were the first words she had spoken since refusing his offer to drive.

"Oh, it don' make any diff'ence w'ere you goin'."

"Then if it don' make any diff'ence w'ere I'm goin', I jus' as well tell you." She hesitated, however. He seemed to have no curiosity and did not urge her.

"I'm goin' to get married," she said.

He uttered some kind of an exclamation; it was nothing articulate—more like the tone of an animal that gets a sudden knife thrust And now he felt how dark the forest was. An instant before it had seemed a sweet, black paradise; better than any heaven he had ever heard of.

"W'y can't you get married at home?" This was not the first thing that occurred to him to say, but this was the first thing he said.

"Ah, b'en oui! with perfec' mules fo' a father an' mother! it's good enough to talk."

"W'y couldn' he come an' get you? W'at kine of a scound'el is that to let you go through the woods at night by yo'se'f?"

"You betta wait till you know who you talkin' about. He didn' come an' get me because he knows I ain't 'fraid; an' because he's got too much pride to ride in Jules Trodon's buckboard afta he done been put out o' Jules Trodon's house."

"W'at's his name an' w'ere you goin' to fine 'im?"

"Yonda on the other side the woods up at ole Wat Gibson's—a kine of justice the peace or something. Anyhow he's goin' to marry us.

An' afta we done married those têtes-de-mulets yonda on bayou de Glaize can say w'at they want."

"W'at's his name?"

"André Pascal."

The name meant nothing to Telèsphore. For all he knew, André Pascal might be one of the shining lights of Avoyelles; but he doubted it.

"You betta turn 'roun'," he said. It was an unselfish impulse that prompted the suggestion. It was the thought of this girl married to a man whom even Jules Trodon would not suffer to enter his house.

"I done give my word," she answered.

"W'at's the matta with 'im? W'y don't yo' father and mother want you to marry 'im?"

"W'y? Because it's always the same tune! W'en a man's down eve'ybody's got stones to throw at 'im. They say he's lazy. A man that will walk from St. Landry plumb to Rapides lookin' fo' work; an' they call that lazy! Then, somebody's been spreadin' yonda on the Bayou that he drinks. I don' b'lieve it. I neva saw 'im drinkin', me. Anyway, he won't drink afta he's married to me; he's too fon' of me fo' that. He say he'll blow out his brains if I don' marry 'im."

"I reckon you betta turn roun'."

"No, I done give my word." And they went creeping on through the woods in silence.

"W'at time is it?" she asked after an interval. He lit a match and looked at his watch.

"It's quarta to one. W'at time did he say?"

"I tole 'im I'd come about one o'clock. I knew that was a good time to get away f'om the ball."

She would have hurried a little but the pony could not be induced to do so. He dragged himself, seemingly ready at any moment to give up the breath of life. But once out of the woods he made up for lost time. They were on the open prairie again, and he fairly ripped the air; some flying demon must have changed skins with him.

It was a few minutes of one o'clock when they drew up before Wat Gibson's house. It was not much more than a rude shelter, and in the dim starlight it seemed isolated, as if standing alone in the middle of the black, far-reaching prairie. As they halted at the gate a dog within set up a furious barking; and an old negro who had been smoking his pipe at that ghostly hour, advanced toward them from the shelter of the gallery. Telèsphore descended and helped his companion to alight.

"We want to see Mr. Gibson," spoke up Zaïda. The old fellow had already opened the gate. There was no light in the house.

"Marse Gibson, he yonda to ole Mr. Bodel's playin' kairds. But he neva' stay atter one o'clock. Come in, ma'am; come in, suh; walk right 'long in." He had drawn his own conclusions to explain their appearance. They stood upon the narrow porch waiting while he went inside to light the lamp.

Although the house was small, as it comprised but one room, that room was comparatively a large one. It looked to Telèsphore and Zaïda very large and gloomy when they entered it. The lamp was on a table that stood against the wall, and that held further a rusty looking ink bottle, a pen and an old blank book. A narrow bed was off in the corner. The brick chimney extended into the room and formed a ledge that served as mantel shelf. From the big, low-hanging rafters swung an assortment of fishing tackle, a gun, some discarded articles of clothing and a string of red peppers. The boards of the floor were broad, rough and loosely joined together.

Telèsphore and Zaïda seated themselves on opposite sides of the table and the negro went out to the wood pile to gather chips and pieces of bois-gras with which to kindle a small fire.

It was a little chilly; he supposed the two would want coffee and he knew that Wat Gibson would ask for a cup the first thing on his arrival.

"I wonder w'at's keepin' 'im," muttered Zaïda impatiently. Telèsphore looked at his watch. He had been looking at it at intervals of one minute straight along.

"It's ten minutes pas' one," he said. He offered no further comment.

At twelve minutes past one Zaïda's restlessness again broke into speech.

"I can't imagine, me, w'at's become of André! He said he'd be yere sho' at one." The old negro was kneeling before the fire that he had kindled, contemplating the cheerful blaze. He rolled his eyes toward Zaïda.

"You talkin' 'bout Mr. André Pascal? No need to look fo' him. Mr. Andre he b'en down to de P'int all day raisin' Cain."

"That's a lie," said Zaïda. Telèsphore said nothing.

"Tain't no lie, ma'am; he b'en sho' raisin' de ole Nick." She looked at him, too contemptuous to reply.

The negro told no lie so far as his bald statement was concerned. He was simply mistaken in his estimate of André Pascal's ability to "raise Cain" during an entire afternoon and evening and still keep a rendezvous with a lady at one o'clock in the morning. For André was even then at hand, as the loud and menacing howl of the dog testified. The negro hastened out to admit him.

André did not enter at once; he stayed a while outside abusing the dog and communicating to the negro his intention of coming out to shoot the animal after he had attended to more pressing business that was awaiting him within.

Zaïda arose, a little flurried and excited when he entered. Telèsphore remained seated.

Pascal was partially sober. There had evidently been an attempt at dressing for the occasion at some early part of the previous day, but such evidences had almost wholly vanished. His linen was soiled and his whole appearance was that of a man who, by an effort, had aroused himself from a debauch. He was a little taller than Telèsphore, and more loosely put together. Most women would have called him a handsomer man. It was easy to imagine that when sober, he might betray by some subtle grace of speech or manner, evidences of gentle blood.

"W'y did you keep me waitin', André? w'en you knew—" she got no further, but backed up against the table and stared at him with earnest, startled eyes.

"Keep you waiting, Zaïda? my dear li'le Zaïdé, how can you say such a thing! I started up yere an hour ago an' that—w'ere's that damned ole Gibson?" He had approached Zaïda with the evident intention of embracing her, but she seized his wrist and held him at arm's length away. In casting his eyes about for old Gibson his glance alighted upon Telèsphore.

The sight of the 'Cadian seemed to fill him with astonishment. He stood back and began to contemplate the young fellow and lose himself in speculation and conjecture before him, as if before some unlabeled wax figure. He turned for information to Zaïda.

"Say, Zaïda, w'at you call this? W'at kine of damn fool you got sitting yere? Who let him in? W'at you reckon he's lookin' fo'? trouble?"

Telèsphore said nothing; he was awaiting his cue from Zaïda.

"André Pascal," she said, "you jus' as well take the do' an' go. You might stan' yere till the day o' judgment on yo' knees befo' me; an' blow out yo' brains if you a mine to. I ain't neva goin' to marry you."

"The hell you ain't!"

He had hardly more than uttered the words when he lay prone on his back. Telèsphore had knocked him down. The blow seemed to complete the process of sobering that had begun in him. He gathered himself together and rose to his feet; in doing so he reached back for his pistol. His hold was not yet steady, however, and the weapon slipped from his grasp and fell to the floor. Zaïda picked it up and laid it on the table behind her. She was going to see fair play.

The brute instinct that drives men at each other's throat was awake and stirring in these two. Each saw in the other a thing to be wiped out of his way—out of existence if need be. Passion and blind rage directed the blows which they dealt, and steeled the tension of muscles and clutch of fingers. They were not skillful blows, however.

The fire blazed cheerily; the kettle which the negro had placed upon the coals was steaming and singing. The man had gone in search of his master. Zaïda had placed the lamp out of harm's way on the high mantel ledge and she leaned back with her hands behind her upon the table.

She did not raise her voice or lift her finger to stay the combat that was acting before her. She was motionless, and white to the lips; only her eyes seemed to be alive and burning and blazing. At one moment she felt that André must have strangled Telèsphore; but she said nothing. The next instant she could hardly doubt that the blow from Telèsphore's doubled fist could be less than a killing one; but she did nothing.

How the loose boards swayed and creaked beneath the weight of the struggling men! the very old rafters seemed to groan; and she felt that the house shook.

The combat, if fierce, was short, and it ended out on the gallery whither they had staggered through the open door—or one had dragged the other—she could not tell. But she knew when it was over, for there was a long moment of utter stillness. Then she heard one of the men descend the steps and go away, for the gate slammed after him. The other went out to the cistern; the sound of the tin bucket splashing in the water reached her where she stood. He must have been endeavoring to remove traces of the encounter.

Presently Telèsphore entered the room. The elegance of his apparel had been somewhat marred; the men over at the 'Cadian ball would hardly have taken exception now to his appearance.

"W'ere is André?" the girl asked.

"He's gone," said Telèsphore.

She had never changed her position and now when she drew herself up her wrists ached and she rubbed them a little. She was no longer pale; the blood had come back into her cheeks and lips, staining them crimson. She held out her hand to him. He took it gratefully enough, but he did not know what to do with it; that is, he did not know what he might dare to do with it, so he let it drop gently away and went to the fire.

"I reckon we betta be goin', too," she said. He stooped and poured some of the bubbling water from the kettle upon the coffee which the negro had set upon the hearth.

"I'll make a li'le coffee firs'," he proposed, "an' anyhow we betta wait till ole man w'at's-his-name comes back. It wouldn't look well to leave his house that way without some kine of excuse or explanation."

She made no reply, but seated herself submissively beside the table.

Her will, which had been overmastering and aggressive, seemed to have grown numb under the disturbing spell of the past few hours. An illusion had gone from her, and had carried her love with it. The absence of regret revealed this to her. She realized, but could not comprehend it, not knowing that the love had been part of the illusion. She was tired in body and spirit, and it was with a sense of restfulness that she sat all drooping and relaxed and watched Telèsphore make the coffee.

He made enough for them both and a cup for old Wat Gibson when he should come in, and also one for the negro. He supposed the cups, the sugar and spoons were in the safe over there in the corner, and that is where he found them.

When he finally said to Zaïda, "Come, I'm going to take you home now," and drew her shawl around her, pinning it under the chin, she was like a little child and followed whither he led in all confidence.

It was Telèsphore who drove on the way back, and he let the pony cut no capers, but held him to a steady and tempered gait. The girl was still quiet and silent; she was thinking tenderly—a little tearfully of those two old têtes-de-mulets yonder on Bayou de Glaize.

How they crept through the woods! and how dark it was and how still!

"W'at time it is?" whispered Zaïda. Alas! he could not tell her; his watch was broken. But almost for the first time in his life, Telèsphore did not care what time it was.

Athénaïse

Athénaïse

I.

ATHÉNAÏSE went away in the morning
to make a visit to her parents, ten
miles back on rigolet de Bon Dieu.
She did not return in the evening, and
Cazeau, her husband, fretted not a little. He did not worry much about Athénaïse, who, he suspected, was resting only
too content in the bosom of her family; his chief
solicitude was manifestly for the pony she had
ridden. He felt sure those "lazy pigs," her
brothers, were capable of neglecting it seriously. This misgiving Cazeau communicated
to his servant, old Félicité, who waited upon
him at supper.

His voice was low pitched, and even softer
than Félicité's. He was tall, sinewy, swarthy,
and altogether severe looking. His thick black
hair waved, and it gleamed like the breast of
a crow. The sweep of his mustache, which

was not so black, outlined the broad contour of the mouth. Beneath the under lip grew a small tuft which he was much given to twisting, and which he permitted to grow, apparently for no other purpose. Cazeau's eyes were dark blue, narrow and overshadowed. His hands were coarse and stiff from close acquaintance with farming tools and implements, and he handled his fork and knife clumsily. But he was distinguished looking, and succeeded in commanding a good deal of respect, and even fear sometimes.

He ate his supper alone, by the light of a single coal-oil lamp that but faintly illuminated the big room, with its bare floor and huge rafters, and its heavy pieces of furniture that loomed dimly in the gloom of the apartment. Félicité, ministering to his wants, hovered about the table like a little, bent, restless shadow.

She served him with a dish of sunfish fried crisp and brown. There was nothing else set before him beside the bread and butter and the bottle of red wine which she locked carefully in the buffet after he had poured his second glass. She was occupied with her mis-

tress's absence, and kept reverting to it after
he had expressed his solicitude about the pony.

"Dat beat me! on'y marry two mont', an'
got de head turn' a'ready to go 'broad. C'est
pas Chrétien, ténez!"

Cazeau shrugged his shoulders for answer,
after he had drained his glass and pushed aside
his plate. Félicité's opinion of the unchristian-
like behavior of his wife in leaving him thus
alone after two months of marriage weighed
little with him. He was used to solitude, and
did not mind a day or a night or two of it.
He had lived alone ten years, since his first
wife died, and Félicité might have known better than to suppose that he cared. He told her
she was a fool. It sounded like a compliment
in his modulated, caressing voice. She grumbled to herself as she set about clearing the
table, and Cazeau arose and walked outside on
the gallery; his spur, which he had not removed upon entering the house, jangled at
every step.

The night was beginning to deepen, and to
gather black about the clusters of trees and
shrubs that were grouped in the yard. In the
beam of light from the open kitchen door a

black boy stood feeding a brace of snarling, hungry dogs; further away, on the steps of a cabin, some one was playing the accordion; and in still another direction a little negro baby was crying lustily. Cazeau walked around to the front of the house, which was square, squat and one-story.

A belated wagon was driving in at the gate, and the impatient driver was swearing hoarsely at his jaded oxen. Félicité stepped out on the gallery, glass and polishing towel in hand, to investigate, and to wonder, too, who could be singing out on the river. It was a party of young people paddling around, waiting for the moon to rise, and they were singing Juanita, their voices coming tempered and melodious through the distance and the night.

Cazeau's horse was waiting, saddled, ready to be mounted, for Cazeau had many things to attend to before bed-time; so many things that there was not left to him a moment in which to think of Athénaïse. He felt her absence, though, like a dull, insistent pain.

However, before he slept that night he was visited by the thought of her, and by a vision of her fair young face with its drooping lips and sullen and averted eyes. The marriage had been a blunder; he had only to look into her eyes to feel that, to discover her growing aversion. But it was a thing not by any possibility to be undone. He was quite prepared to make the best of it, and expected no less than a like effort on her part. The less she revisited the rigolet, the better. He would find means to keep her at home hereafter.

These unpleasant reflections kept Cazeau awake far into the night, notwithstanding the craving of his whole body for rest and sleep. The moon was shining, and its pale effulgence reached dimly into the room, and with it a touch of the cool breath of the spring night. There was an unusual stillness abroad; no sound to be heard save the distant, tireless, plaintive notes of the accordion.

II.

Athénaïse did not return the following day, even though her husband sent her word to do so by her brother, Montéclin, who passed on his way to the village early in the morning.

On the third day Cazeau saddled his horse
and went himself in search of her. She had
sent no word, no message, explaining her absence, and he felt that he had good cause to
be offended. It was rather awkward to have
to leave his work, even though late in the afternoon,—Cazeau had always so much to do;
but among the many urgent calls upon him,
the task of bringing his wife back to a sense of
her duty seemed to him for the moment paramount.

The Michés, Athénaïse's parents, lived on
the old Gotrain place. It did not belong to
them; they were "running" it for a merchant
in Alexandria. The house was far too big
for their use. One of the lower rooms served
for the storing of wood and tools; the person
"occupying" the place before Miché having
pulled up the flooring in despair of being able
to patch it. Upstairs, the rooms were so large,
so bare, that they offered a constant temptation
to lovers of the dance, whose importunities
Madame Miché was accustomed to meet with
amiable indulgence. A dance at Miché's and
a plate of Madame Miché's gumbo filé at midnight were pleasures not to be neglected or

despised, unless by such serious souls as Cazeau.

Long before Cazeau reached the house his approach had been observed, for there was nothing to obstruct the view of the outer road; vegetation was not yet abundantly advanced, and there was but a patchy, straggling stand of cotton and corn in Miché's field.

Madame Miché, who had been seated on the gallery in a rocking-chair, stood up to greet him as he drew near. She was short and fat, and wore a black skirt and loose muslin sack fastened at the throat with a hair brooch. Her own hair, brown and glossy, showed but a few threads of silver. Her round pink face was cheery, and her eyes were bright and good humored. But she was plainly perturbed and ill at ease as Cazeau advanced.

Montéclin, who was there too, was not ill at ease, and made no attempt to disguise the dislike with which his brother-in-law inspired him. He was a slim, wiry fellow of twenty-five, short of stature like his mother, and resembling her in feature. He was in shirt-sleeves, half leaning, half sitting, on the inse-

cure railing of the gallery, and fanning himself
with his broad-rimmed felt hat.

"Cochon!" he muttered under his breath
as Cazeau mounted the stairs,— "sacré cochon!"

"Cochon" had sufficiently characterized the
man who had once on a time declined to lend
Montéclin money. But when this same man
had had the presumption to propose marriage
to his well-beloved sister, Athénaïse, and the
honor to be accepted by her, Montéclin felt
that a qualifying epithet was needed fully to
express his estimate of Cazeau.

Miché and his oldest son were absent. They
both esteemed Cazeau highly, and talked much
of his qualities of head and heart, and thought
much of his excellent standing with city merchants.

Athénaïse had shut herself up in her room.
Cazeau had seen her rise and enter the house
at perceiving him. He was a good deal mys-
tified, but no one could have guessed it when
he shook hands with Madame Miché. He had
only nodded to Montéclin, with a muttered
"Comment ça va?"

"Tiens! something tole me you were coming to-day!" exclaimed Madame Miché, with a little blustering appearance of being cordial and at ease, as she offered Cazeau a chair.

He ventured a short laugh as he seated himself.

"You know, nothing would do," she went on, with much gesture of her small, plump hands, "nothing would do but Athénaïse mus' stay las' night fo' a li'le dance. The boys wouldn' year to their sister leaving."

Cazeau shrugged his shoulders significantly, telling as plainly as words that he knew nothing about it.

"Comment. Montéclin didn' tell you we were going to keep Athénaïse?" Montéclin had evidently told nothing.

"An' how about the night befo'," questioned Cazeau, "an' las' night? It isn't possible you dance every night out yere on the Bon Dieu!"

Madame Miché laughed, with amiable appreciation of the sarcasm; and turning to her son, "Montéclin, my boy, go tell yo' sister that Monsieur Cazeau is yere."

Montéclin did not stir except to shift his position and settle himself more securely on the railing.

"Did you year me, Montéclin?"

"Oh yes, I yeard you plain enough," responded her son, "but you know as well as me it's no use to tell 'Thénaïse anything. You been talkin' to her yo'se'f since Monday; an' pa's preached himse'f hoa'se on the subject; an' you even had uncle Achille down yere yesterday to reason with her. W'en 'Thénaïse said she wasn' goin' to set her foot back in Cazeau's house, she meant it."

This speech, which Montéclin delivered with thorough unconcern, threw his mother into a condition of painful but dumb embarrassment. It brought two fiery red spots to Cazeau's cheeks, and for the space of a moment he looked wicked.

What Montéclin had spoken was quite true, though his taste in the manner and choice of time and place in saying it were not of the best. Athénaïse, upon the first day of her arrival, had announced that she came to stay, having no intention of returning under Cazeau's roof. The announcement had scattered consternation, as she knew it would. She had been implored, scolded, entreated, stormed at, until she felt herself like a dragging sail that all the winds of heaven had beaten upon. Why in the name of God had she married Cazeau? Her father had lashed her with the question a dozen times. Why indeed? It was difficult now for her to understand why, unless because she supposed it was customary for girls to marry when the right opportunity came. Cazeau, she knew, would make life more comfortable for her; and again, she had liked him, and had even been rather flustered when he pressed her hands and kissed them, and kissed her lips and cheeks and eyes, when she accepted him.

Montéclin himself had taken her aside to talk the thing over. The turn of affairs was delighting him.

"Come, now, 'Thénaïse, you mus' explain to me all about it, so we can settle on a good cause, an' secu' a separation fo' you. Has he been mistreating an' abusing you, the sacré cochon?" They were alone together in her room, whither she had taken refuge from the angry domestic elements.

"You please to reserve yo' disgusting expressions, Montéclin. No, he has not abused me in any way that I can think."

"Does he drink?   Come 'Thénaïse, think well over it.   Does he ever get drunk?"

"Drunk!   Oh, mercy, no,—Cazeau never gets drunk."

"I see; it's jus' simply you feel like me; you hate him."

"No, I don't hate him," she returned reflectively; adding with a sudden impulse, "It's jus' being married that I detes' an' despise. I hate being Mrs. Cazeau, an' would want to be Athénaïse Miché again.   I can't stan' to live with a man; to have him always there; his coats an' pantaloons hanging in my room; his ugly bare feet—washing them in my tub, befo' my very eyes, ugh!"   She shuddered with recollections, and resumed, with a sigh that was almost a sob: "Mon Dieu, mon Dieu! Sister Marie Angélique knew w'at she was saying; she knew me better than myse'f w'en she said God had sent me a vocation an' I was turning deaf ears.   W'en I think of a blessed life in the convent, at peace!   Oh, w'at was I dreaming of!" and then the tears came.

Montéclin felt disconcerted and greatly disappointed at having obtained evidence that would carry no weight with a court of justice.

The day had not come when a young woman might ask the court's permission to return to her mamma on the sweeping ground of a constitutional disinclination for marriage. But if there was no way of untying this Gordian knot of marriage, there was surely a way of cutting it.

"Well, 'Thénaïse, I'm mighty durn sorry yo got no better groun's 'an w'at you say. But you can count on me to stan' by you w'atever you do. God knows I don' blame you fo' not wantin' to live with Cazeau."

And now there was Cazeau himself, with the red spots flaming in his swarthy cheeks, looking and feeling as if he wanted to thrash Montéclin into some semblance of decency. He arose abruptly, and approaching the room which he had seen his wife enter, thrust open the door after a hasty preliminary knock. Athénaïse, who was standing erect at a far window, turned at his entrance.

She appeared neither angry nor frightened, but thoroughly unhappy, with an appeal in her soft dark eyes and a tremor on her lips that seemed to him expressions of unjust reproach, that wounded and maddened him at once. But

whatever he might feel, Cazeau knew only one
way to act toward a woman.

"Athénaïse, you are not ready?" he asked in
his quiet tones. "It's getting late; we havn'
any time to lose."

She knew that Montéclin had spoken out,
and she had hoped for a wordy interview, a
stormy scene, in which she might have held
her own as she had held it for the past three
days against her family, with Montéclin's aid.
But she had no weapon with which to combat subtlety. Her husband's looks, his tones,
his mere presence, brought to her a sudden
sense of hopelessness, an instinctive realization of the futility of rebellion against a social
and sacred institution.

Cazeau said nothing further, but stood waiting in the doorway. Madame Miché had
walked to the far end of the gallery, and pretended to be occupied with having a chicken
driven from her parterre. Montéclin stood by,
exasperated, fuming, ready to burst out.

Athénaïse went and reached for her riding
skirt that hung against the wall. She was
rather tall, with a figure which, though not robust, seemed perfect in its fine proportions.

"La fille de son père," she was often called, which was a great compliment to Miché. Her brown hair was brushed all fluffily back from her temples and low forehead, and about her features and expression lurked a softness, a prettiness, a dewiness, that were perhaps too childlike, that savored of immaturity.

She slipped the riding-skirt, which was of black alpaca, over her head, and with impatient fingers hooked it at the waist over her pink linen-lawn. Then she fastened on her white sunbonnet and reached for her gloves on the mantelpiece.

"If you don' wan' to go, you know w'at you got to do, 'Thénaïse," fumed Montéclin. "You don' set yo' feet back on Cane River, by God, unless you want to,—not w'ile I'm alive."

Cazeau looked at him as if he were a monkey whose antics fell short of being amusing.

Athénaïse still made no reply, said not a word. She walked rapidly past her husband, past her brother; bidding good-bye to no one, not even to her mother. She descended the stairs, and without assistance from any one mounted the pony, which Cazeau had ordered to be saddled upon his arrival. In this way

she obtained a fair start of her husband, whose
departure was far more leisurely, and for the
greater part of the way she managed to keep an
appreciable gap between them. She rode almost madly at first, with the wind inflating her
skirt balloon-like about her knees, and her sunbonnet falling back between her shoulders.

At no time did Cazeau make an effort to
overtake her until traversing an old fallow
meadow that was level and hard as a table.
The sight of a great solitary oak-tree, with
its seemingly immutable outlines, that had
been a landmark for ages—or was it the odor
of elderberry stealing up from the gully to the
south? or what was it that brought vividly
back to Cazeau, by some association of ideas,
a scene of many years ago? He had passed
that old live-oak hundreds of times, but it
was only now that the memory of one day
came back to him. He was a very small boy
that day, seated before his father on horse-
back. They were proceeding slowly, and
Black Gabe was moving on before them at a
little dog-trot. Black Gabe had run away, and
had been discovered back in the Gotrain
swamp. They had halted beneath this big oak

to enable the negro to take breath; for Cazeau's father was a kind and considerate master, and every one had agreed at the time that Black Gabe was a fool, a great idiot indeed, for wanting to run away from him.

The whole impression was for some reason hideous, and to dispel it Cazeau spurred his horse to a swift gallop. Overtaking his wife, he rode the remainder of the way at her side in silence.

It was late when they reached home. Félicité was standing on the grassy edge of the road, in the moonlight, waiting for them.

Cazeau once more ate his supper alone; for Athénaïse went to her room, and there she was crying again.

III.

Athénaïse was not one to accept the inevitable with patient resignation, a talent born in the souls of many women; neither was she the one to accept it with philosophical resignation, like her husband. Her sensibilities were alive and keen and responsive. She met the pleasurable things of life with frank, open appreciation, and against distasteful conditions she rebelled.

Dissimulation was as foreign to her nature as
guile to the breast of a babe, and her rebellious
outbreaks, by no means rare, had hitherto been
quite open and aboveboard. People often said
that Athénaïse would know her own mind
some day, which was equivalent to saying that
she was at present unacquainted with it.　If
she ever came to such knowledge, it would be
by no intellectual research, by no subtle analy-
ses or tracing the motives of actions to their
source.　It would come to her as the song
to the bird, the perfume and color to the flower.

Her parents had hoped—not without reason
and justice—that marriage would bring the
poise, the desirable pose, so glaringly lacking
in Athénaïse's character. Marriage they knew
to be a wonderful and powerful agent in the
development and formation of a woman's character; they had seen its effect too often to
doubt it.

"And if this marriage does nothing else,"
exclaimed Miché in an outburst of sudden ex-
asperation, "it will rid us of Athénaïse; for I
am at the end of my patience with her!　You
have never had the firmness to manage her,"—
he was speaking to his wife,—"I have not had

the time, the leisure, to devote to her training; and what good we might have accomplished, that maudit Montéclin—Well, Cazeau is the one! It takes just such a steady hand to guide a disposition like Athénaïse's, a master hand, a strong will that compels obedience."

And now, when they had hoped for so much, here was Athénaïse, with gathered and fierce vehemence, beside which her former outbursts appeared mild, declaring that she would not, and she would not, and she would not continue to enact the rôle of wife to Cazeau. If she had had a reason! as Madame Miché lamented; but it could not be discovered that she had any sane one. He had never scolded, or called names, or deprived her of comforts, or been guilty of any of the many reprehensible acts commonly attributed to objectionable husbands. He did not slight nor neglect her. Indeed, Cazeau's chief offense seemed to be that he loved her, and Athénaïse was not the woman to be loved against her will. She called marriage a trap set for the feet of unwary and unsuspecting girls, and in round, unmeasured terms reproached her mother with treachery and deceit.

"I told you Cazeau was the man," chuckled Miché, when his wife had related the scene that had accompanied and influenced Athénaïse's departure.

Athénaïse again hoped, in the morning, that Cazeau would scold or make some sort of a scene, but he apparently did not dream of it. It was exasperating that he should take her acquiescence so for granted. It is true he had been up and over the fields and across the river and back long before she was out of bed, and he may have been thinking of something else, which was no excuse, which was even in some sense an aggravation. But he did say to her at breakfast, "That brother of yo's, that Montéclin, is unbearable."

"Montéclin?   Par exemple!"

Athénaïse, seated opposite to her husband, was attired in a white morning wrapper. She wore a somewhat abused, long face, it is true, —an expression of countenance familiar to some husbands,—but the expression was not sufficiently pronounced to mar the charm of her youthful freshness.   She had little heart to eat, only playing with the food before her, and she

felt a pang of resentment at her husband's
healthy appetite.

"Yes, Montéclin," he reasserted: "He's developed into a firs'-class nuisance; an' you better tell him, Athénaïse,—unless you want me
to tell him,—to confine his energies after this
to matters that concern him. I have no use
fo' him or fo' his interference in w'at regards
you an' me alone."

This was said with unusual asperity. It was
the little breach that Athénaïse had been
watching for, and she charged rapidly: "It's
strange, if you detes' Montéclin so heartily,
that you would desire to marry his sister." She
knew it was a silly thing to say, and was not
surprised when he told her so. It gave her
a little foothold for further attack, however. "I
don't see, anyhow, w'at reason you had to
marry me, w'en there were so many others,"
she complained, as if accusing him of perse-
cution and injury. "There was Marianne running after you fo' the las' five years till it was
disgraceful; an' any one of the Dortrand girls
would have been glad to marry you. But no,
nothing would do; you mus' come out on the
rigolet fo' me." Her complaint was pathetic,

and at the same time so amusing that Cazeau
was forced to smile.

"I can't see w'at the Dortrand girls or Marianne have to do with it," he rejoined; adding,
with no trace of amusement, "I married you
because I loved you; because you were the
woman I wanted to marry, an' the only one.
I reckon I tole you that befo'. I thought—
of co'se I was a fool fo' taking things fo' granted—but I did think that I might make you
happy in making things easier an' mo' comfortable fo' you. I expected—I was even that
big a fool—I believed that yo' coming yere
to me would be like the sun shining out of the
clouds, an' that our days would be like w'at the
story-books promise after the wedding. I was
mistaken. But I can't imagine w'at induced
you to marry me. W'atever it was, I reckon
you foun' out you made a mistake, too. I
don' see anything to do but make the best of
a bad bargain, an' shake han's over it." He
had arisen from the table, and, approaching,
held out his hand to her. What he had said
was commonplace enough, but it was significant, coming from Cazeau, who was not often
so unreserved in expressing himself.

Athénaïse ignored the hand held out to her.
She was resting her chin in her palm, and kept
her eyes fixed moodily upon the table.   He
rested his hand, that she would not touch, upon
her head for an instant, and walked away out
of the room.

She heard him giving orders to workmen
who had been waiting for him out on the gallery, and she heard him mount his horse and
ride away.   A hundred things would distract
him and engage his attention during the day.
She felt that he had perhaps put her and her
grievance from his thoughts when he crossed
the threshold; whilst she—

Old Félicité was standing there holding a
shining tin pail, asking for flour and lard and
eggs from the storeroom, and meal for the
chicks.

Athénaïse seized the bunch of keys which
hung from her belt and flung them at
Félicité's feet.

"Tiens! tu vas les garder comme tu as jadis
fait.   Je ne veux plus de ce train là, moi!"

The old woman stooped and picked up the
keys from the floor.   It was really all one to

her that her mistress returned them to her keeping, and refused to take further account of the ménage.

IV.

It seemed now to Athénaïse that Montéclin was the only friend left to her in the world. Her father and mother had turned from her in what appeared to be her hour of need. Her friends laughed at her, and refused to take seriously the hints which she threw out,—feeling her way to discover if marriage were as distasteful to other women as to herself. Montéclin alone understood her. He alone had always been ready to act for her and with her, to comfort and solace her with his sympathy and his support. Her only hope for rescue from her hateful surroundings lay in Montéclin. Of herself she felt powerless to plan, to act, even to conceive a way out of this pitfall into which the whole world seemed to have conspired to thrust her.

She had a great desire to see her brother, and wrote asking him to come to her. But it better suited Montéclin's spirit of adventure to appoint a meeting-place at the turn of the lane, where Athénaïse might appear to be walking leisurely for health and recreation, and where he might seem to be riding along, bent on some errand of business or pleasure.

There had been a shower, a sudden downpour, short as it was sudden, that had laid the dust in the road. It had freshened the pointed leaves of the live-oaks, and brightened up the big fields of cotton on either side of the lane till they seemed carpeted with green, glittering gems.

Athénaïse walked along the grassy edge of the road, lifting her crisp skirts with one hand, and with the other twirling a gay sunshade over her bare head. The scent of the fields after the rain was delicious. She inhaled long breaths of their freshness and perfume, that soothed and quieted her for the moment. There were birds splashing and spluttering in the pools, pluming themselves on the fence-rails, and sending out little sharp cries, twitters, and shrill rhapsodies of delight.

She saw Montéclin approaching from a great distance,—almost as far away as the turn of the woods. But she could not feel sure it was he; it appeared too tall for Montéclin, but

that was because he was riding a large horse.
She waved her parasol to him; she was so glad
to see him. She had never been so glad to
see Montéclin before; not even the day when
he had taken her out of the convent, against
her parents' wishes, because she had expressed
a desire to remain there no longer. He
seemed to her, as he drew near, the embodi-
ment of kindness, of bravery, of chivalry, even
of wisdom; for she had never known Montéclin at a loss to extricate himself from a disagreeable situation.

He dismounted, and, leading his horse by
the bridle, started to walk beside her, after he
had kissed her affectionately and asked her
what she was crying about. She protested that
she was not crying, for she was laughing,
though drying her eyes at the same time on
her handkerchief, rolled in a soft mop for the
purpose.

She took Montéclin's arm, and they strolled
slowly down the lane; they could not seat
themselves for a comfortable chat, as they
would have liked, with the grass all sparkling
and bristling wet.

Yes, she was quite as wretched as ever, she told him. The week which had gone by since she saw him had in no wise lightened the burden of her discontent. There had even been some additional provocations laid upon her, and she told Montéclin all about them,—about the keys, for instance, which in a fit of temper she had returned to Félicité's keeping; and she told how Cazeau had brought them back to her as if they were something she had accidentally lost, and he had recovered; and how he had said, in that aggravating tone of his, that it was not the custom on Cane river for the negro servants to carry the keys, when there was a mistress at the head of the household.

But Athénaïse could not tell Montéclin anything to increase the disrespect which he already entertained for his brother-in-law; and it was then he unfolded to her a plan which he had conceived and worked out for her deliverance from this galling matrimonial yoke.

It was not a plan which met with instant favor, which she was at once ready to accept, for it involved secrecy and dissimulation, hateful alternatives, both of them. But she was filled with admiration for Montéclin's resources and wonderful talent for contrivance. She accepted the plan; not with the immediate determination to act upon it, rather with the intention to sleep and to dream upon it.

Three days later she wrote to Montéclin that she had abandoned herself to his counsel. Displeasing as it might be to her sense of honesty, it would yet be less trying than to live on with a soul full of bitterness and revolt, as she had done for the past two months.

V.

When Cazeau awoke, one morning at his usual very early hour, it was to find the place at his side vacant. This did not surprise him until he discovered that Athénaïse was not in the adjoining room, where he had often found her sleeping in the morning on the lounge. She had perhaps gone out for an early stroll, he reflected, for her jacket and hat were not on the rack where she had hung them the night before. But there were other things absent,— a gown or two from the armoire; and there was a great gap in the piles of lingerie on the shelf; and her traveling-bag was missing, and so were her bits of jewelry from the toilet tray —and Athénaïse was gone!

But the absurdity of going during the night, as if she had been a prisoner, and he the keeper of a dungeon! So much secrecy and mystery, to go sojourning out on the Bon Dieu? Well, the Michés might keep their daughter after this. For the companionship of no woman on earth would he again undergo the humiliating sensation of baseness that had overtaken him in passing the old oak-tree in the fallow meadow.

But a terrible sense of loss overwhelmed Cazeau. It was not new or sudden; he had felt it for weeks growing upon him, and it seemed to culminate with Athénaïse's flight from home. He knew that he could again compel her return as he had done once before,—compel her to return to the shelter of his roof, compel her cold and unwilling submission to his love and passionate transports; but the loss of self-respect seemed to him too dear a price to pay for a wife.

He could not comprehend why she had seemed to prefer him above others; why she had attracted him with eyes, with voice, with a hundred womanly ways, and finally distracted him with love which she seemed, in her timid, maidenly fashion, to return. The great sense of loss came from the realization of having missed a chance for happiness,—a chance that would come his way again only through a miracle. He could not think of himself loving any other woman, and could not think of Athénaïse ever—even at some remote date—caring for him.

He wrote her a letter, in which he disclaimed any further intention of forcing his commands upon her. He did not desire her presence ever again in his home unless she came of her free will, uninfluenced by family or friends; unless she could be the companion he had hoped for in marrying her, and in some measure return affection and respect for the love which he continued and would always continue to feel for her. This letter he sent out to the rigolet by a messenger early in the day. But she was not out on the rigolet, and had not been there.

The family turned instinctively to Monté-clin, and almost literally fell upon him for an explanation; he had been absent from home all night. There was much mystification in his answers, and a plain desire to mislead in his assurances of ignorance and innocence.

But with Cazeau there was no doubt or speculation when he accosted the young fellow. "Montéclin, w'at have you done with Athénaïse?" he questioned bluntly. They had met in the open road on horseback, just as Cazeau ascended the river bank before his house.

"W'at have you done to Athénaïse?" returned Montéclin for answer.

"I don't reckon you've considered yo' conduct by any light of decency an' propriety in encouraging yo' sister to such an action, but let me tell you"—

"Voyons! you can let me alone with yo' decency an' morality an' fiddlesticks. I know you mus' 'a' done Athénaïse pretty mean that she can't live with you; an' fo' my part, I'm mighty durn glad she had the spirit to quit you."

"I ain't in the humor to take any notice of yo' impertinence, Montéclin; but let me remine you that Athénaïse is nothing but a chile in character; besides that, she's my wife, an'

I hole you responsible fo' her safety an' welfare. If any harm of any description happens
to her, I'll strangle you, by God, like a rat, and
fling you in Cane river, if I have to hang fo'
it!" He had not lifted his voice. The only sign
of anger was a savage gleam in his eyes.

"I reckon you better keep yo' big talk fo'
the women, Cazeau," replied Montéclin, riding
away.

But he went doubly armed after that, and in-
timated that the precaution was not needless,
in view of the threats and menaces that were
abroad touching his personal safety.

VI.

Athénaïse reached her destination sound of
skin and limb, but a good deal flustered, a little frightened, and altogether excited and in-
terested by her unusual experiences.

Her destination was the house of Sylvie, on
Dauphine Street, in New Orleans,—a three-
story gray brick, standing directly on the banquette, with three broad stone steps leading to
the deep front entrance. From the second-story
balcony swung a small sign, conveying to pass-

ers-by the intelligence that within were "*chambres garnies.*"

It was one morning in the last week of April that Athénaïse presented herself at the Dauphine Street house. Sylvie was expecting her, and introduced her at once to her apartment, which was in the second story of the back ell, and accessible by an open, outside gallery. There was a yard below, paved with broad stone flagging; many fragrant flowering shrubs and plants grew in a bed along the side of the opposite wall, and others were distributed about in tubs and green boxes.

It was a plain but large enough room into which Athénaïse was ushered, with matting on the floor, green shades and Nottingham-lace curtains at the windows that looked out on the gallery, and furnished with a cheap walnut suit. But everything looked exquisitely clean, and the whole place smelled of cleanliness.

Athénaïse at once fell into the rocking-chair, with the air of exhaustion and intense relief of one who has come to the end of her troubles. Sylvie, entering behind her, laid the big traveling-bag on the floor and deposited the jacket on the bed.

She was a portly quadroon of fifty or there-about, clad in an ample *volante* of the old-fashioned purple calico so much affected by her class. She wore large golden hoop-earrings, and her hair was combed plainly, with every appearance of effort to smooth out the kinks. She had broad, coarse features, with a nose that turned up, exposing the wide nostrils, and that seemed to emphasize the loftiness and command of her bearing,—a dignity that in the presence of white people assumed a character of respectfulness, but never of obsequiousness. Sylvie believed firmly in maintaining the color-line, and would not suffer a white person, even a child, to call her "Madame Sylvie,"—a title which she exacted religiously, however, from those of her own race.

"I hope you be please' wid yo' room, ma-dame," she observed amiably. "Dat's de same room w'at yo' brother, M'sieur Miché, all time like w'en he come to New Orlean'. He well, M'sieur Miché? I receive' his letter las' week, an' dat same day a gent'man want I give 'im dat room. I say, 'No, dat room already in-gage'.' Ev-body like dat room on 'count it so quite (quiet). M'sieur Gouvernail, dere in nax' room, you can't pay 'im! He been stay t'ree year' in dat room; but all fix' up fine wid his own furn'ture an' books, 'tel you can't see! I say to 'im plenty time', 'M'sieur Gouvernail, w'y you don't take dat t'ree-story front, now, long it's empty?' He tells me, 'Leave me 'lone, Sylvie; I know a good room w'en I fine it, me.' "

She had been moving slowly and majestic-ally about the apartment, straightening and smoothing down bed and pillows, peering into ewer and basin, evidently casting an eye around to make sure that everything was as it should be.

"I sen' you some fresh water, madame," she offered upon retiring from the room. "An' w'en you want an't'ing, you jus' go out on de gall'ry an' call Pousette: she year you plain, —she right down dere in de kitchen."

Athénaïse was really not so exhausted as she had every reason to be after that interminable and circuitous way by which Montéclin had seen fit to have her conveyed to the city.

Would she ever forget that dark and truly dangerous midnight ride along the "coast" to the mouth of Cane river! There Montéclin had parted with her, after seeing her aboard the St. Louis and Shreveport packet which he knew would pass there before dawn. She had received instructions to disembark at the mouth of Red river, and there transfer to the first south-bound steamer for New Orleans; all of which instructions she had followed implicitly, even to making her way at once to Sylvie's upon her arrival in the city. Montéclin had enjoined secrecy and much caution; the clandestine nature of the affair gave it a savor of adventure which was highly pleasing to him. Eloping with his sister was only a little less engaging than eloping with some one else's sister.

But Montéclin did not do the *grand seigneur* by halves. He had paid Sylvie a whole month in advance for Athénaïse's board and lodging. Part of the sum he had been forced to borrow, it is true, but he was not niggardly.

Athénaïse was to take her meals in the house, which none of the other lodgers did; the one exception being that Mr. Gouvernail was served with breakfast on Sunday mornings.

Sylvie's clientèle came chiefly from the southern parishes; for the most part, people spending but a few days in the city. She prided herself upon the quality and highly respectable character of her patrons, who came and went unobtrusively.

The large parlor opening upon the front balcony was seldom used. Her guests were permitted to entertain in this sanctuary of elegance,—but they never did. She often rented it for the night to parties of respectable and discreet gentlemen desiring to enjoy a quiet game of cards outside the bosom of their families. The second-story hall also led by a long window out on the balcony. And Sylvie advised Athénaïse, when she grew weary of her back room, to go and sit on the front balcony, which was shady in the afternoon, and where she might find diversion in the sounds and sights of the street below.

Athénaïse refreshed herself with a bath, and was soon unpacking her few belongings, which she ranged neatly away in the bureau drawers and the armoire.

She had revolved certain plans in her mind during the past hour or so. Her present in-

tention was to live on indefinitely in this big,
cool, clean back room on Dauphine street. She
had thought seriously, for moments, of the convent, with all readiness to embrace the vows
of poverty and chastity; but what about obedience? Later, she intended, in some round-
about way, to give her parents and her husband the assurance of her safety and welfare;
reserving the right to remain unmolested and
lost to them. To live on at the expense of
Montéclin's generosity was wholly out of the
question, and Athénaïse meant to look about
for some suitable and agreeable employment.

The imperative thing to be done at present,
however, was to go out in search of material
for an inexpensive gown or two; for she found
herself in the painful predicament of a young
woman having almost literally nothing to wear.
She decided upon pure white for one, and some
sort of a sprigged muslin for the other.

VII.

On Sunday morning, two days after Athénaïse's arrival in the city, she went in to breakfast somewhat later than usual, to find two

covers laid at table instead of the one to which
she was accustomed.   She had been to mass,
and did not remove her hat, but put her fan,
parasol, and prayer-book aside.   The dining-
room was situated just beneath her own apartment, and, like all rooms of the house, was
large and airy; the floor was covered with a
glistening oil-cloth.

The small, round table, immaculately set,
was drawn near the open window.   There were
some tall plants in boxes on the gallery outside; and Pousette, a little, old, intensely black
woman, was splashing and dashing buckets of
water on the flagging, and talking loud in her
Creole patois to no one in particular.

A dish piled with delicate river-shrimps and
crushed ice was on the table; a caraffe of
crystal-clear water, a few *hors d'œuvres*, beside a small golden-brown crusty loaf of French
bread at each plate.   A half-bottle of wine and
the morning paper were set at the place opposite Athénaïse.

She had almost completed her breakfast
when Gouvernail came in and seated himself
at table.   He felt annoyed at finding his cher-
ished privacy invaded.   Sylvie was removing

the remains of a mutton-chop from before
Athénaïse, and serving her with a cup of café
au lait.

"M'sieur Gouvernail," offered Sylvie in her
most insinuating and impressive manner, "you
please leave me make you acquaint' wid Madame Cazeau. Dat's M'sieur Miché's sister;
you meet 'im two t'ree time', you rec'lec', an'
been one day to de race wid 'im. Madame
Cazeau, you please leave me make you acquaint' wid M'sieur Gouvernail."

Gouvernail expressed himself greatly pleased
to meet the sister of Monsieur Miché, of whom
he had not the slightest recollection. He inquired after Monsieur Miché's health, and politely offered Athénaïse a part of his newspaper,—the part which contained the Woman's
Page and the social gossip.

Athénaïse faintly remembered that Sylvie
had spoken of a Monsieur Gouvernail occupying the room adjoining hers, living amid luxu-
rious surroundings and a multitude of books.
She had not thought of him further than to
picture him a stout, middle-aged gentleman,
with a bushy beard turning gray, wearing large
gold-rimmed spectacles, and stooping some-

what from much bending over books and writing material. She had confused him in her mind with the likeness of some literary celebrity that she had run across in the advertising pages of a magazine.

Gouvernail's appearance was, in truth, in no sense striking. He looked older than thirty and younger than forty, was of medium height and weight, with a quiet, unobtrusive manner which seemed to ask that he be let alone. His hair was light brown, brushed carefully and parted in the middle. His mustache was brown, and so were his eyes, which had a mild, penetrating quality. He was neatly dressed in the fashion of the day; and his hands seemed to Athénaïse remarkably white and soft for a man's.

He had been buried in the contents of his newspaper, when he suddenly realized that some further little attention might be due to Miché's sister. He started to offer her a glass of wine, when he was surprised and relieved to find that she had quietly slipped away while he was absorbed in his own editorial on Corrupt Legislation.

Gouvernail finished his paper and smoked his cigar out on the gallery. He lounged about, gathered a rose for his buttonhole, and had his regular Sunday-morning confab with Pousette, to whom he paid a weekly stipend for brushing his shoes and clothing. He made a great pretense of haggling over the transaction, only to enjoy her uneasiness and garrulous excitement.

He worked or read in his room for a few hours, and when he quitted the house, at three in the afternoon, it was to return no more till late at night. It was his almost invariable custom to spend Sunday evenings out in the American quarter, among a congenial set of men and women,—*des esprits forts*, all of them, whose lives were irreproachable, yet whose opinions would startle even the traditional "sapeur," for whom "nothing is sacred." But for all his "advanced" opinions, Gouvernail was a liberal-minded fellow; a man or woman lost nothing of his respect by being married.

When he left the house in the afternoon, Athénaïse had already ensconced herself on the front balcony. He could see her through the jalousies when he passed on his way to the front entrance. She had not yet grown lonesome or homesick; the newness of her surroundings made them sufficiently entertaining. She found it diverting to sit there on the front balcony watching people pass by, even though there was no one to talk to. And then the comforting, comfortable sense of not being married!

She watched Gouvernail walk down the street, and could find no fault with his bearing. He could hear the sound of her rockers for some little distance. He wondered what the "poor little thing" was doing in the city, and meant to ask Sylvie about her when he should happen to think of it.

VIII.

The following morning, towards noon, when Gouvernail quitted his room, he was confronted by Athénaïse, exhibiting some confusion and trepidation at being forced to request a favor of him at so early a stage of their acquaintance. She stood in her doorway, and had evidently been sewing, as the thimble on her finger testified, as well as a long-threaded needle thrust in the bosom of her gown. She held a stamped but unaddressed letter in her hand.

And would Mr. Gouvernail be so kind as to address the letter to her brother, Mr. Montéclin Miché? She would hate to detain him with explanations this morning,—another time, perhaps,—but now she begged that he would give himself the trouble.

He assured her that it made no difference, that it was no trouble whatever; and he drew a fountain pen from his pocket and addressed the letter at her dictation, resting it on the inverted rim of his straw hat. She wondered a little at a man of his supposed erudition stumbling over the spelling of "Montéclin" and "Miché."

She demurred at overwhelming him with the additional trouble of posting it, but he succeeded in convincing her that so simple a task as the posting of a letter would not add an iota to the burden of the day. Moreover, he promised to carry it in his hand, and thus avoid any possible risk of forgetting it in his pocket.

After that, and after a second repetition of the favor, when she had told him that she had had a letter from Montéclin, and looked as if she wanted to tell him more, he felt that he knew her better. He felt that he knew her well enough to join her out on the balcony, one night, when he found her sitting there alone. He was not one who deliberately sought the society of women, but he was not wholly a bear. A little commiseration for Athénaïse's aloneness, perhaps some curiosity to know further what manner of woman she was, and the natural influence of her feminine charm were equal unconfessed factors in turning his steps towards the balcony when he discovered the shimmer of her white gown through the open hall window.

It was already quite late, but the day had been intensely hot, and neighboring balconies and doorways were occupied by chattering groups of humanity, loath to abandon the grateful freshness of the outer air. The voices about her served to reveal to Athénaïse the feeling of loneliness that was gradually coming over her.   Notwithstanding certain dormant impulses, she craved human sympathy and companionship.

She shook hands impulsively with Gouvernail, and told him how glad she was to see him. He was not prepared for such an admission, but it pleased him immensely, detecting as he did that the expression was as sincere as it was outspoken. He drew a chair up within comfortable conversational distance of Athénaïse, though he had no intention of talking more than was barely necessary to encourage Madame— He had actually forgotten her name!

He leaned an elbow on the balcony rail, and would have offered an opening remark about the oppressive heat of the day, but Athénaïse did not give him the opportunity. How glad she was to talk to some one, and how she talked!

An hour later she had gone to her room, and Gouvernail stayed smoking on the balcony. He knew her quite well after that hour's talk. It was not so much what she had said as what her half saying had revealed to his quick intelligence. He knew that she adored Montéclin, and he suspected that she adored Cazeau without being herself aware of it. He had gathered that she was self-willed, impulsive, innocent, ignorant, unsatisfied, dissatisfied; for had she not complained that things seemed all

wrongly arranged in this world, and no one
was permitted to be happy in his own way?
And he told her he was sorry she had discovered that primordial fact of existence so early
in life.

He commiserated her loneliness, and scanned
his bookshelves next morning for something to
lend her to read, rejecting everything that offered itself to his view. Philosophy was out
of the question, and so was poetry; that is,
such poetry as he possessed. He had not
sounded her literary tastes, and strongly suspected she had none; that she would have re-
jected The Duchess as readily as Mrs. Hum-
phry Ward. He compromised on a magazine.

It had entertained her passably, she admitted,
upon returning it. A New England story had
puzzled her, it was true, and a Creole tale had
offended her, but the pictures had pleased her
greatly, especially one which had reminded her
so strongly of Montéclin after a hard day's
ride that she was loath to give it up. It was
one of Remington's Cowboys, and Gouvernail
insisted upon her keeping it,—keeping the
magazine.

He spoke to her daily after that, and was always eager to render her some service or to do something towards her entertainment.

One afternoon he took her out to the lake end. She had been there once, some years before, but in winter, so the trip was comparatively new and strange to her. The large expanse of water studded with pleasure-boats, the sight of children playing merrily along the grassy palisades, the music, all enchanted her. Gouvernail thought her the most beautiful woman he had ever seen. Even her gown—the sprigged muslin—appeared to him the most charming one imaginable. Nor could anything be more becoming than the arrangement of her brown hair under the white sailor hat, all rolled back in a soft puff from her radiant face. And she carried her parasol and lifted her skirts and used her fan in ways that seemed quite unique and peculiar to herself, and which he considered almost worthy of study and imitation.

They did not dine out there at the water's edge, as they might have done, but returned early to the city to avoid the crowd. Athénaïse wanted to go home, for she said Sylvie would have dinner prepared and would be expecting her. But it was not difficult to persuade her to dine instead in the quiet little restaurant that he knew and liked, with its sanded floor, its secluded atmosphere, its delicious menu, and its obsequious waiter wanting to know what he might have the honor of serving to "monsieur et madame." No wonder he made the mistake, with Gouvernail assuming such an air of proprietorship! But Athénaïse was very tired after it all; the sparkle went out of her face, and she hung draggingly on his arm in walking home.

He was reluctant to part from her when she bade him good-night at her door and thanked him for the agreeable evening. He had hoped she would sit outside until it was time for him to regain the newspaper office. He knew that she would undress and get into her peignoir and lie upon her bed; and what he wanted to do, what he would have given much to do, was to go and sit beside her, read to her something restful, soothe her, do her bidding, whatever it might be. Of course there was no use in thinking of that. But he was surprised at his growing desire to be serving her. She gave him an opportunity sooner than he looked for.

"Mr. Gouvernail," she called from her room, "will you be so kine as to call Pousette an' tell her she fo'got to bring my ice-water?"

He was indignant at Pousette's negligence, and called severely to her over the banisters. He was sitting before his own door, smoking. He knew that Athénaïse had gone to bed, for her room was dark, and she had opened the slats of the door and windows. Her bed was near a window.

Pousette came flopping up with the ice-water, and with a hundred excuses: "Mo pa oua vou à tab c'te lanuite, mo cri vou pé gagni déja là-bas; parole! Vou pas cri conté ça Madame Sylvie?" She had not seen Athénaïse at table, and thought she was gone. She swore to this, and hoped Madame Sylvie would not be informed of her remissness.

A little later Athénaïse lifted her voice again: "Mr. Gouvernail, did you remark that young man sitting on the opposite side from us, coming in, with a gray coat an' a blue ban' aroun' his hat?"

Of course Gouvernail had not noticed any such individual, but he assured Athénaïse that he had observed the young fellow particularly.

"Don't you think he looked something,— not very much, of co'se,—but don't you think he had a little faux-air of Montéclin?"

"I think he looked strikingly like Monté-clin," asserted Gouvernail, with the one idea of prolonging the conversation. "I meant to call your attention to the resemblance, and something drove it out of my head."

"The same with me," returned Athénaïse. "Ah, my dear Montéclin! I wonder w'at he is doing now?"

"Did you receive any news, any letter from him to-day?" asked Gouvernail, determined that if the conversation ceased it should not be through lack of effort on his part to sustain it.

"Not to-day, but yesterday. He tells me that maman was so distracted with uneasiness that finally, to pacify her, he was fo'ced to con-fess that he knew w'ere I was, but that he was boun' by a vow of secrecy not to reveal it. But Cazeau has not noticed him or spoken to him since he threaten' to throw po' Montéclin in Cane river. You know Cazeau wrote me a

letter the morning I lef', thinking I had gone
to the rigolet. An' maman opened it, an' said
it was full of the mos' noble sentiments, an' she
wanted Montéclin to sen' it to me; but Montéclin refuse' poin' blank, so he wrote to me."

Gouvernail preferred to talk of Montéclin.
He pictured Cazeau as unbearable, and did not
like to think of him.

A little later Athénaïse called out, "Good-
night, Mr. Gouvernail."

"Good-night," he returned reluctantly. And
when he thought that she was sleeping, he got
up and went away to the midnight pandemon-
ium of his newspaper office.

IX.

Athénaïse could not have held out through
the month had it not been for Gouvernail. With
the need of caution and secrecy always uppermost in her mind, she made no new acquaintances, and she did not seek out persons already known to her; however, she knew so few,
it required little effort to keep out of their way.
As for Sylvie, almost every moment of her
time was occupied in looking after her house;

and, moreover, her deferential attitude towards
her lodgers forbade anything like the gossipy
chats in which Athénaïse might have conde-
scended sometimes to indulge with her land-
lady. The transient lodgers, who came and
went, she never had occasion to meet. Hence
she was entirely dependent upon Gouvernail
for company.

He appreciated the situation fully; and every
moment that he could spare from his work he
devoted to her entertainment. She liked to be
out of doors, and they strolled together in the
summer twilight through the mazes of the old
French quarter. They went again to the lake
end, and stayed for hours on the water; returning so late that the streets through which they
passed were silent and deserted. On Sunday
morning he arose at an unconscionable hour to
take her to the French market, knowing that
the sights and sounds there would interest her.
And he did not join the intellectual coterie in
the afternoon, as he usually did, but placed
himself all day at the disposition and service of
Athénaïse.

Notwithstanding all, his manner toward her
was tactful, and evinced intelligence and a deep

knowledge of her character, surprising upon so brief an acquaintance. For the time he was everything to her that she would have him; he replaced home and friends. Sometimes she wondered if he had ever loved a woman. She could not fancy him loving any one passionately, rudely, offensively, as Cazeau loved her. Once she was so naïve as to ask him outright if he had ever been in love, and he assured her promptly that he had not. She thought it an admirable trait in his character, and esteemed him greatly therefor.

He found her crying one night, not openly or violently. She was leaning over the gallery rail, watching the toads that hopped about in the moonlight, down on the damp flagstones of the courtyard. There was an oppressively sweet odor rising from the cape jessamine. Pousette was down there, mumbling and quarreling with some one, and seeming to be having it all her own way,—as well she might, when her companion was only a black cat that had come in from a neighboring yard to keep her company.

Athénaïse did admit feeling heart-sick, body-sick, when he questioned her; she supposed it

was nothing but homesick. A letter from Montéclin had stirred her all up. She longed for
her mother, for Montéclin; she was sick for a
sight of the cotton-fields, the scent of the
ploughed earth, for the dim, mysterious charm
of the woods, and the old tumble-down home
on the Bon Dieu.

As Gouvernail listened to her, a wave of pity
and tenderness swept through him. He took
her hands and pressed them against him. He
wondered what would happen if he were to
put his arms around her.

He was hardly prepared for what happened,
but he stood it courageously. She twined her
arms around his neck and wept outright on
his shoulder; the hot tears scalding his cheek
and neck, and her whole body shaken in his
arms. The impulse was powerful to strain her
to him; the temptation was fierce to seek her
lips; but he did neither.

He understood a thousand times better than
she herself understood it that he was acting as
substitute for Montéclin. Bitter as the conviction was, he accepted it. He was patient;
he could wait. He hoped some day to hold

her with a lover's arms. That she was married
made no particle of difference to Gouvernail.
He could not conceive or dream of it making
a difference. When the time came that she
wanted him,—as he hoped and believed it
would come,—he felt he would have a right
to her. So long as she did not want him, he
had no right to her,—no more than her husband had. It was very hard to feel her warm
breath and tears upon his cheek, and her struggling bosom pressed against him and her soft
arms clinging to him and his whole body and
soul aching for her, and yet to make no sign.

He tried to think what Montéclin would
have said and done, and to act accord-
ingly. He stroked her hair, and held her in a
gentle embrace, until the tears dried and the
sobs ended. Before releasing herself she kissed
him against the neck; she had to love somebody in her own way! Even that he endured
like a stoic. But it was well he left her, to
plunge into the thick of rapid, breathless, exacting work till nearly dawn.

Athénaïse was greatly soothed, and slept
well. The touch of friendly hands and caress-

ing arms had been very grateful. Henceforward she would not be lonely and unhappy, with Gouvernail there to comfort her.

X.

The fourth week of Athénaïse's stay in the city was drawing to a close. Keeping in view the intention which she had of finding some suitable and agreeable employment, she had made a few tentatives in that direction. But with the exception of two little girls who had promised to take piano lessons at a price that would be embarrassing to mention, these attempts had been fruitless. Moreover, the homesickness kept coming back, and Gouvernail was not always there to drive it away.

She spent much of her time weeding and pottering among the flowers down in the courtyard. She tried to take an interest in the black cat, and a mockingbird that hung in a cage outside the kitchen door, and a disreputable parrot that belonged to the cook next door, and swore hoarsely all day long in bad French.

Beside, she was not well; she was not herself,
as she told Sylvie. The climate of New Orleans did not agree with her. Sylvie was distressed to learn this, as she felt in some measure
responsible for the health and well-being of
Monsieur Miché's sister; and she made it her
duty to inquire closely into the nature and
character of Athénaïse's malaise.

Sylvie was very wise, and Athénaïse was
very ignorant. The extent of her ignorance
and the depth of her subsequent enlightenment
were bewildering. She stayed a long, long
time quite still, quite stunned, after her interview with Sylvie, except for the short,
uneven breathing that ruffled her bosom.
Her whole being was steeped in a wave of
ecstasy. When she finally arose from the
chair in which she had been seated, and looked
at herself in the mirror, a face met hers which
she seemed to see for the first time, so transfigured was it with wonder and rapture.

One mood quickly followed another, in this
new turmoil of her senses, and the need of action became uppermost. Her mother must
know at once, and her mother must tell Montéclin. And Cazeau must know. As she

thought of him, the first purely sensuous tremor of her life swept over her. She half whispered his name, and the sound of it brought red blotches into her cheeks. She spoke it over and over, as if it were some new, sweet sound born out of darkness and confusion, and reaching her for the first time. She was impatient to be with him. Her whole passionate nature was aroused as if by a miracle.

She seated herself to write to her husband. The letter he would get in the morning, and she would be with him at night. What would he say? How would he act? She knew that he would forgive her, for had he not written a letter?—and a pang of resentment toward Montéclin shot through her. What did he mean by withholding that letter? How dared he not have sent it?

Athénaïse attired herself for the street, and went out to post the letter which she had penned with a single thought, a spontaneous impulse. It would have seemed incoherent to most people, but Cazeau would understand.

She walked along the street as if she had fallen heir to some magnificent inheritance. On her face was a look of pride and satisfaction

that passers-by noticed and admired.   She
wanted to talk to some one, to tell some person; and she stopped at the corner and told
the oyster-woman, who was Irish, and who
God-blessed her, and wished prosperity to the
race of Cazeaus for generations to come. She
held the oyster-woman's fat, dirty little baby in
her arms and scanned it curiously and observ-
ingly, as if a baby were a phenomenon that she
encountered for the first time in life.   She even
kissed it!

Then what a relief it was to Athénaïse to
walk the streets without dread of being seen
and recognized by some chance acquaintance
from Red river!   No one could have said now
that she did not know her own mind.

She went directly from the oyster-woman's
to the office of Harding & Offdean, her husband's merchants; and it was with such an air
of partnership, almost proprietorship, that she
demanded a sum of money on her husband's
account, they gave it to her as unhesitatingly as
they would have handed it over to Cazeau himself. When Mr. Harding, who knew her,
asked politely after her health, she turned so
rosy and looked so conscious, he thought it a

great pity for so pretty a woman to be such a little goose.

Athénaïse entered a dry-goods store and bought all manner of things,—little presents for nearly everybody she knew. She bought whole bolts of sheerest, softest, downiest white stuff; and when the clerk, in trying to meet her wishes, asked if she intended it for infant's use, she could have sunk through the floor, and wondered how he might have suspected it.

As it was Montéclin who had taken her away from her husband, she wanted it to be Montéclin who should take her back to him. So she wrote him a very curt note,—in fact it was a postal card,—asking that he meet her at the train on the evening following. She felt convinced that after what had gone before, Cazeau would await her at their own home; and she preferred it so.

Then there was the agreeable excitement of getting ready to leave, of packing up her things. Pousette kept coming and going, coming and going; and each time that she quitted the room it was with something that Athénaïse had given her,—a handkerchief, a petticoat, a pair of stockings with two tiny holes at the toes, some broken prayer-beads, and finally a silver dollar.

Next it was Sylvie who came along bearing a gift of what she called "a set of pattern'," —things of complicated design which never could have been obtained in any new-fangled bazaar or pattern-store, that Sylvie had acquired of a foreign lady of distinction whom she had nursed years before at the St. Charles hotel. Athénaïse accepted and handled them with reverence, fully sensible of the great compliment and favor, and laid them religiously away in the trunk which she had lately acquired.

She was greatly fatigued after the day of unusual exertion, and went early to bed and to sleep. All day long she had not once thought of Gouvernail, and only did think of him when aroused for a brief instant by the sound of his foot-falls on the gallery, as he passed in going to his room. He had hoped to find her up, waiting for him.

But the next morning he knew. Some one must have told him. There was no subject known to her which Sylvie hesitated to discuss in detail with any man of suitable years and discretion.

Athénaïse found Gouvernail waiting with a carriage to convey her to the railway station. A momentary pang visited her for having forgotten him so completely, when he said to her, "Sylvie tells me you are going away this morning."

He was kind, attentive, and amiable, as usual, but respected to the utmost the new dignity and reserve that her manner had developed since yesterday. She kept looking from the carriage window, silent, and embarrassed as Eve after losing her ignorance. He talked of the muddy streets and the murky morning, and of Montéclin. He hoped she would find everything comfortable and pleasant in the country, and trusted she would inform him whenever she came to visit the city again. He talked as if afraid or mistrustful of silence and himself.

At the station she handed him her purse, and he bought her ticket, secured for her a comfortable section, checked her trunk, and got all the bundles and things safely aboard the train. She felt very grateful. He pressed her hand warmly, lifted his hat, and left her. He was a man of intelligence, and took defeat gracefully; that was all. But as he made his way back to the carriage, he was thinking, "By heaven, it hurts, it hurts!"

XI.

Athénaïse spent a day of supreme happiness and expectancy. The fair sight of the country unfolding itself before her was balm to her vision and to her soul. She was charmed with the rather unfamiliar, broad, clean sweep of the sugar plantations, with their monster sugar-houses, their rows of neat cabins like little villages of a single street, and their impressive homes standing apart amid clusters of trees. There were sudden glimpses of a bayou curling between sunny, grassy banks, or creeping sluggishly out from a tangled growth of wood, and brush, and fern, and poison-vines, and palmettos. And passing through the long stretches of monotonous woodlands, she would close her eyes and taste in anticipation the moment of her meeting with Cazeau. She could think of nothing but him.

It was night when she reached her station. There was Montéclin, as she had expected, waiting for her with a two-seated buggy, to which he had hitched his own swift-footed, spirited pony. It was good, he felt, to have her back on any terms; and he had no fault to find since she came of her own choice. He more than suspected the cause of her coming; her eyes and her voice and her foolish little manner went far in revealing the secret that was brimming over in her heart. But after he had deposited her at her own gate, and as he continued his way toward the rigolet, he could not help feeling that the affair had taken a very disappointing, an ordinary, a most commonplace turn, after all. He left her in Cazeau's keeping.

Her husband lifted her out of the buggy, and neither said a word until they stood together within the shelter of the gallery. Even then they did not speak at first. But Athénaïse turned to him with an appealing gesture. As he clasped her in his arms, he felt the yielding of her whole body against him. He felt her lips for the first time respond to the passion of his own.

The country night was dark and warm and still, save for the distant notes of an accordion which some one was playing in a cabin away off. A little negro baby was crying somewhere. As Athénaïse withdrew from her husband's embrace, the sound arrested her.

"Listen, Cazeau! How Juliette's baby is crying! Pauvre ti chou, I wonder w'at is the matter with it?"

After the Winter

After the Winter

I.

TRÉZINIE, the blacksmith's daughter, stepped out upon the gallery just as M'sieur Michel passed by. He did not notice the girl but walked straight on down the village street.

His seven hounds skulked, as usual, about him. At his side hung his powder-horn, and on his shoulder a gunny-bag slackly filled with game that he carried to the store. A broad felt hat shaded his bearded face and in his hand he carelessly swung his old-fashioned rifle. It was doubtless the same with which he had slain so many people, Trézinie shudderingly reflected. For Cami, the cobbler's son—who must have known—had often related to her how this man had killed two Choctaws, as many Texans, a free mulatto and numberless blacks, in that vague locality known as "the hills."

Older people who knew better took little trouble to correct this ghastly record that a younger generation had scored against him. They themselves had come to half-believe that M'sieur Michel might be capable of anything, living as he had, for so many years, apart from humanity, alone with his hounds in a kennel of a cabin on the hill. The time seemed to most of them fainter than a memory when, a lusty young fellow of twenty-five, he had cultivated his strip of land across the lane from Les Chêniers; when home and toil and wife and child were so many benedictions that he humbly thanked heaven for having given him.

But in the early '60's he went with his friend Duplan and the rest of the "Louisiana Tigers." He came back with some of them. He came to find—well, death may lurk in a peaceful valley lying in wait to ensnare the toddling feet of little ones. Then, there are women—there are wives with thoughts that roam and grow wanton with roaming; women whose pulses are stirred by strange voices and eyes that woo; women who forget the claims of yesterday, the hopes of to-morrow, in the impetuous clutch of to-day.

But that was no reason, some people thought, why he should have cursed men who found their blessings where they had left them —cursed God, who had abandoned him.

Persons who met him upon the road had long ago stopped greeting him. What was the use? He never answered them; he spoke to no one; he never so much as looked into men's faces. When he bartered his game and fish at the village store for powder and shot and such scant food as he needed, he did so with few words and less courtesy. Yet feeble as it was, this was the only link that held him to his fellow-beings.

Strange to say, the sight of M'sieur Michel, though more forbidding than ever that delightful spring afternoon, was so suggestive to Trézinie as to be almost an inspiration.

It was Easter eve and the early part of April. The whole earth seemed teeming with new, green, vigorous life everywhere—except the arid spot that immediately surrounded Trézinie. It was no use; she had tried. Nothing would grow among those cinders that filled the yard; in that atmosphere of smoke and flame that was constantly belching from the forge

where her father worked at his trade. There
were wagon wheels, bolts and bars of iron,
plowshares and all manner of unpleasant-look-
ing things littering the bleak, black yard;
nothing green anywhere except a few weeds
that would force themselves into fence corners.
And Trézinie knew that flowers belong to
Easter time, just as dyed eggs do. She had
plenty of eggs; no one had more or prettier
ones; she was not going to grumble about that.
But she did feel distressed because she had not
a flower to help deck the altar on Easter morning.   And every one else seemed to have them
in such abundance! There was 'Dame Suzanne among her roses across the way. She
must have clipped a hundred since noon. An
hour ago Trézinie had seen the carriage from
Les Chêniers pass by on its way to church with
Mamzelle Euphrasie's pretty head looking like
a picture enframed with the Easter lilies that
filled the vehicle.

For the twentieth time Trézinie walked out
upon the gallery. She saw M'sieur Michel
and thought of the pine hill. When she
thought of the hill she thought of the flowers
that grew there—free as sunshine. The girl

gave a joyous spring that changed to a faran-
dole as her feet twinkled across the rough,
loose boards of the gallery.

"Hé, Cami!" she cried, clapping her hands
together.

Cami rose from the bench where he sat peg-
ging away at the clumsy sole of a shoe, and
came lazily to the fence that divided his abode
from Trézinie's.

"Well, w'at?" he inquired with heavy amiability.   She leaned far over the railing to better communicate with him.

"You'll go with me yonda on the hill to pick
flowers fo' Easter, Cami? I'm goin' to take
La Fringante along, too, to he'p with the
baskets. W'at you say?"

"No!" was the stolid reply. "I'm boun' to
finish them shoe', if it is fo' a nigga."

"Not now," she returned impatiently; "to-
morrow mo'nin' at sun-up.   An' I tell you,
Cami, my flowers'll beat all! Look yonda at
'Dame Suzanne pickin' her roses a'ready. An'
Mamzelle Euphraisie she's car'ied her lilies an'
gone, her.   You tell me all that's goin' be fresh
to-moro'!"

"Jus' like you say," agreed the boy, turning to resume his work. "But you want to mine out fo' the ole possum up in the wood. Let M'sieu Michel set eyes on you!" and he raised his arms as if aiming with a gun. "Pim, pam, poum! No mo' Trézinie, no mo' Cami, no mo' La Fringante—all stretch'!"

The possible risk which Cami so vividly foreshadowed but added a zest to Trézinie's projected excursion.

II.

It was hardly sun-up on the following morning when the three children—Trézinie, Cami and the little negress, La Fringante—were filling big, flat Indian baskets from the abundance of brilliant flowers that studded the hill.

In their eagerness they had ascended the slope and penetrated deep into the forest without thought of M'sieur Michel or of his abode. Suddenly, in the dense wood, they came upon his hut—low, forbidding, seeming to scowl rebuke upon them for their intrusion.

La Fringante dropped her basket, and, with a cry, fled. Cami looked as if he wanted to

do the same. But Trézinie, after the first tremor, saw that the ogre himself was away. The
wooden shutter of the one window was closed.
The door, so low that even a small man must
have stooped to enter it, was secured with a
chain. Absolute silence reigned, except for
the whirr of wings in the air, the fitful notes of
a bird in the treetop.

"Can't you see it's nobody there!" cried Trézinie impatiently.

La Fringante, distracted between curiosity
and terror, had crept cautiously back again.
Then they all peeped through the wide chinks
between the logs of which the cabin was built.

M'sieur Michel had evidently begun the construction of his house by felling a huge tree,
whose remaining stump stood in the centre of
the hut, and served him as a table. This prim-
itive table was worn smooth by twenty-five
years of use. Upon it were such humble uten-
sils as the man required. Everything within
the hovel, the sleeping bunk, the one seat,
were as rude as a savage would have fashioned
them.

The stolid Cami could have stayed for hours
with his eyes fastened to the aperture, morbid-

ly seeking some dead, mute sign of that awful pastime with which he believed M'sieur Michel was accustomed to beguile his solitude. But Trézinie was wholly possessed by the thought of her Easter offerings. She wanted flowers and flowers, fresh with the earth and crisp with dew.

When the three youngsters scampered down the hill again there was not a purple verbena left about M'sieur Michel's hut; not a May apple blossom, not a stalk of crimson phlox— hardly a violet.

He was something of a savage, feeling that the solitude belonged to him. Of late there had been forming within his soul a sentiment toward man, keener than indifference, bitter as hate. He was coming to dread even that brief intercourse with others into which his traffic forced him.

So when M'sieur Michel returned to his hut, and with his quick, accustomed eye saw that his woods had been despoiled, rage seized him. It was not that he loved the flowers that were gone more than he loved the stars, or the wind that trailed across the hill, but they belonged to and were a part of that life which he had

made for himself, and which he wanted to live
alone and unmolested.

Did not those flowers help him to keep his
record of time that was passing? They had no
right to vanish until the hot May days were
upon him. How else should he know? Why
had these people, with whom he had nothing in
common, intruded upon his privacy and vio-
lated it? What would they not rob him of
next?

He knew well enough it was Easter; he had
heard and seen signs yesterday in the store
that told him so. And he guessed that his
woods had been rifled to add to the mummery
of the day.

M'sieur Michel sat himself moodily down
beside his table—centuries old—and brooded.
He did not even notice his hounds that were
pleading to be fed. As he revolved in his
mind the event of the morning—innocent as it
was in itself—it grew in importance and assumed a significance not at first apparent. He
could not remain passive under pressure of its
disturbance. He rose to his feet, every impulse aggressive, urging him to activity. He
would go down among those people all gath-

ered together, blacks and whites, and face them
for once and all. He did not know what he
would say to them, but it would be defiance—
something to voice the hate that oppressed
him.

The way down the hill, then across a piece of
flat, swampy woodland and through the lane
to the village was so familiar that it required
no attention from him to follow it.   His
thoughts were left free to revel in the humor
that had driven him from his kennel.

As he walked down the village street he saw
plainly that the place was deserted save for the
appearance of an occasional negress, who
seemed occupied with preparing the midday
meal.   But about the church scores of horses
were fastened; and M'sieur Michel could see
that the edifice was thronged to the very threshold.

He did not once hesitate, but obeying the
force that impelled him to face the people wherever they might be, he was soon standing with
the crowd within the entrance of the church.
His broad, robust shoulders had forced space
for himself, and his leonine head stood higher
than any there.

"Take off yo' hat!"

It was an indignant mulatto who addressed him. M'sieur Michel instinctively did as he was bidden. He saw confusedly that there was a mass of humanity close to him, whose contact and atmosphere affected him strangely. He saw his wild-flowers, too. He saw them plainly, in bunches and festoons, among the Easter lilies and roses and geraniums. He was going to speak out, now; he had the right to and he would, just as soon as that clamor overhead would cease.

"Bonté divine! M'sieur Michel!" whispered 'Dame Suzanne tragically to her neighbor. Trézinie heard. Cami saw. They exchanged an electric glance, and tremblingly bowed their heads low.

M'sieur Michel looked wrathfully down at the puny mulatto who had ordered him to remove his hat. Why had he obeyed? That initial act of compliance had somehow weakened his will, his resolution. But he would regain firmness just as soon as that clamor above gave him chance to speak.

It was the organ filling the small edifice with volumes of sound. It was the voices of men and women mingling in the "Gloria in excelsis Deo!"

The words bore no meaning for him apart from the old familiar strain which he had known as a child and chanted himself in that same organ-loft years ago. How it went on and on! Would it never cease! It was like a menace; like a voice reaching out from the dead past to taunt him.

"Gloria in excelsis Deo!" over and over! How the deep basso rolled it out! How the tenor and alto caught it up and passed it on to be lifted by the high, flute-like ring of the soprano, till all mingled again in the wild pæan, "Gloria in excelsis!"

How insistent was the refrain! and where, what, was that mysterious, hidden quality in it; the power which was overcoming M'sieur Michel, stirring within him a turmoil that bewildered him?

There was no use in trying to speak, or in wanting to. His throat could not have uttered a sound. He wanted to escape, that was all. "Bonæ voluntatis,"—he bent his head as if before a beating storm. "Gloria! Gloria! Gloria!" He must fly; he must save himself, re-

gain his hill where sights and odors and sounds
and saints or devils would cease to molest him.
"In excelsis Deo!" He retreated, forcing his
way backward to the door. He dragged his
hat down over his eyes and staggered away
down the road. But the refrain pursued him
—"Pax! pax! pax!"—fretting him like a lash.
He did not slacken his pace till the tones grew
fainter than an echo, floating, dying away in
an "in excelsis!" When he could hear it no
longer he stopped and breathed a sigh of rest
and relief.

III.

All day long M'sieur Michel stayed about
his hut engaged in some familiar employment
that he hoped might efface the unaccountable
impressions of the morning. But his restlessness was unbounded. A longing had sprung
up within him as sharp as pain and not to be
appeased. At once, on this bright, warm Easter
morning the voices that till now had filled his
solitude became meaningless. He stayed mute
and uncomprehending before them. Their significance had vanished before the driving want

for human sympathy and companionship that
had reawakened in his soul.

When night came on he walked through the
woods down the slant of the hill again.

"It mus' be all fill' up with weeds," muttered M'sieur Michel to himself as he went.
"Ah, Bon Dieu! with trees, Michel, with trees
—in twenty-five years, man."

He had not taken the road to the village,
but was pursuing a different one in which his
feet had not walked for many days. It led him
along the river bank for a distance. The narrow stream, stirred by the restless breeze,
gleamed in the moonlight that was flooding the
land.

As he went on and on, the scent of the new-
plowed earth that had been from the first
keenly perceptible, began to intoxicate him. He
wanted to kneel and bury his face in it. He
wanted to dig into it; turn it over. He
wanted to scatter the seed again as he had done
long ago, and watch the new, green life spring
up as if at his bidding.

When he turned away from the river, and
had walked a piece down the lane that divided
Joe Duplan's plantation from that bit of land

that had once been his, he wiped his eyes to drive away the mist that was making him see things as they surely could not be.

He had wanted to plant a hedge that time before he went away, but he had not done so. Yet there was the hedge before him, just as he had meant it to be, and filling the night with fragrance. A broad, low gate divided its length, and over this he leaned and looked before him in amazement. There were no weeds as he had fancied; no trees except the scattered live oaks that he remembered.

Could that row of hardy fig trees, old, squat and gnarled, be the twigs that he himself had set one day into the ground? One raw December day when there was a fine, cold mist falling. The chill of it breathed again upon him; the memory was so real. The land did not look as if it ever had been plowed for a field. It was a smooth, green meadow, with cattle huddled upon the cool sward, or moving with slow, stately tread as they nibbled the tender shoots.

There was the house unchanged, gleaming white in the moon, seeming to invite him beneath its calm shelter. He wondered who

dwelt within it now. Whoever it was he would
not have them find him, like a prowler, there
at the gate. But he would come again and
again like this at nighttime, to gaze and refresh
his spirit.

A hand had been laid upon M'sieur Michel's
shoulder and some one called his name. Startled, he turned to see who accosted him.

"Duplan!"

The two men who had not exchanged speech
for so many years stood facing each other for
a long moment in silence.

"I knew you would come back some day,
Michel. It was a long time to wait, but you
have come home at last."

M'sieur Michel cowered instinctively and
lifted his hands with expressive deprecatory
gesture. "No, no; it's no place for me, Joe;
no place!"

"Isn't a man's home a place for him, Michel?" It seemed less a question than an assertion, charged with gentle authority.

"Twenty-five years, Duplan; twenty-five
years! It's no use; it's too late."

"You see, I have used it," went on the planter, quietly, ignoring M'sieur Michel's protesta-

tions. "Those are my cattle grazing off there. The house has served me many a time to lodge guests or workmen, for whom I had no room at Les Chêniers. I have not exhausted the soil with any crops. I had not the right to do that. Yet am I in your debt, Michel, and ready to settle en bon ami."

The planter had opened the gate and entered the inclosure, leading M'sieur Michel with him. Together they walked toward the house.

Language did not come readily to either— one so unaccustomed to hold intercourse with men; both so stirred with memories that would have rendered any speech painful. When they had stayed long in a silence which was eloquent of tenderness, Joe Duplan spoke:

"You know how I tried to see you, Michel, to speak with you, and you never would."

M'sieur Michel answered with but a gesture that seemed a supplication.

"Let the past all go, Michel. Begin your new life as if the twenty-five years that are gone had been a long night, from which you have only awakened. Come to me in the morning," he added with quick resolution, "for

a horse and a plow." He had taken the key
of the house from his pocket and placed it in
M'sieur Michel's hand.

"A horse?" M'sieur Michel repeated uncer-
tainly; "a plow! Oh, it's too late, Duplan; too
late."

"It isn't too late. The land has rested all
these years, man; it's fresh, I tell you; and rich
as gold. Your crop will be the finest in the
land." He held out his hand and M'sieur
Michel pressed it without a word in reply,
save a muttered "Mon ami."

Then he stood there watching the planter
disappear behind the high, clipped hedge.

He held out his arms. He could not have
told if it was toward the retreating figure, or in
welcome to an infinite peace that seemed to
descend upon him and envelop him.

All the land was radiant except the hill far
off that was in black shadow against the sky.

Polydore

Polydore

I T was often said that Polydore was the
stupidest boy to be found "from the
mouth of Cane river plumb to Natchitoches." Hence it was an easy matter to persuade him, as meddlesome and mischievous
people sometimes tried to do, that he was an
overworked and much abused individual.

It occurred one morning to Polydore to
wonder what would happen if he did not get
up. He hardly expected the world to stop
turning on its axis; but he did in a way believe
that the machinery of the whole plantation
would come to a standstill.

He had awakened at the usual hour,—about
daybreak,—and instead of getting up at once,
as was his custom, he re-settled himself between the sheets. There he lay, peering out
through the dormer window into the gray
morning that was deliciously cool after the hot

summer night, listening to familiar sounds that came from the barn-yard, the fields and woods beyond, heralding the approach of day.

A little later there were other sounds, no less familiar or significant; the roll of the wagon-wheels; the distant call of a negro's voice; Aunt Siney's shuffling step as she crossed the gallery, bearing to Mamzelle Adélaïde and old Monsieur José their early coffee.

Polydore had formed no plan and had thought only vaguely upon results. He lay in a half-slumber awaiting developments, and philosophically resigned to any turn which the affair might take. Still he was not quite ready with an answer when Jude came and thrust his head in at the door.

"Mista Polydore! O Mista Polydore! You 'sleep?"

"W'at you want?"

"Dan 'low he ain' gwine wait yonda wid de wagon all day. Say does you inspect 'im to pack dat freight f'om de landing by hisse'f?"

"I reckon he got it to do, Jude. I ain' going to get up, me."

"You ain' gwine git up?"

"No; I'm sick. I'm going stay in bed. Go 'long and le' me sleep."

The next one to invade Polydore's privacy was Mamzelle Adélaïde herself. It was no small effort for her to mount the steep, narrow stairway to Polydore's room. She seldom penetrated to these regions under the roof. He could hear the stairs creak beneath her weight, and knew that she was panting at every step. Her presence seemed to crowd the small room; for she was stout and rather tall, and her flowing muslin wrapper swept majestically from side to side as she walked.

Mamzelle Adélaïde had reached middle age, but her face was still fresh with its mignon features; and her brown eyes at the moment were round with astonishment and alarm.

"W'at's that I hear, Polydore? They tell me you're sick!" She went and stood beside the bed, lifting the mosquito bar that settled upon her head and fell about her like a veil.

Polydore's eyes blinked, and he made no attempt to answer. She felt his wrist softly with the tips of her fingers, and rested her hand for a moment on his low forehead beneath the shock of black hair.

"But you don't seem to have any fever, Polydore!"

"No," hesitatingly, feeling himself forced to make some reply. "It's a kine of—a kine of pain, like you might say. It kitch me yere in the knee, and it goes 'long like you stickin' a knife clean down in my heel. Aie! Oh, la-la!" expressions of pain wrung from him by Mamzelle Adélaïde gently pushing aside the covering to examine the afflicted member.

"My patience! but that leg is swollen, yes, Polydore." The limb, in fact, seemed drop-sical, but if Mamzelle Adélaïde had bethought her of comparing it with the other one, she would have found the two corresponding in their proportions to a nicety. Her kind face expressed the utmost concern, and she quitted Polydore feeling pained and ill at ease.

For one of the aims of Mamzelle Adélaïde's existence was to do the right thing by this boy, whose mother, a 'Cadian hill woman, had begged her with dying breath to watch over the temporal and spiritual welfare of her son; above all, to see that he did not follow in the slothful footsteps of an over-indolent father.

Polydore's scheme worked so marvellously to his comfort and pleasure that he wondered at not having thought of it before. He ate with keen relish the breakfast which Jude brought to him on a tray. Even old Monsieur José was concerned, and made his way up to Polydore, bringing a number of picture-papers for his entertainment, a palm-leaf fan and a cow-bell, with which to summon Jude when necessary and which he placed within easy reach.

As Polydore lay on his back fanning luxuriously, it seemed to him that he was enjoying a foretaste of paradise. Only once did he shudder with apprehension. It was when he heard Aunt Siney, with lifted voice, recommending to "wrop the laig up in bacon fat; de oniest way to draw out de misery."

The thought of a healthy leg swathed in bacon fat on a hot day in July was enough to intimidate a braver heart than Polydore's. But the suggestion was evidently not adopted, for he heard no more of the bacon fat. In its stead he became acquainted with the not unpleasant sting of a soothing liniment which

Jude rubbed into the leg at intervals during the day.

He kept the limb propped on a pillow, stiff and motionless, even when alone and unobserved. Toward evening he fancied that it really showed signs of inflammation, and he was quite sure it pained him.

It was a satisfaction to all to see Polydore appear down-stairs the following afternoon. He limped painfully, it is true, and clutched wildly at anything in his way that offered a momentary support. His acting was clumsily overdrawn; and by less guileless souls than Mamzelle Adélaïde and her father would have surely been suspected. But these two only thought with deep concern of means to make him comfortable.

They seated him on the shady back gallery in an easy-chair, with his leg propped up before him.

"He inhe'its dat rheumatism," proclaimed Aunt Siney, who affected the manner of an oracle. "I see dat boy's granpap, many times, all twis' up wid rheumatism twell his head sot down on his body, hine side befo'. He got to keep outen de jew in de mo'nin's, and he 'bleege to w'ar red flannen."

Monsieur José, with flowing white locks enframing his aged face, leaned upon his cane and contemplated the boy with unflagging attention. Polydore was beginning to believe himself a worthy object as a center of interest.

Mamzelle Adélaïde had but just returned from a long drive in the open buggy, from a mission which would have fallen to Polydore had he not been disabled by this unlooked-for illness. She had thoughtlessly driven across the country at an hour when the sun was hottest, and now she sat panting and fanning herself; her face, which she mopped incessantly with her handkerchief, was inflamed from the heat.

Mamzelle Adélaïde ate no supper that night, and went to bed early, with a compress of *eau sédative* bound tightly around her head. She thought it was a simple headache, and that she would be rid of it in the morning; but she was not better in the morning.

She kept her bed that day, and late in the afternoon Jude rode over to town for the doctor, and stopped on the way to tell Mamzelle

Adélaïde's married sister that she was quite ill,
and would like to have her come down to the
plantation for a day or two.

Polydore made round, serious eyes and for-
got to limp. He wanted to go for the doctor
in Jude's stead; but Aunt Siney, assuming a
brief authority, forced him to sit still by the
kitchen door and talked further of bacon fat.

Old Monsieur José moved about uneasily
and restlessly, in and out of his daughter's
room. He looked vacantly at Polydore now,
as if the stout young boy in blue jeans and
a calico shirt were a sort of a transparency.

A dawning anxiety, coupled to the inertia of
the past two days, deprived Polydore of his
usual healthful night's rest. The slightest
noises awoke him. Once it was the married
sister breaking ice down on the gallery. One
of the hands had been sent with the cart for
ice late in the afternoon; and Polydore himself had wrapped the huge chunk in an old
blanket and set it outside of Mamzelle Adélaïde's door.

Troubled and wakeful, he arose from bed
and went and stood by the open window.
There was a round moon in the sky, shedding

its pale glamor over all the country; and the
live-oak branches, stirred by the restless
breeze, flung quivering, grotesque shadows
slanting across the old roof. A mocking-bird
had been singing for hours near Polydore's
window, and farther away there were frogs
croaking. He could see as through a silvery
gauze the level stretch of the cotton-field, ripe
and white; a gleam of water beyond,—that was
the bend of the river,—and farther yet, the
gentle rise of the pine hill.

There was a cabin up there on the hill that
Polydore remembered well. Negroes were
living in it now, but it had been his home once.
Life had been pinched and wretched enough
up there with the little chap. The bright days
had been the days when his godmother, Mamzelle Adélaïde, would come driving her old
white horse over the pine needles and crack-
ling fallen twigs of the deserted hill-road. Her
presence was connected with the earliest recollections of whatever he had known of comfort and well-being.

And one day when death had taken his
mother from him, Mamzelle Adélaïde had
brought him home to live with her always.

Now she was sick down there in her room; very sick, for the doctor had said so, and the married sister had put on her longest face.

Polydore did not think of these things in any connected or very intelligent way. They were only impressions that penetrated him and made his heart swell, and the tears well up to his eyes. He wiped his eyes on the sleeve of his night-gown. The mosquitoes were stinging him and raising great welts on his brown legs. He went and crept back under the mosquito-bar, and soon he was asleep and dreaming that his *nénaine* was dead and he left alone in the cabin upon the pine hill.

In the morning, after the doctor had seen Mamzelle Adélaïde, he went and turned his horse into the lot and prepared to stay with his patient until he could feel it would be prudent to leave her.

Polydore tiptoed into her room and stood at the foot of the bed. Nobody noticed now whether he limped or not. She was talking very loud, and he could not believe at first that she could be as ill as they said, with such strength of voice. But her tones were unna-

tural, and what she said conveyed no meaning
to his ears.

He understood, however, when she thought
she was talking to his mother. She was in a
manner apologizing for his illness; and seemed
to be troubled with the idea that she had in a
way been the indirect cause of it by some over-
sight or neglect.

Polydore felt ashamed, and went outside and
stood by himself near the cistern till some one
told him to go and attend to the doctor's
horse.

Then there was confusion in the household,
when mornings and afternoons seemed turned
around; and meals, which were scarcely tasted,
were served at irregular and unseasonable
hours. And there came one awful night, when
they did not know if Mamzelle Adélaïde would
live or die.

Nobody slept. The doctor snatched moments of rest in the hammock. He and the
priest, who had been summoned, talked a little
together with professional callousness about
the dry weather and the crops.

Old monsieur walked, walked, like a restless, caged animal. The married sister came out

on the gallery every now and then and leaned
up against the post and sobbed in her handkerchief. There were many negroes around,
sitting on the steps and standing in small
groups in the yard.

Polydore crouched on the gallery. It had
finally come to him to comprehend the cause
of his *nénaine's* sickness—that drive in the
sweltering afternoon, when he was shamming
illness. No one there could have compre-
hended the horror of himself, the terror that
possessed him, squatting there outside her door
like a savage. If she died—but he could not
think of that. It was the point at which his
reason was stunned and seemed to swoon.

A week or two later Mamzelle Adélaïde was
sitting outside for the first time since her convalescence began. They had brought her own
rocker around to the side where she could get
a sight and whiff of the flower-garden and the
blossom-laden rose-vine twining in and out of
the banisters. Her former plumpness had not
yet returned, and she looked much older, for
the wrinkles were visible.

She was watching Polydore cross the yard. He had been putting up his pony. He approached with his heavy, clumsy walk; his round, simple face was hot and flushed from the ride. When he had mounted to the gallery he went and leaned against the railing, facing Mamzelle Adélaïde, mopping his face, his hands and neck with his handkerchief. Then he removed his hat and began to fan himself with it.

"You seem to be perfec'ly cu'ed of yo' rheumatism, Polydore. It doesn' hurt you any mo', my boy?" she questioned.

He stamped the foot and extended the leg violently, in proof of its perfect soundness.

"You know w'ere I been, *nénaine?*" he said. "I been to confession."

"That's right. Now you mus' rememba and not take a drink of water to-morrow morning, as you did las' time, and miss yo' communion, my boy. You are a good child, Polydore, to go like that to confession without bein told."

"No, I ain' good," he returned, doggedly. He began to twirl his hat on one finger. "Père Cassimelle say he always yeard I was stupid, but he never knew befo' how bad I been."

"Indeed!" muttered Mamzelle Adélaïde, not over well pleased with the priest's estimate of her protégé.

"He gave me a long penance," continued Polydore. "The 'Litany of the Saint' and the 'Litany of the Blessed Virgin,' and three 'Our Father' and three 'Hail Mary' to say ev'ry mo'ning fo' a week. But he say' that ain' enough."

"My patience! W'at does he expec' mo' from you, I like to know?" Polydore was now creasing and scanning his hat attentively.

"He say' w'at I need, it's to be wo' out with the raw-hide. He say' he knows M'sieur José is too ole and feeble to give it to me like I de-serve; and if you want, he say' he's willing to give me a good tas'e of the raw-hide himse'f."

Mamzelle Adélaïde found it impossible to disguise her indignation:

"Père Cassimelle sho'ly fo'gets himse'f, Poly-dore. Don't repeat to me any further his in-consid'ate remarks."

"He's right, *nénaine.* Père Cassimelle is right."

Since the night he crouched outside her door, Polydore had lived with the weight of his unconfessed fault oppressing every moment of existence. He had tried to rid himself of it in going to Father Cassimelle; but that had only helped by indicating the way. He was awkward and unaccustomed to express emotions with coherent speech. The words would not come.

Suddenly he flung his hat to the ground, and falling on his knees, began to sob, with his face pressed down in Mamzelle Adélaïde's lap. She had never seen him cry before, and in her weak condition it made her tremble.

Then somehow he got it out; he told the whole story of his deceit. He told it simply, in a way that bared his heart to her for the first time. She said nothing; only held his hand close and stroked his hair. But she felt as if a kind of miracle had happened. Hitherto her first thought in caring for this boy had been a desire to fulfill his dead mother's wishes.

But now he seemed to belong to herself, and to be her very own. She knew that a bond of love had been forged that would hold them together always.

"I know I can't he'p being stupid," sighed Polydore, "but it's no call fo' me to be bad."

"Neva mine, Polydore; neva mine, my boy," and she drew him close to her and kissed him as mothers kiss.

Regret

Regret

MAMZELLE Aurélie possessed a good strong figure, ruddy cheeks, hair that was changing from brown to gray, and a determined eye. She wore a man's hat about the farm, and an old blue army overcoat when it was cold, and sometimes topboots.

Mamzelle Aurélie had never thought of marrying. She had never been in love. At the age of twenty she had received a proposal, which she had promptly declined, and at the age of fifty she had not yet lived to regret it.

So she was quite alone in the world, except for her dog Ponto, and the negroes who lived in her cabins and worked her crops, and the fowls, a few cows, a couple of mules, her gun (with which she shot chicken-hawks), and her religion.

One morning Mamzelle Aurélie stood upon her gallery, contemplating, with arms akimbo,

a small band of very small children who, to all
intents and purposes, might have fallen from
the clouds, so unexpected and bewildering
was their coming, and so unwelcome. They
were the children of her nearest neighbor,
Odile, who was not such a near neighbor, after
all.

The young woman had appeared but five
minutes before, accompanied by these four children. In her arms she carried little Elodie;
she dragged Ti Nomme by an unwilling hand;
while Marcéline and Marcélette followed with
irresolute steps.

Her face was red and disfigured from tears
and excitement. She had been summoned to
a neighboring parish by the dangerous illness
of her mother; her husband was away in Texas
—it seemed to her a million miles away; and
Valsin was waiting with the mule-cart to drive
her to the station.

"It's no question, Mamzelle Aurélie; you jus'
got to keep those youngsters fo' me tell I
come back. Dieu sait, I would n' botha you
with 'em if it was any otha way to do! Make
'em mine you, Mamzelle Aurélie; don' spare
'em. Me, there, I'm half crazy between the

chil'ren, an' Léon not home, an' maybe not
even to fine po' maman alive encore!"—a har-
rowing possibility which drove Odile to take
a final hasty and convulsive leave of her disconsolate family.

She left them crowded into the narrow strip
of shade on the porch of the long, low house;
the white sunlight was beating in on the white
old boards; some chickens were scratching in
the grass at the foot of the steps, and one had
boldly mounted, and was stepping heavily,
solemnly, and aimlessly across the gallery.
There was a pleasant odor of pinks in the air,
and the sound of negroes' laughter was coming
across the flowering cotton-field.

Mamzelle Aurélie stood contemplating the
children. She looked with a critical eye upon
Marcéline, who had been left staggering beneath the weight of the chubby Elodie. She
surveyed with the same calculating air Marcélette mingling her silent tears with the au-
dible grief and rebellion of Ti Nomme. During those few contemplative moments she was
collecting herself, determining upon a line of
action which should be identical with a line
of duty. She began by feeding them.

If Mamzelle Aurélie's responsibilities might
have begun and ended there, they could easily
have been dismissed; for her larder was amply
provided against an emergency of this nature.
But little children are not little pigs; they require and demand attentions which were wholly
unexpected by Mamzelle Aurélie, and which
she was ill prepared to give.

She was, indeed, very inapt in her management of Odile's children during the first few
days. How could she know that Marcélette
always wept when spoken to in a loud and
commanding tone of voice? It was a peculi-
arity of Marcélette's. She became acquainted
with Ti Nomme's passion for flowers only
when he had plucked all the choicest gardenias
and pinks for the apparent purpose of critically
studying their botanical construction.

"'Tain't enough to tell 'im, Mamzelle Aurélie," Marcéline instructed her; "you got to tie
'im in a chair. It's w'at maman all time do
w'en he's bad: she tie 'im in a chair." The
chair in which Mamzelle Aurélie tied Ti
Nomme was roomy and comfortable, and he
seized the opportunity to take a nap in it, the
afternoon being warm.

At night, when she ordered them one and all to bed as she would have shooed the chickens into the hen-house, they stayed uncomprehending before her. What about the little white nightgowns that had to be taken from the pillow-slip in which they were brought over, and shaken by some strong hand till they snapped like ox-whips? What about the tub of water which had to be brought and set in the middle of the floor, in which the little tired, dusty, sunbrowned feet had every one to be washed sweet and clean? And it made Marcéline and Marcélette laugh merrily—the idea that Mamzelle Aurélie should for a moment have believed that Ti Nomme could fall asleep without being told the story of *Croque-mitaine* or *Loup-garou*, or both; or that Elodie could fall asleep at all without being rocked and sung to.

"I tell you, Aunt Ruby," Mamzelle Aurélie informed her cook in confidence; "me, I'd rather manage a dozen plantation' than fo' chil'ren. It's terrassent! Bonté! Don't talk to me about chil'ren!"

"'Tain' ispected sich as you would know airy thing 'bout 'em, Mamzelle Aurélie. I see dat plainly yistiddy w'en I spy dat li'le chile playin' wid yo' baskit o' keys. You don' know dat makes chillun grow up hard-headed, to play wid keys? Des like it make 'em teeth hard to look in a lookin'-glass. Them's the things you got to know in the raisin' an' management o' chillun."

Mamzelle Aurélie certainly did not pretend or aspire to such subtle and far-reaching knowledge on the subject as Aunt Ruby possessed, who had "raised five an' bared (buried) six" in her day. She was glad enough to learn a few little mother-tricks to serve the moment's need.

Ti Nomme's sticky fingers compelled her to unearth white aprons that she had not worn for years, and she had to accustom herself to his moist kisses—the expressions of an affectionate and exuberant nature. She got down her sewing-basket, which she seldom used, from the top shelf of the armoire, and placed it within the ready and easy reach which torn slips and buttonless waists demanded. It took her some days to become accustomed to the laughing, the crying, the chattering that echoed through the house and around it all day long. And it was not the first or the second night that she could sleep comfortably with little Elodie's hot, plump body pressed close against her, and the little one's warm breath beating her cheek like the fanning of a bird's wing.

But at the end of two weeks Mamzelle Aurélie had grown quite used to these things, and she no longer complained.

It was also at the end of two weeks that Mamzelle Aurélie, one evening, looking away toward the crib where the cattle were being fed, saw Valsin's blue cart turning the bend of the road. Odile sat beside the mulatto, upright and alert. As they drew near, the young woman's beaming face indicated that her home-coming was a happy one.

But this coming, unannounced and unexpected, threw Mamzelle Aurélie into a flutter that was almost agitation. The children had to be gathered. Where was Ti Nomme? Yonder in the shed, putting an edge on his knife at the grindstone. And Marcéline and Marcélette? Cutting and fashioning doll-rags in the corner of the gallery. As for Elodie, she was safe enough in Mamzelle Aurélie's arms; and she had screamed with delight at sight of

the familiar blue cart which was bringing her
mother back to her.

The excitement was all over, and they were
gone. How still it was when they were gone!
Mamzelle Aurélie stood upon the gallery, looking and listening. She could no longer see the
cart; the red sunset and the blue-gray twilight
had together flung a purple mist across the
fields and road that hid it from her view. She
could no longer hear the wheezing and creaking of its wheels. But she could still faintly
hear the shrill, glad voices of the children.

She turned into the house. There was much
work awaiting her, for the children had left a
sad disorder behind them; but she did not at
once set about the task of righting it. Mamzelle Aurélie seated herself beside the table.
She gave one slow glance through the room,
into which the evening shadows were creeping and deepening around her solitary figure.
She let her head fall down upon her bended
arm, and began to cry. Oh, but she cried!
Not softly, as women often do. She cried like
a man, with sobs that seemed to tear her very
soul. She did not notice Ponto licking her
hand.

A Matter of Prejudice

A Matter of Prejudice

🍃

MADAME Carambeau wanted it strictly understood that she was not to be disturbed by Gustave's birthday party. They carried her big rocking-chair from the back gallery, that looked out upon the garden where the children were going to play, around to the front gallery, which closely faced the green levee bank and the Mississippi coursing almost flush with the top of it.

The house—an old Spanish one, broad, low and completely encircled by a wide gallery—was far down in the French quarter of New Orleans. It stood upon a square of ground that was covered thick with a semi-tropical growth of plants and flowers. An impenetrable board fence, edged with a formidable row of iron spikes, shielded the garden from the prying glances of the occasional passer-by.

Madame Carambeau's widowed daughter, Madame Cécile Lalonde, lived with her. This annual party, given to her little son, Gustave, was the one defiant act of Madame Lalonde's existence. She persisted in it, to her own astonishment and the wonder of those who knew her and her mother.

For old Madame Carambeau was a woman of many prejudices—so many, in fact, that it would be difficult to name them all. She detested dogs, cats, organ-grinders, white servants and children's noises. She despised Americans, Germans and all people of a different faith from her own. Anything not French had, in her opinion, little right to existence.

She had not spoken to her son Henri for ten years because he had married an American girl from Prytania street. She would not permit green tea to be introduced into her house, and those who could not or would not drink coffee might drink tisane of *fleur de Laurier* for all she cared.

Nevertheless, the children seemed to be having it all their own way that day, and the organ-grinders were let loose. Old madame,

in her retired corner, could hear the screams,
the laughter and the music far more distinctly
than she liked. She rocked herself noisily,
and hummed "Partant pour la Syrie."

She was straight and slender. Her hair
was white, and she wore it in puffs on the
temples. Her skin was fair and her eyes blue
and cold.

Suddenly she became aware that footsteps
were approaching, and threatening to invade
her privacy—not only footsteps, but screams!
Then two little children, one in hot pursuit of
the other, darted wildly around the corner
near which she sat.

The child in advance, a pretty little girl,
sprang excitedly into Madame Carambeau's
lap, and threw her arms convulsively around
the old lady's neck. Her companion lightly
struck her a "last tag," and ran laughing glee-
fully away.

The most natural thing for the child to do
then would have been to wriggle down from
madame's lap, without a "thank you" or a
"by your leave," after the manner of small
and thoughtless children. But she did not

do this. She stayed there, panting and fluttering, like a frightened bird.

Madame was greatly annoyed. She moved
as if to put the child away from her, and
scolded her sharply for being boisterous and
rude. The little one, who did not understand
French, was not disturbed by the reprimand,
and stayed on in madame's lap. She rested
her plump little cheek, that was hot and
flushed, against the soft white linen of the old
lady's gown.

Her cheek was very hot and very flushed.
It was dry, too, and so were her hands. The
child's breathing was quick and irregular.
Madame was not long in detecting these signs
of disturbance.

Though she was a creature of prejudice,
she was nevertheless a skillful and accomplished nurse, and a connoisseur in all matters
pertaining to health. She prided herself upon
this talent, and never lost an opportunity of
exercising it. She would have treated an or-
gan-grinder with tender consideration if one
had presented himself in the character of an
invalid.

Madame's manner toward the little one changed immediately. Her arms and her lap were at once adjusted so as to become the most comfortable of resting places. She rocked very gently to and fro. She fanned the child softly with her palm leaf fan, and sang "Partant pour la Syrie" in a low and agreeable tone.

The child was perfectly content to lie still and prattle a little in that language which madame thought hideous. But the brown eyes were soon swimming in drowsiness, and the little body grew heavy with sleep in madame's clasp.

When the little girl slept Madame Carambeau arose, and treading carefully and deliberately, entered her room, that opened near at hand upon the gallery. The room was large, airy and inviting, with its cool matting upon the floor, and its heavy, old, polished mahogany furniture. Madame, with the child still in her arms, pulled a bell-cord; then she stood waiting, swaying gently back and forth. Presently an old black woman answered the summons. She wore gold hoops in her ears, and a bright bandanna knotted fantastically on her head.

"Louise, turn down the bed," commanded madame. "Place that small, soft pillow below the bolster. Here is a poor little unfortunate creature whom Providence must have driven into my arms." She laid the child carefully down.

"Ah, those Americans! Do they deserve to have children? Understanding as little as they do how to take care of them!" said madame, while Louise was mumbling an accompanying assent that would have been unintelligible to any one unacquainted with the negro patois.

"There, you see, Louise, she is burning up," remarked madame; "she is consumed. Unfasten the little bodice while I lift her. Ah, talk to me of such parents! So stupid as not to perceive a fever like that coming on, but they must dress their child up like a monkey to go play and dance to the music of organ-grinders.

"Haven't you better sense, Louise, than to take off a child's shoe as if you were removing the boot from the leg of a cavalry officer?" Madame would have required fairy fingers

to minister to the sick. "Now go to Mamzelle Cécile, and tell her to send me one of
those old, soft, thin nightgowns that Gustave
wore two summers ago."

When the woman retired, madame busied
herself with concocting a cooling pitcher of
orange-flower water, and mixing a fresh supply of *eau sédative* with which agreeably to
sponge the little invalid.

Madame Lalonde came herself with the old,
soft nightgown. She was a pretty, blonde,
plump little woman, with the deprecatory air
of one whose will has become flaccid from
want of use. She was mildly distressed at
what her mother had done.

"But, mamma! But, mamma, the child's
parents will be sending the carriage for her
in a little while. Really, there was no use.
Oh dear! oh dear!"

If the bedpost had spoken to Madame Carambeau, she would have paid more attention,
for speech from such a source would have
been at least surprising if not convincing.
Madame Lalonde did not possess the faculty
of either surprising or convincing her mother.

"Yes, the little one will be quite comfortable in this," said the old lady, taking the garment from her daughter's irresolute hands.

"But, mamma! What shall I say, what shall I do when they send? Oh, dear; oh, dear!"

"That is your business," replied madame, with lofty indifference. "My concern is solely with a sick child that happens to be under my roof. I think I know my duty at this time of life, Cécile."

As Madame Lalonde predicted, the carriage soon came, with a stiff English coachman driving it, and a red-cheeked Irish nurse-maid seated inside. Madame would not even permit the maid to see her little charge. She had an original theory that the Irish voice is distressing to the sick.

Madame Lalonde sent the girl away with a long letter of explanation that must have satis·fied the parents; for the child was left undisturbed in Madame Carambeau's care. She was a sweet child, gentle and affectionate. And, though she cried and fretted a little throughout the night for her mother, she seemed, after all, to take kindly to madame's gentle nursing. It was not much of a fever that afflicted her, and after two days she was well enough to be sent back to her parents.

Madame, in all her varied experience with the sick, had never before nursed so objectionable a character as an American child. But the trouble was that after the little one went away, she could think of nothing really objectionable against her except the accident of her birth, which was, after all, her misfortune; and her ignorance of the French language, which was not her fault.

But the touch of the caressing baby arms; the pressure of the soft little body in the night; the tones of the voice, and the feeling of the hot lips when the child kissed her, believing herself to be with her mother, were impressions that had sunk through the crust of madame's prejudice and reached her heart.

She often walked the length of the gallery, looking out across the wide, majestic river. Sometimes she trod the mazes of her garden where the solitude was almost that of a tropical jungle. It was during such moments that the seed began to work in her soul—the seed planted by the innocent and undesigning hands of a little child.

The first shoot that it sent forth was Doubt. Madame plucked it away once or twice. But it sprouted again, and with it Mistrust and Dissatisfaction. Then from the heart of the seed, and amid the shoots of Doubt and Misgiving, came the flower of Truth. It was a very beautiful flower, and it bloomed on Christmas morning.

As Madame Carambeau and her daughter were about to enter her carriage on that Christmas morning, to be driven to church, the old lady stopped to give an order to her black coachman, François. François had been driving these ladies every Sunday morning to the French Cathedral for so many years —he had forgotten exactly how many, but ever since he had entered their service, when Madame Lalonde was a little girl. His astonishment may therefore be imagined when Madame Carambeau said to him:

"François, to-day you will drive us to one of the American churches."

"Plait-il, madame?" the negro stammered, doubting the evidence of his hearing.

"I say, you will drive us to one of the American churches. Any one of them," she added, with a sweep of her hand. "I suppose they are all alike," and she followed her daughter into the carriage.

Madame Lalonde's surprise and agitation were painful to see, and they deprived her of the ability to question, even if she had possessed the courage to do so.

François, left to his fancy, drove them to St. Patrick's Church on Camp street. Madame Lalonde looked and felt like the proverbial fish out of its element as they entered the edifice. Madame Carambeau, on the contrary, looked as if she had been attending St. Patrick's church all her life. She sat with unruffled calm through the long service and through a lengthy English sermon, of which she did not understand a word.

When the mass was ended and they were about to enter the carriage again, Madame Carambeau turned, as she had done before, to the coachman.

"François," she said, coolly, "you will now drive us to the residence of my son, M. Henri Carambeau. No doubt Mamzelle Cécile can inform you where it is," she added, with a sharply penetrating glance that caused Madame Lalonde to wince.

Yes, her daughter Cécile knew, and so did François, for that matter. They drove out St. Charles avenue—very far out. It was like a strange city to old madame, who had not been in the American quarter since the town had taken on this new and splendid growth.

The morning was a delicious one, soft and mild; and the roses were all in bloom. They were not hidden behind spiked fences. Madame appeared not to notice them, or the beautiful and striking residences that lined the avenue along which they drove. She held a bottle of smelling-salts to her nostrils, as though she were passing through the most unsavory instead of the most beautiful quarter of New Orleans.

Henri's house was a very modern and very handsome one, standing a little distance away from the street. A well-kept lawn, studded with rare and charming plants, surrounded it. The ladies, dismounting, rang the bell, and stood out upon the banquette, waiting for the iron gate to be opened.

A white maid-servant admitted them. Madame did not seem to mind. She handed her a card with all proper ceremony, and followed with her daughter to the house.

Not once did she show a sign of weakness; not even when her son, Henri, came and took her in his arms and sobbed and wept upon her neck as only a warm-hearted Creole could. He was a big, good-looking, honest-faced man, with tender brown eyes like his dead father's and a firm mouth like his mother's.

Young Mrs. Carambeau came, too, her sweet, fresh face transfigured with happiness. She led by the hand her little daughter, the "American child" whom madame had nursed so tenderly a month before, never suspecting the little one to be other than an alien to her.

"What a lucky chance was that fever! What a happy accident!" gurgled Madame Lalonde.

"Cécile, it was no accident, I tell you; it was Providence," spoke madame, reprovingly, and no one contradicted her.

They all drove back together to eat Christmas dinner in the old house by the river. Madame held her little granddaughter upon

her lap; her son Henri sat facing her, and beside her was her daughter-in-law.

Henri sat back in the carriage and could
not speak. His soul was possessed by a pathetic joy that would not admit of speech.
He was going back again to the home where
he was born, after a banishment of ten long
years.

He would hear again the water beat against
the green levee-bank with a sound that was
not quite like any other that he could remember. He would sit within the sweet and solemn shadow of the deep and overhanging
roof; and roam through the wild, rich solitude of the old garden, where he had played
his pranks of boyhood and dreamed his
dreams of youth. He would listen to his
mother's voice calling him, "mon fils," as it
had always done before that day he had had
to choose between mother and wife. No; he
could not speak.

But his wife chatted much and pleasantly—
in a French, however, that must have been
trying to old madame to listen to.

"I am so sorry, ma mère," she said, "that
our little one does not speak French. It is

not my fault, I assure you," and she flushed and hesitated a little. "It—it was Henri who would not permit it."

"That is nothing," replied madame, amiably, drawing the child close to her. "Her grandmother will teach her French; and she will teach her grandmother English. You see, I have no prejudices. I am not like my son. Henri was always a stubborn boy. Heaven only knows how he came by such a character!"

Caline

Caline

THE sun was just far enough in the west
to send inviting shadows. In the centre
of a small field, and in the shade of a
haystack which was there, a girl lay sleeping.
She had slept long and soundly, when something awoke her as suddenly as if it had been a
blow. She opened her eyes and stared a moment up in the cloudless sky. She yawned
and stretched her long brown legs and arms,
lazily. Then she arose, never minding the
bits of straw that clung to her black hair, to
her red bodice, and the blue cotonade skirt
that did not reach her naked ankles.

The log cabin in which she dwelt with her
parents was just outside the enclosure in
which she had been sleeping. Beyond was a
small clearing that did duty as a cotton field.
All else was dense wood, except the long
stretch that curved round the brow of the hill,

and in which glittered the steel rails of the
Texas and Pacific road.

When Caline emerged from the shadow she
saw a long train of passenger coaches standing in view, where they must have stopped
abruptly. It was that sudden stopping which
had awakened her; for such a thing had not
happened before within her recollection, and
she looked stupid, at first, with astonishment.
There seemed to be something wrong with
the engine; and some of the passengers who
dismounted went forward to investigate the
trouble. Others came strolling along in the
direction of the cabin, where Caline stood under an old gnarled mulberry tree, staring.
Her father had halted his mule at the end of
the cotton row, and stood staring also, leaning upon his plow.

There were ladies in the party. They walked
awkwardly in their high-heeled boots over
the rough, uneven ground, and held up their
skirts mincingly. They twirled parasols over
their shoulders, and laughed immoderately at
the funny things which their masculine companions were saying.

They tried to talk to Caline, but could not understand the French patois with which she answered them.

One of the men—a pleasant-faced youngster—drew a sketch book from his pocket and began to make a picture of the girl. She stayed motionless, her hands behind her, and her wide eyes fixed earnestly upon him.

Before he had finished there was a summons from the train; and all went scampering hurriedly away. The engine screeched, it sent a few lazy puffs into the still air, and in another moment or two had vanished, bearing its human cargo with it.

Caline could not feel the same after that. She looked with new and strange interest upon the trains of cars that passed so swiftly back and forth across her vision, each day; and wondered whence these people came, and whither they were going.

Her mother and father could not tell her, except to say that they came from "loin là bas," and were going "Djieu sait é où."

One day she walked miles down the track to talk with the old flagman, who stayed down there by the big water tank. Yes, he

knew. Those people came from the great cities
in the north, and were going to the city
in the south. He knew all about the city; it
was a grand place. He had lived there once.
His sister lived there now; and she would be
glad enough to have so fine a girl as Caline
to help her cook and scrub, and tend the
babies. And he thought Caline might earn
as much as five dollars a month, in the city.

So she went; in a new cotonade, and her
Sunday shoes; with a sacredly guarded scrawl
that the flagman sent to his sister.

The woman lived in a tiny, stuccoed house,
with green blinds, and three wooden steps
leading down to the banquette. There seemed
to be hundreds like it along the street. Over
the house tops loomed the tall masts of ships,
and the hum of the French market could be
heard on a still morning.

Caline was at first bewildered. She had to
readjust all her preconceptions to fit the reality of it. The flagman's sister was a kind
and gentle task-mistress. At the end of a
week or two she wanted to know how the girl
liked it all. Caline liked it very well, for it
was pleasant, on Sunday afternoons, to stroll

with the children under the great, solemn
sugar sheds; or to sit upon the compressed
cotton bales, watching the stately steamers,
the graceful boats, and noisy little tugs that
plied the waters of the Mississippi. And it
filled her with agreeable excitement to go
to the French market, where the handsome
Gascon butchers were eager to present their
compliments and little Sunday bouquets to the
pretty Acadian girl; and to throw fistfuls of
lagniappe into her basket.

When the woman asked her again after another week if she were still pleased, she was
not so sure. And again when she questioned
Caline the girl turned away, and went to sit
behind the big, yellow cistern, to cry unobserved. For she knew now that it was not the
great city and its crowds of people she had
so eagerly sought; but the pleasant-faced boy,
who had made her picture that day under the
mulberry tree.

A Dresden Lady in Dixie

A Dresden Lady in Dixie

MADAME Valtour had been in the sitting-room some time before she noticed the absence of the Dresden china figure from the corner of the mantel-piece, where it had stood for years. Aside from the intrinsic value of the piece, there were some very sad and tender memories associated with it. A baby's lips that were now forever still had loved once to kiss the painted "pitty 'ady"; and the baby arms had often held it in a close and smothered embrace.

Madame Valtour gave a rapid, startled glance around the room, to see perchance if it had been misplaced; but she failed to discover it.

Viny, the house-maid, when summoned, remembered having carefully dusted it that morning, and was rather indignantly positive that she had not broken the thing to bits and secreted the pieces.

"Who has been in the room during my absence?" questioned Madame Valtour, with asperity. Viny abandoned herself to a moment's reflection.

"Pa-Jeff comed in yere wid de mail—" If she had said St. Peter came in with the mail, the fact would have had as little bearing on the case from Madame Valtour's point of view.

Pa-Jeff's uprightness and honesty were so long and firmly established as to have become proverbial on the plantation. He had not served the family faithfully since boyhood and been all through the war with "old Marse Valtour" to descend at his time of life to tampering with household bric-a-brac.

"Has any one else been here?" Madame Valtour naturally inquired.

"On'y Agapie w'at brung you some Creole aiggs. I tole 'er to sot 'em down in de hall. I don' know she comed in de settin'-room o' not."

Yes, there they were; eight, fresh "Creole eggs" reposing on the muslin in the sewing basket. Viny herself had been seated on the gallery brushing her mistress' gowns during the hours of that lady's absence, and could think of no one else having penetrated to the sitting-room.

Madame Valtour did not entertain the thought that Agapie had stolen the relic. Her worst fear was, that the girl, finding herself alone in the room, had handled the frail bit of porcelain and inadvertently broken it.

Agapie came often to the house to play with the children and amuse them—she loved nothing better. Indeed, no other spot known to her on earth so closely embodied her confused idea of paradise, as this home with its atmosphere of love, comfort and good cheer. She was, herself, a cheery bit of humanity, overflowing with kind impulses and animal spirits.

Madame Valtour recalled the fact that Agapie had often admired this Dresden figure (but what had she not admired!); and she remembered having heard the girl's assurance that if ever she became possessed of "fo' bits" to spend as she liked, she would have some one buy her just such a china doll in town or in the city.

Before night, the fact that the Dresden lady had strayed from her proud eminence on the sitting-room mantel, became, through Viny's indiscreet babbling, pretty well known on the place.

The following morning Madame Valtour crossed the field and went over to the Be- dauts' cabin. The cabins on the plantation were not grouped; but each stood isolated upon the section of land which its occupants cultivated. Pa-Jeff's cabin was the only one near enough to the Bedauts to admit of neigh- borly intercourse.

Seraphine Bedaut was sitting on her small gallery, stringing red peppers, when Madame Valtour approached.

"I'm so distressed, Madame Bedaut," be- gan the planter's wife, abruptly. But the 'Cadian woman arose politely and interrupted, offering her visitor a chair.

"Come in, set down, Ma'me Valtour."

"No, no; it's only for a moment. You know, Madame Bedaut, yesterday when I returned from making a visit, I found that an ornament was missing from my sitting-room mantel-piece. It's a thing I prize very, very much —" with sudden tears filling her eyes—"and I would not willingly part with it for many times its value." Seraphine Bedaut was listening, with her mouth partly open, looking, in truth, stupidly puzzled.

"No one entered the room during my absence," continued Madame Valtour, "but Agapie." Seraphine's mouth snapped like a steel trap and her black eyes gleamed with a flash of anger.

"You wan' say Agapie stole some'in' in yo' house!" she cried out in a shrill voice, tremulous from passion.

"No; oh no! I'm sure Agapie is an honest girl and we all love her; but you know how children are. It was a small Dresden figure. She may have handled and broken the thing and perhaps is afraid to say so. She may have thoughtlessly misplaced it; oh, I don't know what! I want to ask if she saw it."

"Come in; you got to come in, Ma'me Valtour," stubbornly insisted Seraphine, leading the way into the cabin. "I sen' 'er to de house yistiddy wid some Creole aiggs," she went on in her rasping voice, "like I all time do, because you all say you can't eat dem sto' aiggs no mo.' Yere de basket w'at I sen' 'em in," reaching for an Indian basket which hung against the wall—and which was partly filled with cotton seed.

"Oh, never mind," interrupted Madame Valtour, now thoroughly distressed at witnessing the woman's agitation.

"Ah, bien non. I got to show you, Agapie en't no mo' thief 'an yo' own child'en is." She led the way into the adjoining room of the hut.

"Yere all her things w'at she 'muse herse'f wid," continued Seraphine, pointing to a soap-box which stood on the floor just beneath the open window. The box was filled with an indescribable assortment of odds and ends, mostly doll-rags. A catechism and a blue-backed speller poked dog-eared corners from out of the confusion; for the Valtour children were making heroic and patient efforts toward Agapie's training.

Seraphine cast herself upon her knees before the box and dived her thin brown hands among its contents. "I wan' show you; I goin' show you," she kept repeating excitedly. Madame Valtour was standing beside her.

Suddenly the woman drew forth from among the rags, the Dresden lady, as dapper, sound, and smiling as ever. Seraphine's hand shook so violently that she was in danger of letting the image fall to the floor. Madame Valtour reached out and took it very quietly from her. Then Seraphine rose tremblingly to her feet and broke into a sob that was pitiful to hear.

Agapie was approaching the cabin. She was a chubby girl of twelve. She walked with bare, callous feet over the rough ground and bare-headed under the hot sun. Her thick, short, black hair covered her head like a mane. She had been dancing along the path, but slackened her pace upon catching sight of the two women who had returned to the gallery. But when she perceived that her mother was crying she darted impetuously forward. In an instant she had her arms around her mother's neck, clinging so tenaciously in her youthful strength as to make the frail woman totter.

Agapie had seen the Dresden figure in Madame Valtour's possession and at once guessed the whole accusation.

"It en't so! I tell you, maman, it en't so! I neva touch' it. Stop cryin'; stop cryin'!" and she began to cry most piteously herself.

"But Agapie, we fine it in yo' box," moaned Seraphine through her sobs.

"Then somebody put it there. Can't you see somebody put it there? 'Ten't so, I tell you."

The scene was extremely painful to Madame Valtour. Whatever she might tell these two later, for the time she felt herself powerless to say anything befitting, and she walked away. But she turned to remark, with a hardness of expression and intention which she seldom displayed: "No one will know of this through me. But, Agapie, you must not come into my house again; on account of the children; I could not allow it."

As she walked away she could hear Agapie comforting her mother with renewed protestations of innocence.

Pa-Jeff began to fail visibly that year.   No wonder, considering his great age, which he computed to be about one hundred.   It was, in fact, some ten years less than that, but a good old age all the same.   It was seldom that he got out into the field; and then, never to do any heavy work—only a little light hoeing.   There were days when the "misery" doubled him up and nailed him down to his chair so that he could not set foot beyond the door of his cabin.   He would sit there courting the sunshine and blinking, as he gazed across the fields with the patience of the savage.

The Bedauts seemed to know almost instinctively when Pa-Jeff was sick.   Agapie would shade her eyes and look searchingly towards the old man's cabin.

"I don' see Pa-Jeff this mo'nin'," or "Pa-Jeff en't open his winda," or "I didn' see no smoke yet yonda to Pa-Jeff's."   And in a little while the girl would be over there with a pail of soup or coffee, or whatever there was at hand which she thought the old negro might fancy.   She had lost all the color out of her cheeks and was pining like a sick bird.

She often sat on the steps of the gallery and talked with the old man while she waited for him to finish his soup from her tin pail.

"I tell you, Pa-Jeff, its neva been no thief in the Bedaut family. My pa say he couldn' hole up his head if he think I been a thief, me. An' maman say it would make her sick in bed, she don' know she could ever git up. Sosthène tell me the chil'en been cryin' fo' me up yonda. Li'le Lulu cry so hard M'sieur Valtour want sen' afta me, an' Ma'me Valtour say no."

And with this, Agapie flung herself at length upon the gallery with her face buried in her arms, and began to cry so hysterically as seriously to alarm Pa-Jeff. It was well he had finished his soup, for he could not have eaten another mouthful.

"Hole up yo' head, chile. God save us! W'at you kiarrin' on dat away?" he exclaimed in great distress. "You gwine to take a fit? Hole up yo' head."

Agapie rose slowly to her feet, and drying her eyes upon the sleeve of her "josie," reached out for the tin bucket. Pa-Jeff handed it to her, but without relinquishing his hold upon it.

"War hit you w'at tuck it?" he questioned in a whisper. "I isn' gwine tell; you knows I isn' gwine tell." She only shook her head, attempting to draw the pail forcibly away from the old man.

"Le' me go, Pa-Jeff. W'at you doin'! Gi' me my bucket!"

He kept his old blinking eyes fastened for a while questioningly upon her disturbed and tear-stained face. Then he let her go and she turned and ran swiftly away towards her home.

He sat very still watching her disappear; only his furrowed old face twitched convulsively, moved by an unaccustomed train of reasoning that was at work in him.

"She w'ite, I is black," he muttered calculatingly. "She young, I is ole; sho I is ole. She good to Pa-Jeff like I her own kin an' color." This line of thought seemed to possess him to the exclusion of every other. Late in the night he was still muttering.

"Sho I is ole. She good to Pa-Jeff, yas."

A few days later, when Pa-Jeff happened to be feeling comparatively well, he presented himself at the house just as the family had assembled at their early dinner. Looking up suddenly, Monsieur Valtour was astonished to see him standing there in the room near the open door. He leaned upon his cane and his grizzled head was bowed upon his breast. There was general satisfaction expressed at seeing Pa-Jeff on his legs once more.

"Why, old man, I'm glad to see you out again," exclaimed the planter, cordially, pouring a glass of wine, which he instructed Viny to hand to the old fellow. Pa-Jeff accepted the glass and set it solemnly down upon a small table near by.

"Marse Albert," he said, "I is come heah to-day fo' to make a statement of de rights an' de wrongs w'at is done hang heavy on my soul dis heah long time. Arter you heahs me an' de missus heahs me an' de chillun an' ev'body, den ef you says: 'Pa-Jeff you kin tech yo' lips to dat glass o' wine,' all well an' right.'"

His manner was impressive and caused the family to exchange surprised and troubled glances. Foreseeing that his recital might be long, a chair was offered to him, but he declined it.

"One day," he began, "w'en I ben hoein' de madam's flower bed close to de fence, Sosthène he ride up, he say: 'Heah, Pa-Jeff, heah de mail.' I takes de mail f'om 'im an' I calls out to Viny w'at settin' on de gallery: 'Heah Marse Albert's mail, gal; come git it.'

"But Viny she answer, pert-like—des like Viny: 'You is got two laigs, Pa-Jeff, des well as me.' I ain't no han' fo' disputin' wid gals, so I brace up an' I come 'long to de house an' goes on in dat settin'-room dah, naix' to de dinin'-room. I lays dat mail down on Marse Albert's table; den I looks roun'.

"Ev'thing do look putty, sho! De lace cu'-tains was a-flappin' an' de flowers was a-smell-in' sweet, an' de pictures a-settin' back on de wall. I keep on lookin' roun'. To reckly my eye hit fall on de li'le gal w'at al'ays sets on de een' o' de mantel-shelf. She do look mighty sassy dat day, wid 'er toe a-stickin' out, des so; an' holdin' her skirt des dat away; an' lookin' at me wid her head twis'.

"I laff out. Viny mus' heahed me. I say,
'g'long 'way f'om dah, gal.' She keep on
smilin'. I reaches out my han'. Den Satan
an' de good Sperrit, dey begins to wrastle in
me. De Sperrit say: 'You ole fool-nigga,
you; mine w'at you about.' Satan keep on
shovin' my han'—des so—keep on shovin'.
Satan he mighty powerful dat day, an' he
win de fight. I kiar dat li'le trick home in
my pocket."

Pa-Jeff lowered his head for a moment in
bitter confusion. His hearers were moved
with distressful astonishment. They would
have had him stop the recital right there, but
Pa-Jeff resumed, with an effort:

"Come dat night I heah tell how dat li'le
trick, wo'th heap money; how madam, she
cryin' 'cause her li'le blessed lamb was use' to
play wid dat, an' kiar-on ov' it. Den I git
scared. I say, 'w'at I gwine do?' An' up
jump Satan an' de Sperrit a-wrastlin' again.

"De Sperrit say: 'Kiar hit back whar it
come f'om, Pa-Jeff.' Satan 'low: 'Fling it
in de bayeh, you ole fool.' De Sperrit say:
'You won't fling dat in de bayeh, whar de
madam kain't neva sot eyes on hit no mo''?'

Den Satan he kine give in; he 'low he plumb sick o' disputin' so long; tell me go hide it some 'eres whar dey nachelly gwine fine it. Satan he win dat fight.

"Des w'en de day g'ine break, I creeps out an' goes 'long de fiel' road. I pass by Ma'me Bedaut's house. I riclic how dey says li'le Bedaut gal ben in de sittin'-room, too, day befo'. De winda war open. Ev'body sleepin'. I tres' in my head, des like a dog w'at shame hisse'f. I sees dat box o' rags befo' my eyes; an' I drops dat li'le imp'dence 'mongst dem rags.

"Mebby yo' all t'ink Satan an' de Sperrit lef' me 'lone, arter dat?" continued Pa-Jeff, straightening himself from the relaxed position in which his members seemed to have settled.

"No, suh; dey ben desputin' straight 'long. Las' night dey come nigh onto en'in' me up. De Sperrit cay: 'Come 'long, I gittin' tired dis heah, you g'long up yonda an' tell de truf an' shame de devil.' Satan 'low: 'Stay whar you is; you heah me!' Dey clutches me. Dey twis'es an' twines me. Dey dashes me down an' jerks me up. But de Sperrit he win dat fight in de en', an' heah I is, mist'ess, master, chillun'; heah I is."

Years later Pa-Jeff was still telling the story of his temptation and fall.   The negroes especially seemed never to tire of hearing him relate it.   He enlarged greatly upon the theme as he went, adding new and dramatic features which gave fresh interest to its every telling.

Agapie grew up to deserve the confidence and favors of the family.   She redoubled her acts of kindness toward Pa-Jeff; but somehow she could not look into his face again.

Yet she need not have feared.   Long before the end came, poor old Pa-Jeff, confused, bewildered, believed the story himself as firmly as those who had heard him tell it over and over for so many years.

Nég Créol

Nég Créol

❦

AT the remote period of his birth he
had been named César François Xavier,
but no one ever thought of calling him
anything but Chicot, or Nég, or Maringouin.
Down at the French market, where he worked
among the fishmongers, they called him Chicot, when they were not calling him names
that are written less freely than they are spok-
en. But one felt privileged to call him almost anything, he was so black, lean, lame,
and shriveled. He wore a head-kerchief, and
whatever other rags the fishermen and their
wives chose to bestow upon him. Throughout one whole winter he wore a woman's discarded jacket with puffed sleeves.

Among some startling beliefs entertained
by Chicot was one that "Michié St. Pierre et
Michié St. Paul" had created him. Of
"Michié bon Dieu" he held his own private

opinion, and not a too flattering one at that.
This fantastic notion concerning the origin of
his being he owed to the early teaching of his
young master, a lax believer, and a great
farceur in his day. Chicot had once been
thrashed by a robust young Irish priest for
expressing his religious views, and at another
time knifed by a Sicilian. So he had come to
hold his peace upon that subject.

Upon another theme he talked freely and
harped continuously. For years he had tried
to convince his associates that his master had
left a progeny, rich, cultured, powerful, and
numerous beyond belief. This prosperous
race of beings inhabited the most imposing
mansions in the city of New Orleans. Men
of note and position, whose names were familiar to the public, he swore were grandchildren,
great-grandchildren, or, less frequently, distant relatives of his master, long deceased,
Ladies who came to the market in carriages,
or whose elegance of attire attracted the attention and admiration of the fishwomen, were
all *des 'tites cousines* to his former master,
Jean Boisduré. He never looked for recognition from any of these superior beings, but

delighted to discourse by the hour upon their dignity and pride of birth and wealth.

Chicot always carried an old gunny-sack, and into this went his earnings. He cleaned stalls at the market, scaled fish, and did many odd offices for the itinerant merchants, who usually paid in trade for his service. Occasionally he saw the color of silver and got his clutch upon a coin, but he accepted anything, and seldom made terms. He was glad to get a handkerchief from the Hebrew, and grateful if the Choctaws would trade him a bottle of *filé* for it. The butcher flung him a soup bone, and the fishmonger a few crabs or a paper bag of shrimps. It was the big *mulatresse, vendeuse de café*, who cared for his inner man.

Once Chicot was accused by a shoe-vender of attempting to steal a pair of ladies' shoes. He declared he was only examining them. The clamor raised in the market was terrific. Young Dagoes assembled and squealed like rats; a couple of Gascon butchers bellowed like bulls. Matteo's wife shook her fist in the accuser's face and called him incomprehensible names. The Choctaw women, where they squatted, turned their slow eyes in the direction of the fray, taking no further notice; while a policeman jerked Chicot around by the puffed sleeve and brandished a club. It was a narrow escape.

Nobody knew where Chicot lived. A man —even a nég créol—who lives among the reeds and willows of Bayou St. John, in a deserted chicken-coop constructed chiefly of tarred paper, is not going to boast of his habitation or to invite attention to his domestic appointments. When, after market hours, he vanished in the direction of St. Philip street, limping, seemingly bent under the weight of his gunny-bag, it was like the disappearance from the stage of some petty actor whom the audience does not follow in imagination beyond the wings, or think of till his return in another scene.

There was one to whom Chicot's coming or going meant more than this. In *la maison grise* they called her La Chouette, for no earthly reason unless that she perched high under the roof of the old rookery and scolded in shrill sudden outbursts. Forty or fifty years before, when for a little while she acted minor parts with a company of French players (an escapade that had brought her grandmother to the grave), she was known as Mademoiselle de Montallaine. Seventy-five years before she had been christened Aglaé Boisduré.

No matter at what hour the old negro appeared at her threshold, Mamzelle Aglaé always kept him waiting till she finished her prayers. She opened the door for him and silently motioned him to a seat, returning to prostrate herself upon her knees before a crucifix, and a shell filled with holy water that stood on a small table; it represented in her imagination an altar. Chicot knew that she did it to aggravate him; he was convinced that she timed her devotions to begin when she heard his footsteps on the stairs. He would sit with sullen eyes contemplating her long, spare, poorly clad figure as she knelt and read from her book or finished her prayers. Bitter was the religious warfare that had raged for years between them, and Mamzelle Aglaé had grown, on her side, as intolerant as Chicot. She had come to hold St. Peter and St. Paul in such utter detestation that she had cut their pictures out of her prayer-book.

Then Mamzelle Aglaé pretended not to care what Chicot had in his bag. He drew forth a small hunk of beef and laid it in her basket that stood on the bare floor. She looked from the corner of her eye, and went on dusting the table. He brought out a handful of potatoes, some pieces of sliced fish, a few herbs, a yard of calico, and a small pat of butter wrapped in lettuce leaves. He was proud of the butter, and wanted her to notice it. He held it out and asked her for something to put it on. She handed him a saucer, and looked indifferent and resigned, with lifted eyebrows.

"Pas d' sucre, Nég?"

Chicot shook his head and scratched it, and looked like a black picture of distress and mortification. No sugar! But tomorrow he would get a pinch here and a pinch there, and would bring as much as a cupful.

Mamzelle Aglaé then sat down, and talked to Chicot uninterruptedly and confidentially. She complained bitterly, and it was all about a pain that lodged in her leg; that crept and acted like a live, stinging serpent, twining about her waist and up her spine, and coiling round the shoulder-blade. And then *les rheumatismes* in her fingers! He could see for himself how they were knotted. She could not bend them; she could hold nothing in her hands, and had let a saucer fall that morning and broken it in pieces. And if she were to tell him that she had slept a wink through the night, she would be a liar, deserving of perdition. She had sat at the window *la nuit blanche*, hearing the hours strike and the market-wagons rumble. Chicot nodded, and kept up a running fire of sympathetic comment and suggestive remedies for rheumatism and insomnia: herbs, or *tisanes*, or *grigris*, or all three. As if he knew! There was Purgatory Mary, a perambulating soul whose office in life was to pray for the shades in purgatory,— she had brought Mamzelle Aglaé a bottle of *eau de Lourdes*, but so little of it! She might have kept her water of Lourdes, for all the good it did,—a drop! Not so much as would cure a fly or a mosquito! Mamzelle Aglaé was going to show Purgatory Mary the door when she came again, not only because of her avarice with the Lourdes water, but, beside that, she brought in on her feet dirt that could only be removed with a shovel after she left.

And Mamzelle Aglaé wanted to inform Chicot that there would be slaughter and bloodshed in *la maison grise* if the people below stairs did not mend their ways. She was convinced that they lived for no other purpose than to torture and molest her. The woman kept a bucket of dirty water constantly on the landing with the hope of Mamzelle Aglaé falling over it or into it. And she knew that the children were instructed to gather in the hall and on the stairway, and scream and make a noise and jump up and down like galloping horses, with the intention of driving her to suicide. Chicot should notify the policeman on the beat, and have them arrested, if possible, and thrust into the parish prison, where they belonged.

Chicot would have been extremely alarmed if he had ever chanced to find Mamzelle Aglaé in an uncomplaining mood. It never occurred to him that she might be otherwise. He felt that she had a right to quarrel with fate, if ever mortal had. Her poverty was a disgrace, and he hung his head before it and felt ashamed.

One day he found Mamzelle Aglaé stretched on the bed, with her head tied up in a handkerchief. Her sole complaint that day was, "Aïe—aïe—aïe! Aïe—aïe—aïe!" uttered with every breath. He had seen her so before, especially when the weather was damp.

"Vous pas bézouin tisane, Mamzelle Aglaé? Vous pas veux mo cri gagni docteur?"

She desired nothing. "Aïe—aïe—aïe!"

He emptied his bag very quietly, so as not to disturb her; and he wanted to stay there with her and lie down on the floor in case she needed him, but the woman from below had come up. She was an Irishwoman with rolled sleeves.

"It's a shtout shtick I'm afther giving her, Nég, and she do but knock on the flure it's me or Janie or wan of us that'll be hearing her."

"You too good, Brigitte. Aïe—aïe—aïe! Une goutte d'eau sucré, Nég! That Purg'-tory Marie,—you see hair, ma bonne Brigitte, you tell hair go say li'le prayer là-bas au Cathédral. Aïe—aïe—aïe!"

Nég could hear her lamentation as he descended the stairs. It followed him as he limped his way through the city streets, and seemed part of the city's noise; he could hear it in the rumble of wheels and jangle of car-bells, and in the voices of those passing by.

He stopped at Mimotte the Voudou's shanty and bought a *grigri*—a cheap one for fifteen cents. Mimotte held her charms at all prices. This he intended to introduce next day into Mamzelle Anglaé's room,—somewhere about the altar,—to the confusion and discomfort of "Michié bon Dieu," who persistently declined to concern himself with the welfare of a Boisduré.

At night, among the reeds on the bayou, Chicot could still hear the woman's wail, mingled now with the croaking of the frogs. If he could have been convinced that giving up his life down there in the water would in any way have bettered her condition, he would not have hesitated to sacrifice the remnant of his existence that was wholly devoted to her. He lived but to serve her. He did not know it himself; but Chicot knew so little, and that little in such a distorted way! He could scarcely have been expected, even in his most lucid moments, to give himself over to self-analysis.

Chicot gathered an uncommon amount of dainties at market the following day. He had to work hard, and scheme and whine a little; but he got hold of an orange and a lump of ice and a *chou-fleur*. He did not drink his cup of *café au lait*, but asked Mimi Lambeau to put it in the little new tin pail that the Hebrew notion-vender had just given him in exchange for a mess of shrimps. This time, however, Chicot had his trouble for nothing. When he reached the upper room of *la maison grise*, it was to find that Mamzelle Aglaé had died during the night. He set his bag down in the middle of the floor, and stood shaking, and whined low like a dog in pain.

Everything had been done. The Irish-woman had gone for the doctor, and Purgatory Mary had summoned a priest. Furthermore, the woman had arranged Mamzelle Aglaé decently. She had covered the table with a white cloth, and had placed it at the head of the bed, with the crucifix and two lighted candles in silver candlesticks upon it; the lit-

tle bit of ornamentation brightened and em-
bellished the poor room. Purgatory Mary,
dressed in shabby black, fat and breathing
hard, sat reading half audibly from a prayer-
book. She was watching the dead and the
silver candlesticks, which she had borrowed
from a benevolent society, and for which she
held herself responsible. A young man was
just leaving,— a reporter snuffing the air for
items, who had scented one up there in the
top room of *la maison grise*.

All the morning Janie had been escorting a
procession of street Arabs up and down the
stairs to view the remains. One of them—a
little girl, who had had her face washed and
had made a species of toilet for the occasion
—refused to be dragged away. She stayed
seated as if at an entertainment, fascinated al-
ternately by the long, still figure of Mamzelle
Aglaé, the mumbling lips of Purgatory Mary,
and the silver candlesticks.

"Will ye get down on yer knees, man, and
say a prayer for the dead!" commanded the
woman.

But Chicot only shook his head, and refused to obey. He approached the bed, and

laid a little black paw for a moment on the stiffened body of Mamzelle Aglaé. There was nothing for him to do here. He picked up his old ragged hat and his bag and went away.

"The black h'athen!" the woman muttered. "Shut the dure, child."

The little girl slid down from her chair, and went on tiptoe to shut the door which Chicot had left open. Having resumed her seat, she fastened her eyes upon Purgatory Mary's heaving chest.

"You, Chicot!" cried Matteo's wife the next morning. "My man, he read in paper 'bout woman name' Boisduré, use' b'long to big-a famny. She die roun' on St. Philip—po', same-a like church rat. It's any them Boisdurés you alla talk 'bout?"

Chicot shook his head in slow but emphatic denial. No, indeed, the woman was not of kin to his Boisdurés. He surely had told Matteo's wife often enough—how many times did he have to repeat it!—of their wealth, their social standing. It was doubtless some Boisduré of *les Attakapas;* it was none of his.

The next day there was a small funeral procession passing a little distance away,—a hearse and a carriage or two. There was the priest who had attended Mamzelle Aglaé, and a benevolent Creole gentleman whose father had known the Boisdurés in his youth. There was a couple of player-folk, who, having got wind of the story, had thrust their hands into their pockets.

"Look, Chicot!" cried Matteo's wife. "Yonda go the fune'al. Mus-a be that-a Boisduré woman we talken 'bout yesaday."

But Chicot paid no heed. What was to him the funeral of a woman who had died in St. Philip street? He did not even turn his head in the direction of the moving procession. He went on scaling his red-snapper.

The Lilies

The Lilies

THAT little vagabond Mamouche amused himself one afternoon by letting down the fence rails that protected Mr. Billy's young crop of cotton and corn. He had first looked carefully about him to make sure there was no witness to this piece of rascality. Then he crossed the lane and did the same with the Widow Angèle's fence, thereby liberating Toto, the white calf who stood disconsolately penned up on the other side.

It was not ten seconds before Toto was frolicking madly in Mr. Billy's crop, and Mamouche—the young scamp—was running swiftly down the lane, laughing fiendishly to himself as he went.

He could not at first decide whether there could be more fun in letting Toto demolish things at his pleasure, or in warning Mr. Billy of the calf's presence in the field. But the latter course commended itself as possessing a certain refinement of perfidy.

"Ho, the'a, you!" called out Mamouche to one of Mr. Billy's hands, when he got around to where the men were at work; "you betta go yon'a an' see 'bout that calf o' Ma'me Angèle; he done broke in the fiel' an' 'bout to finish the crop, him." Then Mamouche went and sat behind a big tree, where, unobserved, he could laugh to his heart's content.

Mr. Billy's fury was unbounded when he learned that Madame Angèle's calf was eating up and trampling down his corn. At once he sent a detachment of men and boys to expel the animal from the field. Others were required to repair the damaged fence; while he himself, boiling with wrath, rode up the lane on his wicked black charger.

But merely to look upon the devastation was not enough for Mr. Billy. He dismounted from his horse, and strode belligerently up to Madame Angèle's door, upon which he gave, with his riding-whip, a couple of sharp raps that plainly indicated the condition of his mind

Mr. Billy looked taller and broader than ever as he squared himself on the gallery of Madame Angèle's small and modest house. She herself half-opened the door, a pale, sweet-looking woman, somewhat bewildered, and holding a piece of sewing in her hands. Little Marie Louise was beside her, with big, inquiring, frightened eyes.

"Well, Madam!" blustered Mr. Billy, "this is a pretty piece of work! That young beast of yours is a fence-breaker, Madam, and ought to be shot."

"Oh, non, non, M'sieur. Toto's too li'le; I'm sho he can't break any fence, him."

"Don't contradict me, Madam. I say he's a fence-breaker. There's the proof before your eyes. He ought to be shot, I say, and —don't let it occur again, Madam." And Mr. Billy turned and stamped down the steps with a great clatter of spurs as he went.

Madame Angèle was at the time in desperate haste to finish a young lady's Easter dress, and she could not afford to let Toto's escapade occupy her to any extent, much as she regretted it. But little Marie Louise was greatly impressed by the affair. She went out

in the yard to Toto, who was under the fig-
tree, looking not half so shamefaced as he
ought. The child, with arms clasped around
the little fellow's white shaggy neck, scolded
him roundly.

"Ain't you shame', Toto, to go eat up Mr.
Billy's cotton an' co'n? W'at Mr. Billy ev'a
done to you, to go do him that way? If you
been hungry, Toto, w'y you did'n' come like
always an' put yo' head in the winda? I'm
goin' tell yo' maman w'en she come back
f'om the woods to 's'evenin', M'sieur.

Marie Louise only ceased her mild rebuke
when she fancied she saw a penitential look in
Toto's big soft eyes.

She had a keen instinct of right and justice
for so young a little maid. And all the afternoon, and long into the night, she was disturbed by the thought of the unfortunate accident. Of course, there could be no question
of repaying Mr. Billy with money; she and
her mother had none. Neither had they cotton and corn with which to make good the
loss he had sustained through them.

But had they not something far more beautiful and precious than cotton and corn?

Marie Louise thought with delight of that
row of Easter lilies on their tall green stems,
ranged thick along the sunny side of the
house.

The assurance that she would, after all, be
able to satisfy Mr. Billy's just anger, was a
very sweet one. And soothed by it, Marie
Louise soon fell asleep and dreamt a grotesque dream: that the lilies were having a
stately dance on the green in the moonlight,
and were inviting Mr. Billy to join them.

The following day, when it was nearing noon,
Marie Louise said to her mamma: "Maman,
can I have some of the Easter lily, to do with
like I want?"

Madame Angèle was just then testing the
heat of an iron with which to press out the
seams in the young lady's Easter dress, and
she answered a shade impatiently:

"Yes, yes; va t'en, chérie," thinking that
her little girl wanted to pluck a lily or two.

So the child took a pair of old shears from
her mother's basket, and out she went to
where the tall, perfumed lilies were nodding,
and shaking off from their glistening petals

the rain-drops with which a passing cloud had just laughingly pelted them.

Snip, snap, went the shears here and there, and never did Marie Louise stop plying them till scores of those long-stemmed lilies lay upon the ground. There were far more than she could hold in her small hands, so she literally clasped the great bunch in her arms, and staggered to her feet with it.

Marie Louise was intent upon her purpose, and lost no time in its accomplishment. She was soon trudging earnestly down the lane with her sweet burden, never stopping, and only one glancing aside to cast a reproachful look at Toto, whom she had not wholly forgiven.

She did not in the least mind that the dogs barked, or that the darkies laughed at her. She went straight on to Mr. Billy's big house, and right into the dining-room, where Mr. Billy sat eating his dinner all alone.

It was a finely-furnished room, but disorderly—very disorderly, as an old bachelor's personal surroundings sometimes are. A black boy stood waiting upon the table. When little Marie Louise suddenly appeared, with that armful of lilies, Mr. Billy seemed for a moment transfixed at the sight.

"Well—bless—my soul! what's all this? What's all this?" he questioned, with staring eyes.

Marie Louise had already made a little courtesy. Her sunbonnet had fallen back, leaving exposed her pretty round head; and her sweet brown eyes were full of confidence as they looked into Mr. Billy's.

"I'm bring some lilies to pay back fo' yo' cotton an' co'n w'at Toto eat all up, M'sieur."

Mr. Billy turned savagely upon Pompey. "What are you laughing at, you black rascal? Leave the room!"

Pompey, who out of mistaken zeal had doubled himself with merriment, was too accustomed to the admonition to heed it literally, and he only made a pretense of withdrawing from Mr. Billy's elbow.

"Lilies! well, upon my—isn't it the little one from across the lane?"

"Dat's who," affirmed Pompey, cautiously insinuating himself again into favor.

"Lilies! who ever heard the like? Why, the baby's buried under 'em. Set 'em down

somewhere, little one; anywhere." And
Marie Louise, glad to be relieved from the
weight of the great cluster, dumped them all
on the table close to Mr. Billy.

The perfume that came from the damp,
massed flowers was heavy and almost sicken-
ing in its pungency. Mr. Billy quivered a
little, and drew involuntarily back, as if from
an unexpected assailant, when the odor
reached him. He had been making cotton
and corn for so many years, he had forgotten
there were such things as lilies in the world.

"Kiar 'em out? fling 'em 'way?" questioned
Pompey, who had observed his master cun-
ningly.

"Let 'em alone! Keep your hands off
them! Leave the room, you outlandish black
scamp! What are you standing there for?
Can't you set the Mamzelle a place at table,
and draw up a chair?"

So Marie Louise—perched upon a fine old-
fashioned chair, supplemented by a Webster's
Unabridged—sat down to dine with Mr.
Billy.

She had never eaten in company with so
peculiar a gentleman before; so irascible to-

ward the inoffensive Pompey, and so courteous to herself. But she was not ill at ease, and conducted herself properly as her mamma had taught her how.

Mr. Billy was anxious that she should enjoy her dinner, and began by helping her generously to Jambalaya. When she had tasted it she made no remark, only laid down her fork, and looked composedly before her.

"Why, bless me! what ails the little one? You don't eat your rice."

"It ain't cook', M'sieur," replied Marie Louise politely.

Pompey nearly strangled in his attempt to smother an explosion.

"Of course it isn't cooked," echoed Mr. Billy, excitedly, pushing away his plate. "What do you mean, setting a mess of that sort before human beings? Do you take us for a couple of—of rice-birds? What are you standing there for; can't you look up some jam or something to keep the young one from starving? Where's all that jam I saw stewing a while back, here?"

Pompey withdrew, and soon returned with a platter of black-looking jam. Mr. Billy ordered cream for it. Pompey reported there was none.

"No cream, with twenty-five cows on the plantation if there's one!" cried Mr. Billy, almost springing from his chair with indignation.

"Aunt Printy 'low she sot de pan o' cream on de winda-sell, suh, an' Unc' Jonah come 'long an' tu'n it cl'ar ova; neva lef' a drap in de pan."

But evidently the jam, with or without cream, was as distasteful to Marie Louise as the rice was; for after tasting it gingerly she laid away her spoon as she had done before.

"O, no! little one; you don't tell me it isn't cooked this time," laughed Mr. Billy. "I saw the thing boiling a day and a half. Wasn't it a day and a half, Pompey? if you know how to tell the truth."

"Aunt Printy alluz do cooks her p'esarves tell dey plumb done, sho," agreed Pompey.

"It's burn', M'sieur," said Marie Louise, politely, but decidedly, to the utter confusion of Mr. Billy, who was as mortified as could be at the failure of his dinner to please his fastidious little visitor.

Well, Mr. Billy thought of Marie Louise a good deal after that; as long as the lilies lasted. And they lasted long, for he had the whole household employed in taking care of them. Often he would chuckle to himself: "The little rogue, with her black eyes and her lilies! And the rice wasn't cooked, if you please; and the jam was burnt. And the best of it is, she was right."

But when the lilies withered finally, and had to be thrown away, Mr. Billy donned his best suit, a starched shirt and fine silk necktie. Thus attired, he crossed the lane to carry his somewhat tardy apologies to Madame Angèle and Mamzelle Marie Louise, and to pay them a first visit.

Azélie

Azélie

A ZÉLIE crossed the yard with slow, hesitating steps. She wore a pink sunbonnet and a faded calico dress that had
been made the summer before, and was now
too small for her in every way. She carried a
large tin pail on her arm. When within a few
yards of the house she stopped under a china-
berry-tree, quite still, except for the occasional
slow turning of her head from side to side.

Mr. Mathurin, from his elevation upon the
upper gallery, laughed when he saw her; for
he knew she would stay there, motionless, till
some one noticed and questioned her.

The planter was just home from the city,
and was therefore in an excellent humor, as
he always was, on getting back to what he
called *le grand air*, the space and stillness of
the country, and the scent of the fields. He
was in shirtsleeves, walking around the gal-

lery that encircled the big square white house. Beneath was a brick-paved portico upon which the lower rooms opened. At wide intervals were large whitewashed pillars that supported the upper gallery.

In one corner of the lower house was the store, which was in no sense a store for the general public, but maintained only to supply the needs of Mr. Mathurin's "hands."

"Eh bien! what do you want, Azélie?" the planter finally called out to the girl in French. She advanced a few paces, and, pushing back her sunbonnet, looked up at him with a gentle, inoffensive face—"to which you would give the good God without confession," he once described it.

"Bon jou', M'si' Mathurin," she replied; and continued in English: "I come git a li'le piece o' meat. We plumb out o' meat home."

"Well, well, the meat is n' going to walk to you, my chile: it has n' got feet. Go fine Mr. 'Polyte. He's yonda mending his buggy unda the shed." She turned away with an alert little step, and went in search of Mr. 'Polyte.

"That's you again!" the young man exclaimed, with a pretended air of annoyance,
when he saw her. He straightened himself,
and looked down at her and her pail with a
comprehending glance. The sweat was
standing in shining beads on his brown, good-
looking face. He was in his shirt-sleeves, and
the legs of his trousers were thrust into the
tops of his fine, high-heeled boots. He wore
his straw hat very much on one side, and
had an air that was altogether *fanfaron*. He
reached to a back pocket for the store key,
which was as large as the pistol that he sometimes carried in the same place. She followed
him across the thick, tufted grass of the yard
with quick, short steps that strove to keep
pace with his longer, swinging ones.

When he had unlocked and opened the
heavy door of the store, there escaped from
the close room the strong, pungent odor of
the varied wares and provisions massed within. Azélie seemed to like the odor, and, lifting her head, snuffed the air as people sometimes do upon entering a conservatory filled
with fragrant flowers.

A broad ray of light streamed in through the open door, illumining the dingy interior. The double wooden shutters of the windows were all closed, and secured on the inside by iron hooks.

"Well, w'at you want, Azélie?" asked 'Polyte, going behind the counter with an air of hurry and importance. "I ain't got time to fool. Make has'e; say w'at you want."

Her reply was precisely the same that she had made to Mr. Mathurin.

"I come git a li'le piece o' meat. We plumb out o' meat home."

He seemed exasperated.

"Bonté! w'at you all do with meat yonda? You don't reflec' you about to eat up yo' crop befo' it's good out o' the groun', you all. I like to know w'y yo' pa don't go he'p with the killin' once aw'ile, an' git some fresh meat fo' a change."

She answered in an unshaded, unmodulated voice that was penetrating, like a child's: "Popa he do go he'p wid the killin'; but he say he can't work 'less he got salt meat. He got plenty to feed—him. He's got to hire he'p wid his crop, an' he's boun' to feed 'em;

they won't year no diffe'nt. An' he's got
gra'ma to feed, an' Sauterelle, an' me—"

"An' all the lazy-bone 'Cadians in the country that know w'ere they goin' to fine the cof-
fee-pot always in the corna of the fire," grumbled 'Polyte.

With an iron hook he lifted a small piece of
salt meat from the pork barrel, weighed it,
and placed it in her pail.   Then she wanted a
little coffee.   He gave it to her reluctantly.
He was still more loath to let her have sugar;
and when she asked for lard, he refused flatly.

She had taken off her sunbonnet, and was
fanning herself with it, as she leaned with her
elbows upon the counter, and let her eyes
travel lingeringly along the well-lined shelves.
'Polyte stood staring into her face with a sense
of aggravation that her presence, her manner,
always stirred up in him.

The face was colorless but for the red,
curved line of the lips.   Her eyes were dark,
wide, innocent, questioning eyes, and her
black hair was plastered smooth back from
the forehead and temples.   There was no
trace of any intention of coquetry in her manner.   He resented this as a token of indiffer-

ence toward his sex, and thought it inexcus-
able.

"Well, Azélie, if it's anything you don't see,
ask fo' it," he suggested, with what he flat-
ered himself was humor. But there was no
responsive humor in Azélie's composition. She
seriously drew a small flask from her pocket.

"Popa say, if you want to let him have a
li'le dram, 'count o' his pains that's 'bout to
cripple him."

"Yo' pa knows as well as I do we don't
sell w'isky. Mr. Mathurin don't carry no li-
cense."

"I know· He say if you want to give 'im
a li'le dram, he's willin' to do some work fo'
you."

"No! Once fo' all, no!" And 'Polyte
reached for the day-book, in which to enter
the articles he had given to her.

But Azélie's needs were not yet satisfied.
She wanted tobacco; he would not give it to
her. A spool of thread; he rolled one up, together with two sticks of peppermint candy,
and placed it in her pail. When she asked
for a bottle of coal-oil, he grudgingly con-
sented, but assured her it would be useless to

cudgel her brain further, for he would posi-
tively let her have nothing more. He disappeared toward the coal-oil tank, which was
hidden from view behind the piled-up boxes
on the counter. When she heard him searching for an empty quart bottle, and making a
clatter with the tin funnels, she herself withdrew from the counter against which she had
been leaning.

After they quitted the store, 'Polyte, with a
perplexed expression upon his face, leaned for
a moment against one of the whitewashed
pillars, watching the girl cross the yard. She
had folded her sunbonnet into a pad, which
she placed beneath the heavy pail that she
balanced upon her head. She walked upright,
with a slow, careful tread. Two of the yard
dogs that had stood a moment before upon
the threshold of the store door, quivering and
wagging their tails, were following her now,
with a little businesslike trot. 'Polyte called
them back.

The cabin which the girl occupied with her
father, her grandmother, and her little brother
Sauterelle, was removed some distance from
the plantation house, and only its pointed roof

could be discerned like a speck far away across the field of cotton, which was all in bloom. Her figure soon disappeared from view, and 'Polyte emerged from the shelter of the gallery, and started again toward his interrupted task. He turned to say to the planter, who was keeping up his measured tramp above:

"Mr. Mathurin, ain't it 'mos' time to stop givin' credit to Arsène Pauché. Look like that crop o' his ain't goin' to start to pay his account. I don't see, me, anyway, how you come to take that triflin' Li'le river gang on the place."

"I know it was a mistake, 'Polyte, but que voulez-vous?" the planter returned, with a good-natured shrug. "Now they are yere, we can't let them starve, my frien'. Push them to work all you can. Hole back all supplies that are not necessary, an' nex' year we will let some one else enjoy the privilege of feeding them," he ended, with a laugh.

"I wish they was all back on Li'le river," 'Polyte muttered under his breath as he turned and walked slowly away.

Directly back of the store was the young man's sleeping-room. He had made himself quite comfortable there in his corner. He had screened his windows and doors; planted Madeira vines, which now formed a thick green curtain between the two pillars that faced his room; and had swung a hammock out there, in which he liked well to repose himself after the fatigues of the day.

He lay long in the hammock that evening, thinking over the day's happenings and the morrow's work, half dozing, half dreaming, and wholly possessed by the charm of the night, the warm, sweeping air that blew through the long corridor, and the almost unbroken stillness that enveloped him.

At times his random thoughts formed themselves into an almost inaudible speech: "I wish she would go 'way f'om yere."

One of the dogs came and thrust his cool, moist muzzle against 'Polyte's cheek. He caressed the fellow's shaggy head. "I don't know w'at's the matta with her," he sighed; "I don' b'lieve she's got good sense."

It was a long time afterward that he murmured again: "I wish to God she'd go 'way f'om yere!"

The edge of the moon crept up—a keen, curved blade of light above the dark line of the cotton-field. 'Polyte roused himself when he saw it. "I didn' know it was so late," he said to himself—or to his dog. He entered his room at once, and was soon in bed, sleeping soundly.

It was some hours later that 'Polyte was roused from his sleep by—he did not know what; his senses were too scattered and confused to determine at once. There was at first no sound; then so faint a one that he wondered how he could have heard it. A door of his room communicated with the store, but this door was never used, and was almost completely blocked by wares piled up on the other side. The faint noise that 'Polyte heard, and which came from within the store, was followed by a flare of light that he could discern through the chinks, and that lasted as long as a match might burn.

He was now fully aware that some one was in the store. How the intruder had entered he could not guess, for the key was under his pillow with his watch and his pistol.

As cautiously as he could he donned an extra garment, thrust his bare feet into slippers, and crept out into the portico, pistol in hand.

The shutters of one of the store windows were open. He stood close to it, and waited, which he considered surer and safer than to enter the dark and crowded confines of the store to engage in what might prove a bootless struggle with the intruder.

He had not long to wait. In a few moments some one darted through the open window as nimbly as a cat. 'Polyte staggered back as if a heavy blow had stunned him. His first thought and his first exclamation were: "My God! how close I come to killin' you!"

It was Azélie. She uttered no cry, but made one quick effort to run when she saw him. He seized her arm and held her with a brutal grip. He put the pistol back into his pocket. He was shaking like a man with the palsy. One by one he took from her the parcels she was carrying, and flung them back into the store. There were not many: some packages of tobacco, a cheap pipe, some fishing-tackle, and the flask which she had brought with her in the afternoon. This he threw into the yard. It was still empty, for she had not been able to find the "key" to the whisky-barrel.

"So—so, you a thief!" he muttered savagely under his breath.

"You hurtin' me, Mr. 'Polyte," she complained, squirming. He somewhat relaxed, but did not relinquish, his hold upon her.

"I ain't no thief," she blurted.

"You was stealin'," he contradicted her sharply.

"I wasn' stealin'. I was jus' takin' a few li'le things you all too mean to gi' me. You all treat my popa like he was a dog. It's on'y las' week Mr. Mathurin sen' 'way to the city to fetch a fine buckboa'd fo' Son Ambroise, an' he's on'y a nigga, après tout. An' my popa he want a picayune tobacca? It's 'No'—" She spoke loud in her monotonous, shrill voice. 'Polyte kept saying: "Hush, I tell you! Hush! Somebody'll year you. Hush! It's enough you broke in the sto'—how you got in the sto'?" he added, looking from her to the open window.

"It was w'en you was behine the boxes to the coal-oil tank—I unhook' it," she explained sullenly.

"An' you don' know I could sen' you to Baton Rouge fo' that?" He shook her as though trying to rouse her to a comprehension of her grievous fault.

"Jus' fo' a li'le picayune o' tobacca!" she whimpered.

He suddenly abandoned his hold upon her, and left her free. She mechanically rubbed the arm that he had grasped so violently.

Between the long row of pillars the moon was sending pale beams of light. In one of these they were standing.

"Azélie," he said, "go 'way f'om yere quick; some one might fine you yere. W'en you want something in the sto', fo' yo'se'f or fo' yo' pa —I don' care—ask me fo' it. But you—but you can't neva set yo' foot inside that sto' again. Co 'way f'om yere quick as you can, I tell you!"

She tried in no way to conciliate him. She turned and walked away over the same ground she had crossed before. One of the big dogs started to follow her. 'Polyte did not call him

back this time.   He knew no harm could
come to her, going through those lonely
fields, while the animal was at her side.

He went at once to his room for the store
key that was beneath his pillow. He entered
the store, and refastened the window. When
he had made everything once more secure,
he sat dejectedly down upon a bench that was
in the portico. He sat for a long time motionless. Then, overcome by some powerful
feeling that was at work within him, he buried
his face in his hands and wept, his whole body
shaken by the violence of his sobs.

After that night 'Polyte loved Azélie desper-
ately. The very action which should have
revolted him had seemed, on the contrary, to
inflame him with love. He felt that love to
be a degradation—something that he was almost ashamed to acknowledge to himself; and
he knew that he was hopelessly unable to
stifle it.

He watched now in a tremor for her coming. She came very often, for she remembered every word he had said; and she did not
hesitate to ask him for those luxuries which
she considered necessities to her "popa's" ex-

istence. She never attempted to enter the store, but always waited outside, of her own accord, laughing, and playing with the dogs. She seemed to have no shame or regret for what she had done, and plainly did not realize that it was a disgraceful act. 'Polyte often shuddered with disgust to discern in her a being so wholly devoid of moral sense.

He had always been an industrious, bustling fellow, never idle. Now there were hours and hours in which he did nothing but long for the sight of Azélie. Even when at work there was that gnawing want at his heart to see her, often so urgent that he would leave everything to wander down by her cabin with the hope of seeing her. It was even something if he could catch a glimpse of Sauterelle playing in the weeds, or of Arsène lazily dragging himself about, and smoking the pipe which rarely left his lips now that he was kept so well supplied with tobacco.

Once, down the bank of the bayou, when 'Polyte came upon Azélie unexpectedly, and was therefore unprepared to resist the shock of her sudden appearance, he seized her in his arms, and covered her face with kisses. She was not indignant; she was not flustered or agitated, as might have been a susceptible, coquettish girl; she was only astonished, and annoyed.

"W'at you doin', Mr. 'Polyte?" she cried, struggling. "Leave me 'lone, I say! Leave me go!"

"I love you, I love you, I love you!" he stammered helplessly over and over in her face.

"You mus' los' yo' head," she told him, red from the effort of the struggle, when he released her.

"You right, Azélie; I b'lieve I los' my head," and he climbed up the bank of the bayou as fast as he could.

After that his behavior was shameful, and he knew it, and he did not care. He invented pretexts that would enable him to touch her hand with his. He wanted to kiss her again, and told her she might come into the store as she used to do. There was no need for her to unhook a window now; he gave her whatever she asked for, charging it always to his own account on the books. She permitted his caresses without returning them, and yet that was all he seemed to live for now. He gave her a little gold ring.

He was looking eagerly forward to the close of the season, when Arsène would go back to Little River. He had arranged to ask Azélie to marry him. He would keep her with him when the others went away. He longed to rescue her from what he felt to be the demoralizing influences of her family and her surroundings. 'Polyte believed he would be able to awaken Azélie to finer, better impulses when he should have her apart to himself.

But when the time came to propose it, Azélie looked at him in amazement. "Ah, b'en, no. I ain't goin' to stay yere wid you, Mr. 'Polyte; I'm goin' yonda on Li'le river wid my popa."

This resolve frightened him, but he pretended not to believe it.

"You jokin', Azélie; you mus' care a li'le about me. It looked to me all along like you cared some about me."

"An' my popa, donc? Ah, b'en, no."

"You don' rememba how lonesome it is on Li'le river, Azélie," he pleaded. "W'en-ever I think 'bout Li'le river it always make me sad—like I think about a graveyard. To me it's like a person mus' die, one way or otha, w'en they go on Li'le river. Oh, I hate it! Stay with me, Azélie; don' go 'way f'om me."

She said little, one way or the other, after that, when she had fully understood his wishes, and her reserve led him to believe, since he hoped it, that he had prevailed with her and that she had determined to stay with him and be his wife.

It was a cool, crisp morning in December that they went away. In a ramshackle wagon, drawn by an ill-mated team, Arsène Pauché and his family left Mr. Mathurin's plantation for their old familiar haunts on Little river. The grandmother, looking like a witch, with a black shawl tied over her head, sat upon a roll of bedding in the bottom of the wagon. Sauterelle's bead-like eyes glittered with mischief as he peeped over the side. Azélie, with the pink sunbonnet completely hiding her round young face, sat beside her father, who drove.

'Polyte caught one glimpse of the group as they passed in the road. Turning, he hurried into his room, and locked himself in.

It soon became evident that 'Polyte's services were going to count for little. He himself was the first to realize this. One day he approached the planter, and said: "Mr. Mathurin, befo' we start anotha year togetha, I betta tell you I'm goin' to quit." 'Polyte stood upon the steps, and leaned back against the railing. The planter was a little above on the gallery.

"W'at in the name o' sense are you talking about, 'Polyte!" he exclaimed in astonishment.

"It's jus' that; I'm boun' to quit."

"You had a better offer?"

"No; I ain't had no offa."

"Then explain yo'se'f, my frien'—explain yo'se'f," requested Mr. Mathurin, with something of offended dignity. "If you leave me, w'ere are you going?"

'Polyte was beating his leg with his limp felt hat. "I reckon I jus' as well go yonda on Li'le river—w'ere Azélie," he said.

Mamouche

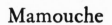

Mamouche

M AMOUCHE stood within the open doorway, which he had just entered. It was night; the rain was falling in torrents, and the water trickled from him as it would have done from an umbrella, if he had carried one.

Old Doctor John-Luis, who was toasting his feet before a blazing hickory-wood fire, turned to. gaze at the youngster through his spectacles. Marshall, the old negro who had opened the door at the boy's knock, also looked down at him, and indignantly said:

"G'long back on de gall'ry an' drip yo'se'f! W'at Cynthy gwine say tomorrow w'en she see dat flo' mess' up dat away?"

"Come to the fire and sit down," said Doctor John-Luis.

Doctor John-Luis was a bachelor. He was small and thin; he wore snuff-colored clothes that were a little too large for him, and spectacles. Time had not deprived him of an abundant crop of hair that had once been red, and was not now more than half-bleached.

The boy looked irresolutely from master to man; then went and sat down beside the fire on a splint-bottom chair. He sat so close to the blaze that had he been an apple he would have roasted. As he was but a small boy, clothed in wet rags, he only steamed.

Marshall grumbled audibly, and Doctor John-Luis continued to inspect the boy through his glasses.

"Marsh, bring him something to eat," he commanded, tentatively.

Marshall hesitated, and challenged the child with a speculating look.

"Is you w'ite o' is you black?" he asked. "Dat w'at I wants ter know 'fo' I kiar' victuals to yo in de settin'-room."

"I'm w'ite, me," the boy responded, promptly.

"I ain't disputin'; go ahead. All right fer dem w'at wants ter take yo' wud fer it." Doctor John-Luis coughed behind his hand and said nothing.

Marshall brought a platter of cold food to the boy, who rested the dish upon his knees and ate from it with keen appetite.

"Where do you come from?" asked Doctor John-Luis, when his caller stopped for breath. Mamouche turned a pair of big, soft, dark eyes upon his questioner.

"I come frum Cloutierville this mo'nin'. I been try to git to the twenty-fo'-mile ferry w'en de rain ketch me."

"What were you going to do at the twenty-four-mile ferry?"

The boy gazed absently into the fire. "I don' know w'at I was goin' to do yonda to the twenty-fo'-mile ferry," he said.

"Then you must be a tramp, to be wandering aimlessly about the country in that way!" exclaimed the doctor.

"No; I don' b'lieve I'm a tramp, me." Mamouche was wriggling his toes with enjoyment of the warmth and palatable food.

"Well, what's your name?" continued Doctor John-Luis.

"My name it's Mamouche."

" 'Mamouche.' Fiddlesticks! That's no name."

The boy looked as if he regretted the fact, while not being able to help it.

"But my pa, his name it was Mathurin Peloté," he offered in some palliation.

"Peloté! Peloté!" mused Doctor John-Luis. "Any kin to Théodule Peloté who lived formerly in Avoyelles parish?"

"W'y, yas!" laughed Mamouche. "Théodule Peloté, it was my gran'pa."

"Your grandfather? Well, upon my word!" He looked again, critically, at the youngster's rags. "Then Stéphanie Galopin must have been your grandmother!"

"Yas," responded Mamouche, complacently; "that who was my gran'ma. She die two year ago down by Alexandria."

"Marsh," called Doctor John-Luis, turning in his chair, "bring him a mug of milk and another piece of pie!"

When Mamouche had eaten all the good things that were set before him, he found that one side of him was quite dry, and he transferred himself over to the other corner of the fire so as to turn to the blaze the side which was still wet.

The action seemed to amuse Doctor John-Luis, whose old head began to fill with recollections.

"That reminds me of Théodule," he laughed. "Ah, he was a great fellow, your father, Théodule!"

"My gran'pa," corrected Mamouche.

"Yes, yes, your grandfather. He was handsome; I tell you, he was good-looking. And the way he could dance and play the fiddle and sing! Let me see, how did that song go that he used to sing when we went out serenading: 'A ta—à ta—'

     ' A ta fenêtre
       Daignes paraître—tra la la la!' "

Doctor John-Luis's voice, even in his youth, could not have been agreeable; and now it bore no resemblance to any sound that Mamouche had ever heard issue from a human throat. The boy kicked his heels and rolled sideward on his chair with enjoyment. Doctor John-Luis laughed even more heartily, finished the stanza, and sang another one through.

"That's what turned the girls' heads, I tell you, my boy," said he, when he had recovered his breath; "that fiddling and dancing and tra la la."

During the next hour the old man lived again through his youth; through any number of alluring experiences with his friend Théodule, that merry fellow who had never done a steady week's work in his life; and Stéphanie, the pretty Acadian girl, whom he had never wholly understood, even to this day.

It was quite late when Doctor John-Luis climbed the stairs that led from the sitting-room up to his bedchamber. As he went, followed by the ever attentive Marshall, he was singing:

> "A ta fenêtre
> Daignes paraître,"

but very low, so as not to awaken Mamouche, whom he left sleeping upon a bed that Marshall at his order had prepared for the boy beside the sitting-room fire.

At a very early hour next morning Marshall appeared at his master's bedside with the accustomed morning coffee.

"What is he doing?" asked Doctor John-Luis, as he sugared and stirred the tiny cup of black coffee.

"Who dat, sah?"

"Why, the boy, Mamouche. What is he doing?"

"He gone, sah. He done gone."

"Gone!"

"Yas, sah. He roll his bed up in de corner; he onlock de do'; he gone. But de silver an' ev'thing dah; he ain't kiar' nuttin' off."

"Marshall," snapped Doctor John-Luis, ill-humoredly, "there are times when you don't seem to have sense and penetration enough to talk about! I think I'll take another nap" he grumbled, as he turned his back upon Marshall. "Wake me at seven."

It was no ordinary thing for Doctor John-Luis to be in a bad humor, and perhaps it is not strictly true to say that he was now. He was only in a little less amiable mood than usual when he pulled on his high rubber boots and went splashing out in the wet to see what his people were doing.

He might have owned a large plantation had he wished to own one, for a long life of persistent, intelligent work had left him with a comfortable fortune in his old age; but he preferred the farm on which he lived contentedly and raised an abundance to meet his modest wants.

He went down to the orchard, where a couple of men were busying themselves in setting out a line of young fruit-trees.

"Tut, tut, tut!" They were doing it all wrong; the line was not straight; the holes were not deep. It was strange that he had to come down there and discover such things with his old eyes!

He poked his head into the kitchen to complain to Prudence about the ducks that she had not seasoned properly the day before, and to hope that the accident would never occur again.

He tramped over to where a carpenter was working on a gate; securing it—as he meant to secure all the gates upon his place—with great patent clamps and ingenious hinges, intended to baffle utterly the designs of the evil-disposed persons who had lately been tampering with them. For there had been a malicious spirit abroad, who played tricks, it seemed, for pure wantonness upon the farmers and planters, and caused them infinite annoyance.

As Dr. John-Luis contemplated the carpenter at work, and remembered how his gates had recently all been lifted from their hinges one night and left lying upon the ground, the provoking nature of the offense dawned upon him as it had not done before. He turned swiftly, prompted by a sudden determination, and re-entered the house.

Then he proceeded to write out in immense black characters a half-dozen placards. It was an offer of twenty-five dollars' reward for the capture of the person guilty of the malicious offence already described. These placards were sent abroad with the same eager haste that had conceived and executed them.

After a day or two, Doctor John-Luis' ill humor had resolved itself into a pensive melancholy.

"Marsh," he said, "you know, after all, it's rather dreary to be living alone as I do, without any companion—of my own color, you understand."

"I knows dat, sah. It sho' am lonesome," replied the sympathetic Marshall.

"You see, Marsh, I've been thinking lately," and Doctor John-Luis coughed, for he disliked the inaccuracy of that "lately." "I've been thinking that this property and wealth that I've worked so hard to accumulate, are after all doing no permanent, practical good to any one. Now, if I could find some well-disposed boy whom I might train to work, to study, to lead a decent, honest life—a boy of good heart who would care for me in my old age; for I am still comparatively—hem—not old? hey, Marsh?"

"Dey ain't one in de pa'ish hole yo' own like you does, sah."

"That's it. Now, can you think of such a boy? Try to think."

Marshall slowly scratched his head and looked reflective.

"If you can think of such a boy," said Doctor John-Luis, "you might bring him here to spend an evening with me, you know, without hinting at my intentions, of course. In that way I could sound him; study him up, as it were. For a step of such importance is not

to be taken without due consideration,
Marsh."

Well, the first whom Marshall brought was
one of Baptiste Choupic's boys. He was a
very timid child, and sat on the edge of his
chair, fearfully. He replied in jerky mono-
syllables when Doctor John-Luis spoke to
him, "Yas, sah—no, sah," as the case might
be; with a little nervous bob of the head.

His presence made the doctor quite uncom-
fortable. He was glad to be rid of the boy
at nine o'clock, when he sent him home with
some oranges and a few sweetmeats.

Then Marshall had Theodore over; an unfortunate selection that evinced little judgment on Marshall's part. Not to mince matters, the boy was painfully forward. He mon-
opolized the conversation; asked impertinent
questions and handled and inspected everything in the room. Dr. John-Luis sent him
home with an orange and not a single sweet.

Then there was Hyppolite, who was too
ugly to be thought of; and Cami, who was
heavy and stupid, and fell asleep in his chair
with his mouth wide open. And so it went.
If Doctor John-Luis had hoped in the com-

pany of any of these boys to repeat the agreeable evening he had passed with Mamouche, he was sadly deceived.

At last he instructed Marshall to discontinue the search of that ideal companion he had dreamed of. He was resigned to spend the remainder of his days without one.

Then, one day when it was raining again, and very muddy and chill, a red-faced man came driving up to Doctor John-Luis' door in a dilapidated buggy. He lifted a boy from the vehicle, whom he held with a vise-like clutch, and whom he straightway dragged into the astonished presence of Doctor John-Luis.

"Here he is, sir," shouted the red-faced man. "We've got him at last! Here he is."

It was Mamouche, covered with mud, the picture of misery. Doctor John-Luis stood with his back to the fire. He was startled, and visibly and painfully moved at the sight of the boy.

"Is it possible!" he exclaimed. "Then it was you, Mamouche, who did this mischievous thing to me? Lifting my gates from their hinges; letting the chickens in among my flowers to ruin them; and the hogs and cattle to trample and uproot my vegetables!"

"Ha! ha!" laughed the red-faced man, "that game's played out, now;" and Doctor John-Luis looked as if he wanted to strike him.

Mamouche seemed unable to reply. His lower lip was quivering.

"Yas, it's me!" he burst out. "It's me w'at take yo' gates off the hinge. It's me w'at turn loose Mr. Morgin's hoss, w'en Mr. Morgin was passing *veillée* wid his sweetheart. It's me w'at take down Ma'ame Angèle's fence, an' lef her calf loose to tramp in Mr. Billy's cotton. It's me w'at play like a ghos' by the graveyard las' Toussaint to scare the darkies passin' in the road. It's me w'at—"

The confession had burst out from the depth of Mamouche's heart like a torrent, and there is no telling when it would have stopped if Doctor John-Luis had not enjoined silence.

"And pray tell me," he asked, as severely as he could, "why you left my house like a criminal, in the morning, secretly?"

The tears had begun to course down Mamouche's brown cheeks.

"I was 'shame' of myse'f, that's w'y. If you wouldn' gave me no suppa, an' no bed, an' no fire, I don' say.' I wouldn' been 'shame' then."

"Well, sir," interrupted the red-faced man, "you've got a pretty square case against him, I see. Not only for malicious trespass, but of theft. See this bolt?" producing a piece of iron from his coat pocket. "That's what gave him away."

"I en't no thief!" blurted Mamouche, indignantly. "It's one piece o' iron w'at I pick up in the road."

"Sir," said Doctor John-Luis with dignity, "I can understand how the grandson of Théodule Peloté might be guilty of such mischievous pranks as this boy has confessed to. But I know that the grandson of Stéphanie Galopin could not be a thief."

And he at once wrote out the check for twenty-five dollars, and handed it to the red-faced man with the tips of his fingers.

It seemed very good to Doctor John-Luis to have the boy sitting again at his fireside; and so natural, too. He seemed to be the incarnation of unspoken hopes; the realization of vague and fitful memories of the past.

When Mamouche kept on crying, Doctor John-Luis wiped away the tears with his own brown silk handkerchief.

"Mamouche," he said, "I want you to stay here; to live here with me always. To learn how to work; to learn how to study; to grow up to be an honorable man. An honorable man, Mamouche, for I want you for my own child."

His voice was pretty low and husky when he said that.

"I shall not take the key from the door to-night," he continued. "If you do not choose to stay and be all this that I say, you may open the door and walk out. I shall use no force to keep you."

"What is he doing, Marsh?" asked Doctor John-Luis the following morning, when he took the coffee that Marshall had brought to him in bed.

"Who dat, sah?"

"Why, the boy Mamouche, of course. What is he doing?"

Marshall laughed.

"He kneelin' down dah on de flo'. He keep on sayin', 'Hail, Mary, full o' grace, de Lord is wid dee. Hail, Mary, full o' grace'— t'ree, fo' times, sah. I tell 'im, 'W'at you sayin' yo' prayer dat away, boy?' He 'low dat w'at his gran'ma larn 'im, ter keep outen mischief. W'en de devil say, 'Take dat gate offen de hinge; do dis; do dat,' he gwine say t'ree Hail Mary, an' de devil gwine tu'n tail an' run."

"Yes, yes," laughed Doctor John-Luis. "That's Stéphanie all over."

"An' I tell 'im: See heah, boy, you drap a couple o' dem Hail Mary, an' quit studyin' 'bout de devil, an' sot yo'se'f down ter wuk. Dat the oniest way to keep outen mischief."

"What business is it of yours to interfere?" broke in Doctor John-Luis, irritably. "Let the boy do as his grandmother instructed him."

"I ain't desputin', sah," apologized Marshall.

"But you know, Marsh," continued the doctor, recovering his usual amiability. "I think we'll be able to do something with the boy. I'm pretty sure of it. For, you see, he has his grandmother's eyes; and his grandmother was a very intelligent woman; a clever woman, Marsh. Her one great mistake was when she married Théodule Peloté."

A Sentimental Soul

A Sentimental Soul

I.

LACODIE stayed longer than was his custom in Mamzelle Fleurette's little store that evening. He had been tempted by the vapid utterances of a conservative bellhanger to loudly voice his radical opinions upon the rights and wrongs of humanity at large and his fellow-workingmen in particular. He was quite in a tremble when he finally laid his picayune down upon Mamzelle Fleurette's counter and helped himself to *l'Abeille* from the top of the diminished pile of newspapers which stood there.

He was small, frail and hollow-chested, but his head was magnificent with its generous adornment of waving black hair; its sunken eyes that glowed darkly and steadily and sometimes flamed, and its moustaches which were formidable.

"Eh bien, Mamzelle Fleurette, à demain, à demain!" and he waved a nervous good-bye as he let himself quickly and noiselessly out.

However violent Lacodie might be in his manner toward conservatives, he was always gentle, courteous and low-voiced with Mamzelle Fleurette, who was much older than he, much taller; who held no opinions, and whom he pitied, and even in a manner revered. Mamzelle Fleurette at once dismissed the bell-hanger, with whom, on general principles, she had no sympathy.

She wanted to close the store, for she was going over to the cathedral to confession. She stayed a moment in the doorway watching Lacodie walk down the opposite side of the street. His step was something between a spring and a jerk, which to her partial eyes seemed the perfection of motion. She watched him until he entered his own small low doorway, over which hung a huge wooden key painted red, the emblem of his trade.

For many months now, Lacodie had been coming daily to Mamzelle Fleurette's little notion store to buy the morning paper, which he only bought and read, however, in the afternoon. Once he had crossed over with his box of keys and tools to open a cupboard, which would unlock for no inducements of its owner. He would not suffer her to pay him for the few moments' work; it was nothing, he assured her; it was a pleasure; he would not dream of accepting payment for so trifling a service from a camarade and fellow-worker. But she need not fear that he would lose by it, he told her with a laugh; he would only charge an extra quarter to the rich lawyer around the corner, or to the top-lofty druggist down the street when these might happen to need his services, as they sometimes did. This was an alternative which seemed far from right and honest to Mamzelle Fleurette. But she held a vague understanding that men were wickeder in many ways than women; that ungodliness was constitutional with them, like their sex, and inseparable from it.

Having watched Lacodie until he disappeared within his shop, she retired to her room, back of the store, and began her preparations to go out. She brushed carefully the black alpaca skirt, which hung in long nun-

like folds around her spare figure. She
smoothed down the brown, ill-fitting basque,
and readjusted the old-fashioned, rusty black
lace collar which she always wore. Her sleek
hair was painfully and suspiciously black. She
powdered her face abundantly with poudre de
riz before starting out, and pinned a dotted
black lace veil over her straw bonnet. There
was little force or character or anything in
her withered face, except a pathetic desire and
appeal to be permitted to exist.

Mamzelle Fleurette did not walk down
Chartres street with her usual composed tread;
she seemed preoccupied and agitated. When
she passed the locksmith's shop over the way
and heard his voice within, she grew trem-
ulously self-conscious, fingering her veil,
swishing the black alpaca and waving her
prayer book about with meaningless intention.

Mamzelle Fleurette was in great trouble;
trouble which was so bitter, so sweet, so bewildering, so terrifying! It had come so
stealthily upon her she had never suspected
what it might be. She thought the world was
growing brighter and more beautiful; she
thought the flowers had redoubled their sweet-

ness and the birds their song, and that the voices of her fellow-creatures had grown kinder and their faces truer.

The day before Lacodie had not come to her for his paper. At six o'clock he was not there, at seven he was not there, nor at eight, and then she knew he would not come. At first, when it was only a little past the time of his coming, she had sat strangely disturbed and distressed in the rear of the store, with her back to the door. When the door opened she turned with fluttering expectancy. It was only an unhappy-looking child, who wanted to buy some foolscap, a pencil and an eraser. The next to come in was an old mulatresse, who was bringing her prayer beads for Mamzelle Fleurette to mend. The next was a gentleman, to buy the Courier des Etats Unis, and then a young girl, who wanted a holy picture for her favorite nun at the Ursulines; it was everybody but Lacodie.

A temptation assailed Mamzelle Fleurette, almost fierce in its intensity, to carry the paper over to his shop herself, when he was not there at seven. She conquered it from sheer moral inability to do anything so daring, so

unprecedented. But to-day, when he had
come back and had stayed so long discours-
ing with the bellhanger, a contentment, a rapture, had settled upon her being which she
could no longer ignore or mistake. She loved
Lacodie. That fact was plain to her now, as
plain as the conviction that every reason ex-
isted why she should not love him. He was
the husband of another woman. To love the
husband of another woman was one of the
deepest sins which Mamzelle Fleurette knew;
murder was perhaps blacker, but she was not
sure. She was going to confession now. She
was going to tell her sin to Almighty God
and Father Fochelle, and ask their forgive-
ness. She was going to pray and beg the
saints and the Holy Virgin to remove the
sweet and subtle poison from her soul. It
was surely a poison, and a deadly one, which
could make her feel that her youth had come
back and taken her by the hand.

II.

Mamzelle Fleurette had been confessing for
many years to old Father Fochelle. In his
secret heart he often thought it a waste of

his time and her own that she should come
with her little babblings, her little nothings to
him, calling them sins. He felt that a wave
of the hand might brush them away, and that
it in a manner compromised the dignity of
holy absolution to pronounce the act over so
innocent a soul.

To-day she had whispered all her short-
comings into his ear through the grating of
the confessional; he knew them so well! There
were many other penitents waiting to be
heard, and he was about to dismiss her with
a hasty blessing when she arrested him, and in
hesitating, faltering accents told him of her
love for the locksmith, the husband of another
woman. A slap in the face would not have
startled Father Fochelle more forcibly or
more painfully. What soul was there on
earth, he wondered, so hedged about with innocence as to be secure from the machinations
of Satan! Oh, the thunder of indignation that
descended upon Mamzelle Fleurette's head!
She bowed down, beaten to earth beneath it.
Then came questions, one, two, three, in quick
succession, that made Mamzelle Fleurette
gasp and clutch blindly before her.   Why was

she not a shadow, a vapor, that she might dissolve from before those angry, penetrating eyes; or a small insect, to creep into some crevice and there hide herself forevermore?

"Oh, father! no, no, no!" she faltered, "he knows nothing, nothing. I would die a hundred deaths before he should know, before anyone should know, besides yourself and the good God of whom I implore pardon."

Father Fochelle breathed more freely, and mopped his face with a flaming bandana, which he took from the ample pocket of his soutane. But he scolded Mamzelle Fleurette roundly, unpityingly; for being a fool, for being a sentimentalist. She had not committed mortal sin, but the occasion was ripe for it; and look to it she must that she keep Satan at bay with watchfulness and prayer. "Go, my child, and sin no more."

Mamzelle Fleurette made a détour in regaining her home by which she would not have to pass the locksmith's shop. She did not even look in that direction when she let herself in at the glass door of her store.

Some time before, when she was yet ignorant of the motive which prompted the act, she had cut from a newspaper a likeness of Lacodie, who had served as foreman of the jury during a prominent murder trial. The likeness happened to be good, and quite did justice to the locksmith's fine physiognomy with its leonine hirsute adornment. This picture Mamzelle Fleurette had kept hitherto between the pages of her prayer book. Here, twice a day, it looked out at her; as she turned the leaves of the holy mass in the morning, and when she read her evening devotions before her own little home altar, over which hung a crucifix and a picture of the Empress Eugénie.

Her first action upon entering her room, even before she unpinned the dotted veil, was to take Lacodie's picture from her prayer book and place it at random between the leaves of a "Dictionnaire de la Langue Francaise," which was the undermost of a pile of old books that stood on the corner of the mantelpiece. Between night and morning, when she would approach the holy sacrament, Mamzelle Fleurette felt it to be her duty to thrust Lacodie from her thoughts by every means and device known to her.

The following day was Sunday, when there was no occasion or opportunity for her to see the locksmith. Moreover, after partaking of holy communion, Mamzelle Fleurette felt invigorated; she was conscious of a new, if fictitious, strength to combat Satan and his wiles.

On Monday, as the hour approached for Lacodie to appear, Mamzelle Fleurette became harassed by indecision. Should she call in the young girl, the neighbor who relieved her on occasion, and deliver the store into the girl's hands for an hour or so? This might be well enough for once in a while, but she could not conveniently resort to this subterfuge daily. After all, she had her living to make, which consideration was paramount. She finally decided that she would retire to her little back room and when she heard the store door open she would call out:

"Is it you, Monsieur Lacodie? I am very busy; please take your paper and leave your cinq sous on the counter." If it happened not to be Lacodie she would come forward and serve the customer in person. She did not, of course, expect to carry out this performance each day; a fresh device would no doubt suggest itself for tomorrow. Mamzelle Fleurette proceeded to carry out her programme to the letter.

"Is it you, Monsieur Lacodie?" she called out from the little back room, when the front door opened. "I am very busy; please take your paper—"

"Ce n'est pas Lacodie, Mamzelle Fleurette. C'est moi, Augustine."

It was Lacodie's wife, a fat, comely young woman, wearing a blue veil thrown carelessly over her kinky black hair, and carrying some grocery parcels clasped close in her arms. Mamzelle Fleurette emerged from the back room, a prey to the most contradictory emotions; relief and disappointment struggling for the mastery with her.

"No Lacodie to-day, Mamzelle Fleurette," Augustine announced with a certain robust ill-humor; "he is there at home shaking with a chill till the very window panes rattle. He had one last Friday" (the day he had not come for his paper) "and now another and a worse one to-day. God knows, if it keeps on—

well, let me have the paper; he will want to
read it to-night when his chill is past."

Mamzelle Fleurette handed the paper to Augustine, feeling like an old woman in a dream
handing a newspaper to a young woman in a
dream. She had never thought of Lacodie
having chills or being ill. It seemed very
strange. And Augustine was no sooner gone
than all the ague remedies she had ever heard
of came crowding to Mamzelle Fleurette's
mind; an egg in black coffee—or was it a
lemon in black coffee? or an egg in vinegar?
She rushed to the door to call Augustine back,
but the young woman was already far down
the street.

III.

Augustine did not come the next day, nor
the next, for the paper. The unhappy looking
child who had returned for more foolscap, informed Mamzelle Fleurette that he had heard
his mother say that Monsieur Lacodie was
very sick, and the bellhanger had sat up all
night with him. The following day Mamzelle
Fleurette saw Choppin's coupé pass clattering
over the cobblestones and stop before the lock-

smith's door. She knew that with her class it was only in a case of extremity that the famous and expensive physician was summoned. For the first time she thought of death. She prayed all day, silently, to herself, even while waiting upon customers.

In the evening she took an *Abeille* from the top of the pile on the counter, and throwing a light shawl over her head, started with the paper over to the locksmith's shop. She did not know if she were committing a sin in so doing. She would ask Father Fochelle on Saturday, when she went to confession. She did not think it could be a sin; she would have called long before on any other sick neighbor, and she intuitively felt that in this distinction might lie the possibility of sin.

The shop was deserted except for the presence of Lacodie's little boy of five, who sat upon the floor playing with the tools and contrivances which all his days he had coveted, and which all his days had been denied to him. Mamzelle Fleurette mounted the narrow stairway in the rear of the shop which led to an upper landing and then into the room of the married couple. She stood a while hesitating upon this landing before venturing to knock softly upon the partly open door through which she could hear their voices.

"I thought," she remarked apologetically to Augustine, "that perhaps Monsieur Lacodie might like to look at the paper and you had no time to come for it, so I brought it myself."

"Come in, come in, Mamzelle Fleurette. It's Mamzelle Fleurette who comes to inquire about you, Lacodie," Augustine called out loudly to her husband, whose half consciousness she somehow confounded with deafness.

Mamzelle Fleurette drew mincingly forward, clasping her thin hands together at the waist line, and she peeped timorously at Lacodie lying lost amid the bedclothes. His black mane was tossed wildly over the pillow and lent a fictitious pallor to the yellow waxiness of his drawn features. An approaching chill was sending incipient shudders through his frame, and making his teeth claque. But he still turned his head courteously in Mamzelle Fleurette's direction.

"Bien bon de votre part, Mamzelle Fleurette—mais c'est fini. J'suis flambé, flambé flambé!"

Oh, the pain of it! to hear him in such extremity thanking her for her visit, assuring her in the same breath that all was over with him. She wondered how Augustine could hear it so composedly. She whisperingly inquired if a priest had been summoned.

"Inutile; il n'en veut pas," was Augustine's reply. So he would have no priest at his bedside, and here was a new weight of bitterness for Mamzelle Fleurette to carry all her days.

She flitted back to her store through the darkness, herself like a slim shadow. The November evening was chill and misty. A dull aureole shot out from the feeble gas jet at the corner, only faintly and for an instant illumining her figure as it glided rapidly and noiselessly along the banquette. Mamzelle Fleurette slept little and prayed much that night. Saturday morning Lacodie died. On Sunday he was buried and Mamzelle Fleurette did not go to the funeral, because Father Fochelle told her plainly she had no business there.

It seemed inexpressibly hard to Mamzelle Fleurette that she was not permitted to hold Lacodie in tender remembrance now that he was dead. But Father Fochelle, with his practical insight, made no compromise with sentimentality; and she did not question his authority, or his ability to master the subtleties of a situation utterly beyond reach of her own powers.

It was no longer a pleasure for Mamzelle Fleurette to go to confession as it had formerly been. Her heart went on loving Lacodie and her soul went on struggling; for she made this delicate and puzzling distinction between heart and soul, and pictured the two as set in a very death struggle against each other.

"I cannot help it, father. I try, but I cannot help it. To love him is like breathing; I do not know how to help it. I pray, and pray, and it does no good, for half of my prayers are for the repose of his soul. It surely cannot be a sin, to pray for the repose of his soul?"

Father Fochelle was heartily sick and tired of Mamzelle Fleurette and her stupidities. Oftentimes he was tempted to drive her from the confessional, and forbid her return until she should have regained a rational state of mind. But he could not withhold absolution from a penitent who, week after week, acknowledged her shortcoming and strove with all her faculties to overcome it and atone for it.

IV.

Augustine had sold out the locksmith's shop and the business, and had removed further down the street over a bakery. Out of her window she had hung a sign, "Blanchisseuse de Fin." Often, in passing by, Mamzelle Fleurette would catch a glimpse of Augustine up at the window, plying the irons; her sleeves rolled to the elbows, baring her round, white arms, and the little black curls all moist and tangled about her face. It was early spring then, and there was a languor in the air; an odor of jasmine in every passing breeze; the sky was blue, unfathomable, and fleecy white; and people along the narrow street laughed, and sang, and called to one another from windows and doorways. Augustine had set a pot of rose-geranium on her window sill and hung out a bird cage.

Once, Mamzelle Fleurette in passing on her way to confession heard her singing roulades, vying with the bird in the cage. Another time she saw the young woman leaning with half her body from the window, exchanging pleasantries with the baker standing beneath on the banquette.

Still, a little later, Mamzelle Fleurette began to notice a handsome young fellow often passing the store. He was jaunty and debonnaire and wore a rich watchchain, and looked prosperous. She knew him quite well as a fine young Gascon, who kept a stall in the French Market, and from whom she had often bought charcuterie. The neighbors told her the young Gascon was paying his addresses to Mme. Lacodie. Mamzelle Fleurette shuddered. She wondered if Lacodie knew! The whole situation seemed suddenly to shift its base, causing Mamzelle Fleurette to stagger. What ground would her poor heart and soul have to do battle upon now?

She had not yet had time to adjust her conscience to the altered conditions when one Saturday afternoon, as she was about to start out to confession, she noticed an unusual movement down the street. The bellhanger, who happened to be presenting himself in the character of a customer, informed her that it was nothing more nor less than Mme. Lacodie returning from her wedding with the Gascon. He was black and bitter with indignation, and thought she might at least have waited for the year to be out. But the charivari was already on foot; and Mamzelle need not feel alarmed if, in the night, she heard sounds and clamor to rouse the dead as far away as Metairie ridge.

Mamzelle Fleurette sank down in a chair, trembling in all her members. She faintly begged the bell hanger to pour her a glass of water from the stone pitcher behind the counter. She fanned herself and loosened her bonnet strings. She sent the bell hanger away.

She nervously pulled off her rusty black kid gloves, and ten times more nervously drew them on again. To a little customer, who came in for chewing gum, she handed a paper of pins.

There was a great, a terrible upheaval taking place in Mamzelle Fleurette's soul. She was preparing for the first time in her life to take her conscience into her own keeping.

When she felt herself sufficiently composed to appear decently upon the street, she started out to confession. She did not go to Father Fochelle. She did not even go to the Cathedral; but to a church which was much farther away, and to reach which she had to spend a picayune for car fare.

Mamzelle Fleurette confessed herself to a priest who was utterly new and strange to her. She told him all her little venial sins, which she had much difficulty in bringing to a number of any dignity and importance whatever. Not once did she mention her love for Lacodie, the dead husband of another woman.

Mamzelle Fleurette did not ride back to her home; she walked. The sensation of walking on air was altogether delicious; she had never experienced it before. A long time she stood contemplative before a shop window in which were displayed wreaths, mottoes, emblems, designed for the embellishment of tombstones. What a sweet comfort it would be, she reflected, on the 1st of November to carry some such delicate offering to Lacodie's last resting place. Might not the sole care of his tomb devolve upon her, after all! The possibility thrilled her and moved her to the heart. What thought would the merry Augustine and her lover-husband have for the dead lying in cemeteries!

When Mamzelle Fleurette reached home she went through the store directly into her little back room. The first thing which she did, even before unpinning the dotted lace veil, was to take the "Dictionnaire de La Langue Francaise" from beneath the pile of old books on the mantelpiece. It was not easy to find Lacodie's picture hidden somewhere in its depths. But the search afforded her almost a sensuous pleasure; turning the leaves slowly back and forth.

When she had secured the likeness she went into the store and from her showcase selected a picture frame—the very handsomest there; one of those which sold for thirty-five cents.

Into the frame Mamzelle Fleurette neatly and deftly pasted Lacodie's picture. Then she re-entered her room and deliberately hung it upon the wall—between the crucifix and the portrait of Empress Eugènie—and she did not care if the Gascon's wife ever saw it or not.

Dead Men's Shoes

Dead Men's Shoes

☙

IT never occurred to any person to wonder what would befall Gilma now that "le vieux Gamiche" was dead. After the burial people went their several ways, some to talk over the old man and his eccentricities, others to forget him before nightfall, and others to wonder what would become of his very nice property, the hundred-acre farm on which he had lived for thirty years, and on which he had just died at the age of seventy.

If Gilma had been a child, more than one motherly heart would have gone out to him. This one and that one would have bethought them of carrying him home with them; to concern themselves with his present comfort, if not his future welfare. But Gilma was not a child. He was a strapping fellow of nineteen, measuring six feet in his stockings, and

as strong as any healthy youth need be. For
ten years he had lived there on the plantation
with Monsieur Gamiche; and he seemed now
to have been the only one with tears to shed
at the old man's funeral.

Gamiche's relatives had come down from
Caddo in a wagon the day after his death, and
had settled themselves in his house. There
was Septime, his nephew, a cripple, so hor-
ribly afflicted that it was distressing to look at
him. And there was Septime's widowed sister, Ma'me Brozé, with her two little girls.
They had remained at the house during the
burial, and Gilma found them still there upon
his return.

The young man went at once to his room
to seek a moment's repose. He had lost
much sleep during Monsieur Gamiche's illness; yet, he was in fact more worn by the
mental than the bodily strain of the past week.

But when he entered his room, there was
something so changed in its aspect that it
seemed no longer to belong to him. In place
of his own apparel which he had left hanging
on the row of pegs, there were a few shabby
little garments and two battered straw hats,

the property of the Brozé children. The bureau drawers were empty, there was not a vestige of anything belonging to him remaining in the room. His first impression was that Ma'me Brozé had been changing things around and had assigned him to some other room.

But Gilma understood the situation better when he discovered every scrap of his personal effects piled up on a bench outside the door, on the back or "false" gallery. His boots and shoes were under the bench, while coats, trousers and underwear were heaped in an indiscriminate mass together.

The blood mounted to his swarthy face and made him look for the moment like an Indian. He had never thought of this. He did not know what he had been thinking of; but he felt that he ought to have been prepared for anything; and it was his own fault if he was not. But it hurt. This spot was "home" to him against the rest of the world. Every tree, every shrub was a friend; he knew every patch in the fences; and the little old house, gray and weather-beaten, that had been the shelter of his youth, he loved as only few

can love inanimate things. A great enmity
arose in him against Ma'me Brozé. She was
walking about the yard, with her nose in the
air, and a shabby black dress trailing behind
her. She held the little girls by the hand.

Gilma could think of nothing better to do
than to mount his horse and ride away—anywhere. The horse was a spirited animal of
great value. Monsieur Gamiche had named
him "Jupiter" on account of his proud bearing, and Gilma had nicknamed him "Jupe,"
which seemed to him more endearing and expressive of his great attachment to the fine
creature. With the bitter resentment of
youth, he felt that "Jupe" was the only friend
remaining to him on earth.

He had thrust a few pieces of clothing in
his saddlebags and had requested Ma'me
Brozé, with assumed indifference, to put his
remaining effects in a place of safety until
he should be able to send for them.

As he rode around by the front of the house,
Septime, who sat on the gallery all doubled
up in his uncle Gamiche's big chair, called
out:

"Hé, Gilma! w'ere you boun' fo'?"

"I'm goin' away," replied Gilma, curtly, reining his horse.

"That's all right; but I reckon you might jus' as well leave that hoss behine you."

"The hoss is mine," returned Gilma, as quickly as he would have returned a blow.

"We'll see 'bout that li'le later, my frien'. I reckon you jus' well turn 'im loose."

Gilma had no more intention of giving up his horse than he had of parting with his own right hand. But Monsieur Gamiche had taught him prudence and respect for the law. He did not wish to invite disagreeable complications. So, controlling his temper by a supreme effort, Gilma dismounted, unsaddled the horse then and there, and led it back to the stable. But as he started to leave the place on foot, he stopped to say to Septime:

"You know, Mr. Septime, that hoss is mine; I can collec' a hundred aff'davits to prove it. I'll bring them yere in a few days with a statement f'om a lawyer; an' I'll expec' the hoss an' saddle to be turned over to me in good condition."

"That's all right. We'll see 'bout that. Won't you stay fo' dinna?"

"No, I thank you, sah; Ma'me Brozé already ask' me." And Gilma strode away, down the beaten footpath that led across the sloping grassplot toward the outer road.

A definite destination and a settled purpose ahead of him seemed to have revived his flagging energies of an hour before. It was with no trace of fatigue that he stepped out bravely along the wagon-road that skirted the bayou.

It was early spring, and the cotton had already a good stand. In some places the negroes were hoeing. Gilma stopped alongside the rail fence and called to an old negress who was plying her hoe at no great distance.

"Hello, Aunt Hal'fax! see yere."

She turned, and immediately quitted her work to go and join him, bringing her hoe with her across her shoulder. She was large-boned and very black. She was dressed in the deshabille of the field.

"I wish you'd come up to yo' cabin with me a minute, Aunt Hally," he said; "I want to get an aff'davit f'om you."

She understood, after a fashion, what an affidavit was; but she couldn't see the good of it.

"I ain't got no aff'davis, boy; you g'long an' don' pesta me."

" 'Twon't take you any time, Aunt Hal'fax. I jus' want you to put yo' mark to a statement I'm goin' to write to the effec' that my hoss, Jupe, is my own prop'ty; that you know it, an' willin' to swear to it."

"Who say Jupe don' b'long to you?" she questioned cautiously, leaning on her hoe.

He motioned toward the house.

"Who? Mista Septime and them?"

"Yes."

"Well, I reckon!" she exclaimed, sympathetically.

"That's it," Gilma went on; "an' nex' thing they'll be sayin' yo' ole mule, Policy, don't b'long to you."

She started violently.

"Who say so?"

"Nobody. But I say, nex' thing, that' w'at they'll be sayin'."

She began to move along the inside of the fence, and he turned to keep pace with her, walking on the grassy edge of the road.

"I'll jus' write the aff'davit, Aunt Hally, an' all you got to do"—

"You know des well as me dat mule mine. I done paid ole Mista Gamiche fo' 'im in good cotton; dat year you falled outen de puckhorn tree; an' he write it down hisse'f in his 'count book."

Gilma did not linger a moment after obtaining the desired statement from Aunt Halifax. With the first of those "hundred affidavits" that he hoped to secure, safe in his pocket, he struck out across the country, seeking the shortest way to town.

Aunt Halifax stayed in the cabin door.

"'Relius," she shouted to a little black boy out in the road, "does you see Pol'cy any-whar? G'long, see ef he 'roun' de ben'. Wouldn' s'prise me ef he broke de fence an' got in yo' pa's corn ag'in." And, shading her eyes to scan the surrounding country, she muttered, uneasily: "Whar dat mule?"

The following morning Gilma entered town and proceeded at once to Lawyer Paxton's office. He had had no difficulty in obtaining the testimony of blacks and whites regarding his ownership of the horse; but he wanted to make his claim as secure as possible by consulting the lawyer and returning to the plantation armed with unassailable evidence.

The lawyer's office was a plain little room opening upon the street. Nobody was there, but the door was open; and Gilma entered and took a seat at the bare round table and waited. It was not long before the lawyer came in; he had been in conversation with some one across the street.

"Good-morning, Mr. Pax'on," said Gilma, rising.

The lawyer knew his face well enough, but could not place him, and only returned: "Good-morning, sir—good-morning."

"I come to see you," began Gilma plunging at once into business, and drawing his handful of nondescript affidavits from his pocket, "about a matter of prope'ty, about regaining possession of my hoss that Mr. Septime, ole Mr. Gamiche's nephew, is holdin' f'om me yonder."

The lawyer took the papers and, adjusting his eye-glasses, began to look them through.

"Yes, yes," he said; "I see."

"Since Mr. Gamiche died on Tuesday"— began Gilma.

"Gamiche died!" repeated Lawyer Paxton, with astonishment. "Why, you don't mean to tell me that vieux Gamiche is dead? Well, well. I hadn't heard of it; I just returned from Shreveport this morning. So le vieux Gamiche is dead, is he? And you say you want to get possession of a horse. What did you say your name was?" drawing a pencil from his pocket.

"Gilma Germain is my name, suh."

"Gilma Germain," repeated the lawyer, a little meditatively, scanning his visitor closely. "Yes, I recall your face now. You are the young fellow whom le vieux Gamiche took to live with him some ten or twelve years ago."

"Ten years ago las' November, suh."

Lawyer Paxton arose and went to his safe, from which, after unlocking it, he took a legal-looking document that he proceeded to read carefully through to himself.

"Well, Mr. Germain, I reckon there won't be any trouble about regaining possession of the horse," laughed Lawyer Paxton. "I'm pleased to inform you, my dear sir, that our old friend, Gamiche, has made you sole heir to his property; that is, his plantation, including live stock, farming implements, machinery, household effects, etc. Quite a pretty piece of property," he proclaimed leisurely, seating himself comfortably for a long talk. "And I may add, a pretty piece of luck, Mr. Germain, for a young fellow just starting out in life; nothing but to step into a dead man's shoes! A great chance—great chance. Do you know, sir, the moment you mentioned your name, it came back to me like a flash, how le vieux Gamiche came in here one day, about three years ago, and wanted to make his will"— And the loquacious lawyer went on with his reminiscences and interesting bits of information, of which Gilma heard scarcely a word.

He was stunned, drunk, with the sudden joy of possession; the thought of what seemed to him great wealth, all his own—his own! It seemed as if a hundred different sensations

were holding him at once, and as if a thous-
and intentions crowded upon him. He felt
like another being who would have to readjust himself to the new conditions, presenting themselves so unexpectedly. The narrow
confines of the office were stifling, and it
seemed as if the lawyer's flow of talk would
never stop. Gilma arose abruptly, and with a
half-uttered apology, plunged from the room
into the outer air.

Two days later Gilma stopped again before
Aunt Halifax's cabin, on his way back to the
plantation. He was walking as before, having declined to avail himself of any one of
the several offers of a mount that had been
tendered him in town and on the way. A
rumor of Gilma's great good fortune had pre-
ceded him, and Aunt Halifax greeted him
with an almost triumphal shout as he approached.

"God knows you desarve it, Mista Gilma!
De Lord knows you does, suh! Come in an'
res' yo'se'f, suh. You, 'Relius! git out dis
heah cabin; crowdin' up dat away!" She
wiped off the best chair available and offered
it to Gilma.

He was glad to rest himself and glad to accept Aunt Halifax's proffer of a cup of coffee, which she was in the act of dripping before a small fire. He sat as far as he could from the fire, for the day was warm; he mopped his face, and fanned himself with his broad-rimmed hat.

"I des' can't he'p laughin' w'en I thinks 'bout it," said the old woman, fairly shaking, as she leaned over the hearth. "I wakes up in de night, even, an' has to laugh."

"How's that, Aunt Hal'fax," asked Gilma, almost tempted to laugh himself at he knew not what.

"G'long, Mista Gilma! like you don' know! It's w'en I thinks 'bout Septime an' them like I gwine see 'em in dat wagon to-mor' mo'nin', on' dey way back to Caddo. Oh, lawsy!"

"That isn' so ver' funny, Aunt Hal'fax," returned Gilma, feeling himself ill at ease as he accepted the cup of coffee which she presented to him with much ceremony on a platter. "I feel pretty sorry for Septime, myse'f."

"I reckon he know now who Jupe b'long to," she went on, ignoring his expression of sympathy; "no need to tell him who Pol'cy b'long to, nuther. An' I tell you, Mista Gilma," she went on, leaning upon the table without seating herself, "dey gwine back to hard times in Caddo. I heah tell dey nuva gits 'nough to eat, yonda. Septime, he can't do nuttin' 'cep' set still all twis' up like a sarpint. An' Ma'me Brozé, she do some kine sewin'; but don't look like she got sense 'nough to do dat halfway. An' dem li'le gals, dey 'bleege to run bar'foot mos' all las' winta', twell dat li'les' gal, she got her heel plum fros' bit, so dey tells me. Oh, lawsy! How dey gwine look to-mor', all trapsin' back to Caddo!"

Gilma had never found Aunt Halifax's company so intensely disagreeable as at that moment. He thanked her for the coffee, and went away so suddenly as to startle her. But her good humor never flagged. She called out to him from the doorway:

"Oh, Mista Gilma! You reckon dey knows who Pol'cy b'longs to now?"

He somehow did not feel quite prepared to face Septime; and he lingered along the road. He even stopped a while to rest, apparently, under the shade of a huge cottonwood tree that overhung the bayou. From the very

first, a subtle uneasiness, a self-dissatisfaction
had mingled with his elation, and he was trying to discover what it meant.

To begin with, the straightforwardness of
his own nature had inwardly resented the sudden change in the bearing of most people toward himself. He was trying to recall, too,
something which the lawyer had said; a little
phrase, out of that multitude of words, that
had fallen in his consciousness. It had stayed
there, generating a little festering sore place
that was beginning to make itself irritatingly
felt. What was it, that little phrase? Something about—in his excitement he had only
half heard it—something about dead men's
shoes.

The exuberant health and strength of his
big body; the courage, virility, endurance of
his whole nature revolted against the expression in itself, and the meaning which it conveyed to him. Dead men's shoes! Were they
not for such afflicted beings as Septime? as
that helpless, dependent woman up there? as
those two little ones, with their poorly fed,
poorly clad bodies and sweet, appealing eyes?

Yet he could not determine how he would act and what he would say to them.

But there was no room left in his heart for hesitancy when he came to face the group. Septime was still crouched in his uncle's chair; he seemed never to have left it since the day of the funeral. Ma'me Brozé had been crying, and so had the children—out of sympathy, perhaps.

"Mr. Septime," said Gilma, approaching, "I brought those aff'davits about the hoss. I hope you about made up yo' mind to turn it over without further trouble."

Septime was trembling, bewildered, almost speechless.

"W'at you mean?" he faltered, looking up with a shifting, sideward glance. "The whole place b'longs to you. You tryin' to make a fool out o' me?"

"Fo' me," returned Gilma, "the place can stay with Mr. Gamiche's own flesh an' blood. I'll see Mr. Pax'on again an' make that according to the law. But I want my hoss."

Gilma took something besides his horse— a picture of le vieux Gamiche, which had stood on his mantelpiece. He thrust it into his pocket. He also took his old benefactor's walking-stick and a gun.

As he rode out of the gate, mounted upon his well-beloved "Jupe," the faithful dog following, Gilma felt as if he had awakened from an intoxicating but depressing dream.

At Chenière Caminada

At Chêniere Caminada

I.

THERE was no clumsier looking fellow
in church that Sunday morning than
Antoine Bocaze—the one they called
Tonie. But Tonie did not really care if
he were clumsy or not. He felt that he
could speak intelligibly to no woman save his
mother; but since he had no desire to inflame
the hearts of any of the island maidens, what
difference did it make?

He knew there was no better fisherman on
the Chênière Caminada than himself, if his
face was too long and bronzed, his limbs too
unmanageable and his eyes too earnest—almost too honest.

It was a midsummer day, with a lazy,
scorching breeze blowing from the Gulf
straight into the church windows. The ribbons on the young girls' hats fluttered like
the wings of birds, and the old women

clutched the flapping ends of the veils that covered their heads.

A few mosquitoes, floating through the blistering air, with their nipping and humming fretted the people to a certain degree of attention and consequent devotion. The measured tones of the priest at the altar rose and fell like a song: "Credo in unum Deum patrem omnipotentem" he chanted. And then the people all looked at one another, suddenly electrified.

Some one was playing upon the organ whose notes no one on the whole island was able to awaken; whose tones had not been heard during the many months since a passing stranger had one day listlessly dragged his fingers across its idle keys. A long, sweet strain of music floated down from the loft and filled the church.

It seemed to most of them—it seemed to Tonie standing there beside his old mother—that some heavenly being must have descended upon the Church of Our Lady of Lourdes and chosen this celestial way of communicating with its people.

But it was no creature from a different sphere; it was only a young lady from Grand Isle. A rather pretty young person with blue eyes and nut-brown hair, who wore a dotted lawn of fine texture and fashionable make, and a white Leghorn sailor-hat.

Tonie saw her standing outside of the church after mass, receiving the priest's voluble praises and thanks for her graceful service.

She had come over to mass from Grand Isle in Baptiste Beaudelet's lugger, with a couple of young men, and two ladies who kept a pension over there. Tonie knew these two ladies —the widow Lebrun and her old mother— but he did not attempt to speak with them; he would not have known what to say. He stood aside gazing at the group, as others were doing, his serious eyes fixed earnestly upon the fair organist.

Tonie was late at dinner that day. His mother must have waited an hour for him, sitting patiently with her coarse hands folded in her lap, in that little still room with its "brick-painted" floor, its gaping chimney and homely furnishings.

He told her that he had been walking—
walking he hardly knew where, and he did
not know why. He must have tramped from
one end of the island to the other; but he
brought her no bit of news or gossip. He did
not know if the Cotures had stopped for dinner with the Avendettes; whether old Pierre
François was worse, or better, or dead, or if
lame Philibert was drinking again this morning. He knew nothing; yet he had crossed
the village, and passed every one of its small
houses that stood close together in a long,
jagged line facing the sea; they were gray
and battered by time and the rude buffets of
the salt sea winds.

He knew nothing, though the Cotures had
all bade him "good day" as they filed into
Avendette's, where a steaming plate of crab
gumbo was waiting for each. He had heard
some woman screaming, and others saying
it was because old Pierre François had just
passed away. But he did not remember this,
nor did he recall the fact that lame Philibert
had staggered against him when he stood absently watching a "fiddler" sidling across the
sun-baked sand. He could tell his mother

nothing of all this; but he said he had noticed that the wind was fair and must have driven Baptiste's boat, like a flying bird, across the water.

Well, that was something to talk about, and old Ma'me Antoine, who was fat, leaned comfortably upon the table after she had helped Tonie to his courtbouillon, and remarked that she found Madame was getting old. Tonie thought that perhaps she was aging and her hair was getting whiter. He seemed glad to talk about her, and reminded his mother of old Madame's kindness and sympathy at the time his father and brothers had perished. It was when he was a little fellow, ten years before, during a squall in Barataria Bay.

Ma'me Antoine declared that she could never forget that sympathy, if she lived till Judgment Day; but all the same she was sorry to see that Madame Lebrun was also not so young or fresh as she used to be. Her chances of getting a husband were surely lessening every year; especially with the young girls around her, budding each spring like flowers to be plucked. The one who had played upon the organ was Mademoiselle Duvigné, Claire

Duvigné, a great belle, the daughter of the
Rampart street. Ma'me Antoine had found
that out during the ten minutes she and
others had stopped after mass to gossip with
the priest.

"Claire Duvigné," muttered Tonie, not even
making a pretense to taste his courtbouillon,
but picking little bits from the half loaf of
crusty brown bread that lay beside his plate.
"Claire Duvigné; that is a pretty name. Don't
you think so, mother? I can't think of anyone on the Chênière who has so pretty a one,
nor at Grand Isle, either, for that matter. And
you say she lives on Rampart street?"

It appeared to him a matter of great importance that he should have his mother repeat all that the priest had told her.

II.

Early the following morning Tonie went out
in search of lame Philibert, than whom there
was no cleverer workman on the island when
he could be caught sober.

Tonie had tried to work on his big lugger
that lay bottom upward under the shed, but

it had seemed impossible. His mind, his
hands, his tools refused to do their office, and
in sudden desperation he desisted. He found
Philibert and set him to work in his own
place under the shed. Then he got into his
small boat with the red lateen-sail and went
over to Grand Isle.

There was no one at hand to warn Tonie
that he was acting the part of a fool. He
had, singularly, never felt those premonitory
symptoms of love which afflict the greater por-
tion of mankind before they reach the age
which he had attained. He did not at first
recognize this powerful impulse that had, without warning, possessed itself of his entire being. He obeyed it without a struggle, as naturally as he would have obeyed the dictates
of hunger and thirst.

Tonie left his boat at the wharf and proceeded at once to Mme. Lebrun's pension,
which consisted of a group of plain, stoutly
built cottages that stood in mid island, about
half a mile from the sea.

The day was bright and beautiful with soft,
velvety gusts of wind blowing from the water.
From a cluster of orange trees a flock of doves

ascended, and Tonie stopped to listen to the beating of their wings and follow their flight toward the water oaks whither he himself was moving.

He walked with a dragging, uncertain step through the yellow, fragrant chamomile, his thoughts traveling before him. In his mind was always the vivid picture of the girl as it had stamped itself there yesterday, connected in some mystical way with that celestial music which had thrilled him and was vibrating yet in his soul.

But she did not look the same to-day. She was returning from the beach when Tonie first saw her, leaning upon the arm of one of the men who had accompanied her yesterday. She was dressed differently—in a dainty blue cotton gown. Her companion held a big white sunshade over them both. They had exchanged hats and were laughing with great abandonment.

Two young men walked behind them and were trying to engage her attention. She glanced at Tonie, who was leaning against a tree when the group passed by; but of course she did not know him. She was speaking

English, a language which he hardly understood.

There were other young people gathered under the water oaks—girls who were, many of them, more beautiful than Mlle. Duvigné; but for Tonie they simply did not exist. His whole universe had suddenly become converted into a glamorous background for the person of Mlle. Duvigné, and the shadowy figures of men who were about her.

Tonie went to Mme. Lebrun and told her he would bring her oranges next day from the Chênière. She was well pleased, and commissioned him to bring her other things from the stores there, which she could not procure át Grand Isle. She did not question his presence, knowing that these summer days were idle ones for the Chênière fishermen. Nor did she seem surprised when he told her that his boat was at the wharf, and would be there every day at her service. She knew his frugal habits, and supposed he wished to hire it, as others did. He intuitively felt that this could be the only way.

And that is how it happened that Tonie spent so little of his time at the Chênière Ca-

minada that summer. Old Ma'me Antoine
grumbled enough about it. She herself had
been twice in her life to Grand Isle and once
to Grand Terre, and each time had been more
than glad to get back to the Chênière. And
why Tonie should want to spend his days, and
even his nights, away from home, was a thing
she could not comprehend, especially as he
would have to be away the whole winter; and
meantime there was much work to be done at
his own hearthside and in the company of his
own mother. She did not know that Tonie
had much, much more to do at Grand Isle
than at the Chênière Caminada.

He had to see how Claire Duvigné sat upon
the gallery in the big rocking chair that she
kept in motion by the impetus of her slender,
slippered foot; turning her head this way and
that way to speak to the men who were always
near her. He had to follow her lithe motions
at tennis or croquet, that she often played
with the children under the trees. Some days
he wanted to see how she spread her bare,
white arms, and walked out to meet the foam-
crested waves. Even here there were men
with her. And then at night, standing alone

like a still shadow under the stars, did he not
have to listen to her voice when she talked
and laughed and sang? Did he not have to
follow her slim figure whirling through the
dance, in the arms of men who must have
loved her and wanted her as he did. He did
not dream that they could help it more than he
could help it. But the days when she stepped
into his boat, the one with the red lateen sail,
and sat for hours within a few feet of him,
were days that he would have given up for
nothing else that he could think of.

III.

There were always others in her company
at such times, young people with jests and
laughter on their lips. Only once she was
alone.

She had foolishly brought a book with her,
thinking she would want to read. But with
the breath of the sea stinging her she could
not read a line. She looked precisely as she
had looked the day he first saw her, standing
outside of the church at Chênière Caminada.

She laid the book down in her lap, and let
her soft eyes sweep dreamily along the line

of the horizon where the sky and water met. Then she looked straight at Tonie, and for the first time spoke directly to him.

She called him Tonie, as she had heard others do, and questioned him about his boat and his work. He trembled, and answered her vaguely and stupidly. She did not mind, but spoke to him anyhow, satisfied to talk herself when she found that he could not or would not. She spoke French, and talked about the Chênière Caminada, its people and its church. She talked of the day she had played upon the organ there, and complained of the instrument being woefully out of tune.

Tonie was perfectly at home in the familiar task of guiding his boat before the wind that bellied its taut, red sail. He did not seem clumsy and awkward as when he sat in church. The girl noticed that he appeared as strong as an ox.

As she looked at him and surprised one of his shifting glances, a glimmer of the truth began to dawn faintly upon her. She remembered how she had encountered him daily in her path, with his earnest, devouring eyes always seeking her out. She recalled—but there was no need to recall anything. There are women whose perception of passion is very keen; they are the women who most inspire it.

A feeling of complacency took possession of her with this conviction. There was some softness and sympathy mingled with it. She would have liked to lean over and pat his big, brown hand, and tell him she felt sorry and would have helped it if she could. With this belief he ceased to be an object of complete indifference in her eyes. She had thought, awhile before, of having him turn about and take her back home. But now it was really piquant to pose for an hour longer before a man—even a rough fisherman—to whom she felt herself to be an object of silent and consuming devotion. She could think of nothing more interesting to do on shore.

She was incapable of conceiving the full force and extent of his infatuation. She did not dream that under the rude, calm exterior before her a man's heart was beating clamorously, and his reason yielding to the savage instinct of his blood.

"I hear the Angelus ringing at Chênière, Tonie," she said. "I didn't know it was so late; let us go back to the island." There had been a long silence which her musical voice interrupted.

Tonie could now faintly hear the Angelus bell himself. A vision of the church came with it, the odor of incense and the sound of the organ. The girl before him was again that celestial being whom our Lady of Lourdes had once offered to his immortal vision.

It was growing dusk when they landed at the pier, and frogs had begun to croak among the reeds in the pools. There were two of Mlle. Duvigné's usual attendants anxiously awaiting her return. But she chose to let Tonie assist her out of the boat. The touch of her hand fired his blood again.

She said to him very low and half-laughing, "I have no money tonight, Tonie; take this instead," pressing into his palm a delicate silver chain, which she had worn twined about her bare wrist. It was purely a spirit of coquetry that prompted the action, and a touch of the sentimentality which most women possess.

She had read in some romance of a young girl doing something like that.

As she walked away between her two attendants she fancied Tonie pressing the chain to his lips. But he was standing quite still, and held it buried in his tightly-closed hand; wanting to hold as long as he might the warmth of the body that still penetrated the bauble when she thrust it into his hand.

He watched her retreating figure like a blotch against the fading sky. He was stirred by a terrible, an overmastering regret, that he had not clasped her in his arms when they were out there alone, and sprung with her into the sea. It was what he had vaguely meant to do when the sound of the Angelus had weakened and palsied his resolution. Now she was going from him, fading away into the mist with those figures on either side of her, leaving him alone. He resolved within himself that if ever again she were out there on the sea at his mercy, she would have to perish in his arms. He would go far, far out where the sound of no bell could reach him. There was some comfort for him in the thought.

But as it happened, Mlle. Duvigné never went out alone in the boat with Tonie again.

IV.

It was one morning in January. Tonie had been collecting a bill from one of the fish-mongers at the French Market, in New Orleans, and had turned his steps toward St. Philip street. The day was chilly; a keen wind was blowing. Tonie mechanically buttoned his rough, warm coat and crossed over into the sun.

There was perhaps not a more wretched-hearted being in the whole district, that morning, than he. For months the woman he so hopelessly loved had been lost to his sight. But all the more she dwelt in his thoughts, preying upon his mental and bodily forces until his unhappy condition became apparent to all who knew him. Before leaving his home for the winter fishing grounds he had opened his whole heart to his mother, and told her of the trouble that was killing him. She hardly expected that he would ever come back to her when he went away. She feared that he would not, for he had spoken wildly of the rest and peace that could only come to him with death.

That morning when Tonie had crossed St. Philip street he found himself accosted by Madame Lebrun and her mother. He had not noticed them approaching, and, moreover, their figures in winter garb appeared unfamiliar to him. He had never seen them elsewhere than at Grand Isle and the Chênière during the summer. They were glad to meet him, and shook his hand cordially. He stood as usual a little helplessly before them. A pulse in his throat was beating and almost choking him, so poignant were the recollections which their presence stirred up.

They were staying in the city this winter, they told him. They wanted to hear the opera as often as possible, and the island was really too dreary with everyone gone. Madame Lebrun had left her son there to keep order and superintend repairs, and so on.

"You are both well?" stammered Tonie.

"In perfect health, my dear Tonie," Madame Lebrun replied. She was wondering at his haggard eyes and thin, gaunt cheeks; but possessed too much tact to mention them.

"And—the young lady who used to go sailing—is she well?" he inquired lamely.

"You mean Mlle. Favette? She was married just after leaving Grand Isle."

"No; I mean the one you called Claire—Mamzelle Duvigné—is she well?"

Mother and daughter exclaimed together: "Impossible! You haven't heard? Why, Tonie," madame continued, "Mlle. Duvigné died three weeks ago. But that was something sad, I tell you!....Her family heartbroken... Simply from a cold caught by standing in thin slippers, waiting for her carriage after the opera....What a warning!"

The two were talking at once. Tonie kept looking from one to the other. He did not know what they were saying, after madame had told him, "Elle est morte."

As in a dream he finally heard that they said good-by to him, and sent their love to his mother.

He stood still in the middle of the banquette when they had left him, watching them go toward the market. He could not stir. Something had happened to him—he did not know what. He wondered if the news was killing him.

Some women passed by, laughing coarsely. He noticed how they laughed and tossed their heads. A mockingbird was singing in a cage which hung from a window above his head. He had not heard it before.

Just beneath the window was the entrance to a barroom. Tonie turned and plunged through its swinging doors. He asked the bartender for whisky. The man thought he was already drunk, but pushed the bottle toward him nevertheless. Tonie poured a great quantity of the fiery liquor into a glass and swallowed it at a draught. The rest of the day he spent among the fishermen and Barataria oystermen; and that night he slept soundly and peacefully until morning.

He did not know why it was so; he could not understand. But from that day he felt that he began to live again, to be once more a part of the moving world about him. He would ask himself over and over again why it was so, and stay bewildered before this truth that he could not answer or explain, and which he began to accept as a holy mystery.

One day in early spring Tonie sat with his mother upon a piece of drift-wood close to the sea.

He had returned that day to the Chênière Caminada. At first she thought he was like his former self again, for all his old strength and courage had returned. But she found that there was a new brightness in his face which had not been there before. It made her think of the Holy Ghost descending and bringing some kind of light to a man.

She knew that Mademoiselle Duvigné was dead, and all along had feared that this knowledge would be the death of Tonie. When she saw him come back to her like a new being, at once she dreaded that he did not know. All day the doubt had been fretting her, and she could bear the uncertainty no longer.

"You know, Tonie—that young lady whom you cared for—well, some one read it to me in the papers—she died last winter." She had tried to speak as cautiously as she could.

"Yes, I know she is dead. I am glad."

It was the first time he had said this in words, and it made his heart beat quicker.

Ma'me Antoine shuddered and drew aside from him. To her it was somehow like murder to say such a thing.

What do you mean? Why are you glad?" she demanded, indignantly.

Tonie was sitting with his elbows on his knees. He wanted to answer his mother, but it would take time; he would have to think. He looked out across the water that glistened gem-like with the sun upon it, but there was nothing there to open his thought. He looked down into his open palm and began to pick at the callous flesh that was hard as a horse's hoof. Whilst he did this his ideas began to gather and take form.

"You see, while she lived I could never hope for anything," he began, slowly feeling his way. "Despair was the only thing for me. There were always men about her. She walked and sang and danced with them. I knew it all the time, even when I didn't see her. But I saw her often enough. I knew that some day one of them would please her and she would give herself to him—she would marry him. That thought haunted me like an evil spirit."

Tonie passed his hand across his forehead as if to sweep away anything of the horror that might have remained there.

"It kept me awake at night," he went on. "But that was not so bad; the worst torture was to sleep, for then I would dream that it was all true.

"Oh, I could see her married to one of them—his wife—coming year after year to Grand Isle and bringing her little children with her! I can't tell you all that I saw—all that was driving me mad! But now"—and Tonie clasped his hands together and smiled as he looked again across the water—"she is where she belongs; there is no difference up there; the curé has often told us there is no difference between men. It is with the soul that we approach each other there. Then she will know who has loved her best. That is why I am so contented. Who knows what may happen up there?"

Ma'me Antoine could not answer. She only took her son's big, rough hand and pressed it against her.

"And now, ma mère," he exclaimed, cheerfully, rising, "I shall go light the fire for your bread; it is a long time since I have done anything for you," and he stooped and pressed a warm kiss on her withered old cheek.

With misty eyes she watched him walk away in the direction of the big brick oven that stood open-mouthed under the lemon trees.

Odalie Misses Mass

.

Odalie Misses Mass

ODALIE sprang down from the mule-cart, shook out her white skirts, and firmly grasping her parasol, which was blue to correspond with her sash, entered Aunt Pinky's gate and proceeded towards the old woman's cabin. She was a thick-waisted young thing who walked with a firm tread and carried her head with a determined poise. Her straight brown hair had been rolled up over night in papillotes, and the artificial curls stood out in clusters, stiff and uncompromising beneath the rim of her white chip hat. Her mother, sister and brother remained seated in the cart before the gate.

It was the fifteenth of August, the great feast of the Assumption, so generally observed in the Catholic parishes of Louisiana. The Chotard family were on their way to mass, and Odalie had insisted upon stopping to "show

herself" to her old friend and protegée, Aunt
Pinky.

The helpless, shrivelled old negress sat in
the depths of a large, rudely-fashioned chair.
A loosely hanging unbleached cotton gown
enveloped her mite of a figure. What was
visible of her hair beneath the bandana tur-
ban, looked like white sheep's wool. She wore
round, silver-rimmed spectacles, which gave
her an air of wisdom and respectability, and
she held in her hand the branch of a hickory
sapling, with which she kept mosquitoes and
flies at bay, and even chickens and pigs that
sometimes penetrated the heart of her domain.

Odalie walked straight up to the old woman
and kissed her on the cheek.

"Well, Aunt Pinky, yere I am," she announced with evident self-complacency, turning herself slowly and stiffly around like a
mechanical dummy. In one hand she held
her prayer-book, fan and handkerchief, in the
other the blue parasol, still open; and on her
plump hands were blue cotton mitts. Aunt
Pinky beamed and chuckled; Odalie hardly
expected her to be able to do more.

"Now you saw me," the child continued. "I reckon you satisfied. I mus' go; I ain't got a minute to was'e." But at the threshold she turned to inquire, bluntly:

"W'ere's Pug?"

"Pug," replied Aunt Pinky, in her tremulous old-woman's voice. "She's gone to chu'ch; done gone; she done gone," nodding her head in seeming approval of Pug's action.

"To church!" echoed Odalie with a look of consternation settling in her round eyes.

"She gone to chu'ch," reiterated Aunt Pinky. "Say she kain't miss chu'ch on de fifteent'; de debble gwine pester her twell jedgment, she miss chu'ch on de fifteent'."

Odalie's plump cheeks fairly quivered with indignation and she stamped her foot. She looked up and down the long, dusty road that skirted the river. Nothing was to be seen save the blue cart with its dejected looking mule and patient occupants. She walked to the end of the gallery and called out to a negro boy whose black bullet-head showed up in bold relief against the white of the cotton patch:

"He, Baptiste! w'ere's yo' ma? Ask yo' ma if she can't come set with Aunt Pinky."

"Mammy, she gone to chu'ch," screamed Baptiste in answer.

"Bonté! w'at's taken you all darkies with yo' 'church' to-day? You come along yere Baptiste an' set with Aunt Pinky. That Pug! I'm goin' to make yo' ma wear her out fo' that trick of hers—leavin' Aunt Pinky like that."

But at the first intimation of what was wanted of him, Baptiste dipped below the cotton like a fish beneath water, leaving no sight nor sound of himself to answer Odalie's repeated calls. Her mother and sister were beginning to show signs of impatience.

"But, I can't go," she cried out to them. "It's nobody to stay with Aunt Pinky. I can't leave Aunt Pinky like that, to fall out of her chair. maybe, like she already fell out once."

"You goin' to miss mass on the fifteenth, you, Odalie! W'at you thinkin' about?" came in shrill rebuke from her sister. But her mother offering no objection, the boy lost not a moment in starting the mule forward at a brisk trot. She watched them disappear in a cloud of dust; and turning with a dejected, almost tearful countenance, re-entered the room.

Aunt Pinky seemed to accept her reappearance as a matter of course; and even evinced no surprise at seeing her remove her hat and mitts, which she laid carefully, almost religiously, on the bed, together with her book, fan and handkerchief.

Then Odalie went and seated herself some distance from the old woman in her own small, low rocking-chair. She rocked herself furiously, making a great clatter with the rockers over the wide, uneven boards of the cabin floor; and she looked out through the open door.

"Puggy, she done gone to chu'ch; done gone. Say de debble gwine pester her twell jedgment—"

"You done tole me that, Aunt Pinky; neva mine; don't le's talk about it."

Aunt Pinky thus rebuked, settled back into silence and Odalie continued to rock and stare out of the door.

Once she arose, and taking the hickory branch from Aunt Pinky's nerveless hand, made a bold and sudden charge upon a little pig that seemed bent upon keeping her company. She pursued him with flying heels and loud cries as far as the road. She came back flushed and breathless and her curls hanging rather limp around her face; she began again to rock herself and gaze silently out of the door.

"You gwine make yo' fus' c'mmunion?"

This seemingly sober inquiry on the part of Aunt Pinky at once shattered Odalie's ill-humor and dispelled every shadow of it. She leaned back and laughed with wild abandonment.

"Mais w'at you thinkin' about, Aunt Pinky? How you don't remember I made my firs' communion las' year, with this same dress w'at maman let out the tuck," holding up the altered skirt for Aunt Pinky's inspection. "An' with this same petticoat w'at maman added this ruffle an' crochet' edge; excep' I had a w'ite sash."

These evidences proved beyond question convincing and seemed to satisfy Aunt Pinky. Odalie rocked as furiously as ever, but she

sang now, and the swaying chair had worked
its way nearer to the old woman.

"You gwine git mar'ied?"

"I declare, Aunt Pinky," said Odalie, when
she had ceased laughing and was wiping her
eyes, "I declare, sometime' I think you gittin'
plumb foolish. How you expec' me to git
married w'en I'm on'y thirteen?"

Evidently Aunt Pinky did not know why
or how she expected anything so preposter-
ous; Odalie's holiday attire that filled her with
contemplative rapture, had doubtless incited
her to these vagaries.

The child now drew her chair quite close
to the old woman's knee after she had gone
out to the rear of the cabin to get herself
some water and had brought a drink to Aunt
Pinky in the gourd dipper.

There was a strong, hot breeze blowing
from the river, and it swept fitfully and in
gusts through the cabin, bringing with it the
weedy smell of cacti that grew thick on the
bank, and occasionally a shower of reddish
dust from the road. Odalie for a while was
greatly occupied in keeping in place her filmy
skirt, which every gust of wind swelled bal-

loon-like about her knees. Aunt Pinky's little black, scrawny hand had found its way
among the droopy curls, and strayed often
caressingly to the child's plump neck and
shoulders.

"You riclics, honey, dat day yo' granpappy
say it wur pinchin' times an' he reckin he
bleege to sell Yallah Tom an' Susan an'
Pinky? Don' know how come he think 'bout
Pinky, 'less caze he sees me playin' an' trapsin' roun' wid you alls, day in an' out. I
riclics yit how you tu'n w'ite like milk an'
fling yo' arms roun' li'le black Pinky; an' you
cries out you don' wan' no saddle-mar'; you
don' wan' no silk dresses and fing' rings an'
sich; an' don' wan' no idication; des wants
Pinky. An' you cries an' screams an' kicks,
an' 'low you gwine kill fus' pusson w'at dar
come an' buy Pinky an' kiars her off. You
riclics dat, honey?"

Odalie had grown accustomed to these
flights of fancy on the part of her old friend;
she liked to humor her as she chose to sometimes humor very small children; so she was
quite used to impersonating one dearly be-
loved but impetuous, "Paulette," who seemed

to have held her place in old Pinky's heart and imagination through all the years of her suffering life.

"I rec'lec' like it was yesterday, Aunt Pinky. How I scream an' kick an' maman gave me some med'cine; an' how you scream an' kick an' Susan took you down to the quarters an' give you 'twenty.' "

"Das so, honey; des like you says," chuckled Aunt Pinky. "But you don' riclic dat time you cotch Pinky cryin' down in de holler behine de gin; an' you say you gwine give me 'twenty' ef I don' tell you w'at I cryin' 'bout?"

"I rec'lec' like it happen'd to-day, Aunt Pinky. You been cryin' because you want to marry Hiram, ole Mr. Benitou's servant."

"Das true like you says, Miss Paulette; an' you goes home an' cries and kiars on an' won' eat, an' breaks dishes, an' pesters yo' gran'pap 'tell he bleedge to buy Hi'um f'om de Benitous."

"Don't talk, Aunt Pink! I can see all that jus' as plain!" responded Odalie sympathetically, yet in truth she took but a languid interest in these reminiscences which she had listened to so often before.

She leaned her flushed cheek against Aunt Pinky's knee.

The air was rippling now, and hot and caressing. There was the hum of bumble bees outside; and busy mud-daubers kept flying in and out through the door. Some chickens had penetrated to the very threshold in their aimless roamings, and the little pig was approaching more cautiously. Sleep was fast overtaking the child, but she could still hear through her drowsiness the familiar tones of Aunt Pinky's voice.

"But Hi'um, he done gone; he nuva come back; an' Yallah Tom nuva come back; an' ole Marster an' de chillun—all gone—nuva come back. Nobody nuva come back to Pinky 'cep you, my honey. You ain' gwine 'way f'om Pinky no mo', is you, Miss Paulette?"

"Don' fret, Aunt Pinky—I'm goin'—to stay with—you."

"No pussun nuva come back 'cep' you."

Odalie was fast asleep. Aunt Pinky was asleep with her head leaning back on her chair and her fingers thrust 'nto the mass of tangled brown hair that swept across her lap. The chickens and little pig walked fearlessly in and out. The sunlight crept close up to the cabin door and stole away again.

Odalie awoke with a start. Her mother was standing over her arousing her from sleep. She sprang up and rubbed her eyes. "Oh, I been asleep!" she exclaimed. The cart was standing in the road waiting. "An' Aunt Pinky, she's asleep, too."

"Yes, chérie, Aunt Pinky is asleep," replied her mother, leading Odalie away. But she spoke low and trod softly as gentle-souled women do, in the presence of the dead.

Cavanelle

Cavanelle

I WAS always sure of hearing something pleasant from Cavanelle across the counter. If he was not mistaking me for the freshest and prettiest girl in New Orleans, he was reserving for me some bit of silk, or lace, or ribbon of a nuance marvelously suited to my complexion, my eyes or my hair! What an innocent, delightful humbug Cavanelle was! How well I knew it and how little I cared! For when he had sold me the confection or bit of dry-goods in question, he always began to talk to me of his sister Mathilde, and then I knew that Cavanelle was an angel.

I had known him long enough to know why he worked so faithfully, so energetically and without rest—it was because Mathilde had a voice. It was because of her voice that his coats were worn till they were out of fashion and almost out at elbows. But for a sister whose voice needed only a little training to rival that of the nightingale, one might do such things without incurring reproach.

"You will believe, madame, that I did not know you las' night at the opera? I remark' to Mathilde, 'tiens! Mademoiselle Montreville,' an' I only rec'nize my mistake when I finally adjust my opera glass......I guarantee you will be satisfied, madame. In a year from now you will come an' thank me for having secu' you that bargain in a poult-de-soie......Yes, yes; as you say, Tolville was in voice. But," with a shrug of the narrow shoulders and a smile of commiseration that wrinkled the lean olive cheeks beneath the thin beard, "but to hear that cavatina render' as I have heard it render' by Mathilde, is another affair! A quality, madame, that moves, that penetrates. Perhaps not yet enough volume, but that will accomplish itself with time, when she will become more robus' in health. It is my intention to sen' her for the summer to Gran' Isle; that good air an' surf bathing will work miracles. An artiste, voyez vous, it is not to be treated like a human being of every day; it needs des petits soins; perfec' res' of body an' mind; good red wine an' plenty......oh yes, madame, the stage; that is our intention; but never with my consent in light opera. Patience is what I counsel to Mathilde. A little more stren'th; a little dev'lopment of the chest to give that soupçon of compass which is lacking, an' gran' opera is what I aspire for my sister."

I was curious to know Mathilde and to hear her sing; and thought it a great pity that a voice so marvelous as she doubtless possessed should not gain the notice that might prove the step toward the attainment of her ambition. It was such curiosity and a half-formed design or desire to interest myself in her career that prompted me to inform Cavanelle that I should greatly like to meet his sister; and I asked permission to call upon her the following Sunday afternoon.

Cavanelle was charmed. He otherwise would not have been Cavanelle. Over and over I was given the most minute directions for finding the house. The green car—or was it the yellow or blue one? I can no longer remember. But it was near Goodchildren street, and would I kindly walk this way and turn that way? At the corner was an ice dealer's. In the middle of the block, their house—one-story; painted yellow; a knocker; a banana tree nodding over the side fence. But indeed, I need not look for the banana tree, the knocker, the number or anything, for if I but turn the corner in the neighborhood of five o'clock I would find him planted at the door awaiting me.

And there he was! Cavanelle himself; but seeming to me not himself; apart from the entourage with which I was accustomed to associate him. Every line of his mobile face, every gesture emphasized the welcome which his kind eyes expressed as he ushered me into the small parlor that opened upon the street.

"Oh, not that chair, madame! I entreat you. This one, by all means. Thousan' times more comfortable."

"Mathilde! Strange; my sister was here but an instant ago. Mathilde! Où es tu donc?" Stupid Cavanelle! He did not know when I had already guessed it—that Mathilde had retired to the adjoining room at my approach, and would appear after a sufficient de-

lay to give an appropriate air of ceremony to
our meeting.

And what a frail little piece of mortality she
was when she did appear! At beholding her
I could easily fancy that when she stepped
outside of the yellow house, the zephyrs would
lift her from her feet and, given a proper ad-
justment of the balloon sleeves, gently waft
her in the direction of Goodchildren street, or
wherever else she might want to go.

Hers was no physique for grand opera—
certainly no stage presence; apparently so
slender a hold upon life that the least tension
might snap it. The voice which could hope
to overcome these glaring disadvantages
would have to be phenomenal.

Mathilde spoke English imperfectly, and
with embarrassment, and was glad to lapse
into French. Her speech was languid, unaf-
fectedly so; and her manner was one of indo-
lent repose; in this respect offering a striking
contrast to that of her brother. Cavanelle
seemed unable to rest. Hardly was I seated
to his satisfaction than he darted from the
room and soon returned followed by a limp-

ing old black woman bringing in a sirop
d'orgeat and layer cake on a tray.

Mathilde's face showed feeble annoyance
at her brother's want of savoir vivre in thus
introducing the refreshments at so early a
stage of my visit.

The servant was one of those cheap black
women who abound in the French quarter,
who speak Creole patois in preference to English, and who would rather work in a petit
ménage in Goodchildren street for five dollars
a month than for fifteen in the fourth district.
Her presence, in some unaccountable manner,
seemed to reveal to me much of the inner
working of this small household. I pictured
her early morning visit to the French market,
where picayunes were doled out sparingly,
and lagniappes gathered in with avidity.

I could see the neatly appointed dinner table; Cavanelle extolling his soup and bouillie
in extravagant terms; Mathilde toying with
her papabotte or chicken-wing, and pouring
herself a demi-verre from her very own half-
bottle of St. Julien; Pouponne, as they called
her, mumbling and grumbling through habit,
and serving them as faithfully as a dog

through instinct. I wondered if they knew that Pouponne "played the lottery" with every spare "quarter" gathered from a judicious management of lagniappe. Perhaps they would not have cared, or have minded, either, that she as often consulted the Voudoo priestess around the corner as her father confessor.

My thoughts had followed Pouponne's limping figure from the room, and it was with an effort I returned to Cavanelle twirling the piano stool this way and that way. Mathilde was languidly turning over musical scores, and the two warmly discussing the merits of a selection which she had evidently decided upon.

The girl seated herself at the piano. Her hands were thin and anæmic, and she touched the keys without firmness or delicacy. When she had played a few introductory bars, she began to sing. Heaven only knows what she sang; it made no difference then, nor can it make any now.

The day was a warm one, but that did not prevent a creepy chilliness seizing hold of me. The feeling was generated by disappointment,

anger, dismay and various other disagreeable
sensations which I cannot find names for.
Had I been intentionally deceived and misled?
Was this some impertinent pleasantry on the
part of Cavanelle? Or rather had not the
girl's voice undergone some hideous transfor-
mation since her brother had listened to it?
I dreaded to look at him, fearing to see horror
and astonishment depicted on his face. When
I did look, his expression was earnestly attentive and beamed approval of the strains to
which he measured time by a slow, satisfied
motion of the hand.

The voice was thin to attenuation, I fear it
was not even true. Perhaps my disappointment exaggerated its simple deficiencies into
monstrous defects. But it was an unsympa-
thetic voice that never could have been a
blessing to possess or to listen to.

I cannot recall what I said at parting—
doubtless conventional things which were not
true. Cavanelle politely escorted me to the
car, and there I left him with a hand-clasp
which from my side was tender with sympathy
and pity.

"Poor Cavanelle! poor Cavanelle!" The
words kept beating time in my brain to the

jingle of the car bells and the regular ring of the mules' hoofs upon the cobble stones. One moment I resolved to have a talk with him in which I would endeavor to open his eyes to the folly of thus casting his hopes and the substance of his labor to the winds. The next instant I had decided that chance would possibly attend to Cavanelle's affair less clumsily than I could. "But all the same," I wondered, "is Cavanelle a fool? is he a lunatic? is he under a hypnotic spell?" And then—strange that I did not think of it before—I realized that Cavanelle loved Mathilde intensely, and we all know that love is blind, but a god just the same.

Two years passed before I saw Cavanelle again. I had been absent that length of time from the city. In the meanwhile Mathilde had died. She and her little voice—the apotheosis of insignificance—were no more. It was perhaps a year after my visit to her that I read an account of her death in a New Orleans paper. Then came a momentary pang of commiseration for my good Cavanelle. Chance had surely acted here the part of a skillful though merciless surgeon; no temporizing, no half measures. A deep, sharp thrust of the scalpel; a moment of agonizing pain; then rest, rest; convalescence; health; happiness! Yes, Mathilde had been dead a year and I was prepared for great changes in Cavanelle.

He had lived like a hampered child who does not recognize the restrictions hedging it about, and lives a life of pathetic contentment in the midst of them. But now all that was altered. He was, doubtless, regaling himself with the half-bottles of St. Julien, which were never before for him; with, perhaps, an occasional petit souper at Moreau's, and there was no telling what little pleasures beside.

Cavanelle would certainly have bought himself a suit of clothes or two of modern fit and finish. I would find him with a brightened eye, a fuller cheek, as became a man of his years; perchance, even, a waxed moustache! So did my imagination run rampant with me.

And after all, the hand which I clasped across the counter was that of the self-same Cavanelle I had left. It was no fuller, no firmer. There were even some additional lines visible through the thin, brown beard.

"Ah, my poor Cavanelle! you have suffered a grievous loss since we parted." I saw in his face that he remembered the circumstances of our last meeting, so there was no use in avoiding the subject. I had rightly conjectured that the wound had been a cruel one, but in a year such wounds heal with a healthy soul.

He could have talked for hours of Mathilde's unhappy taking-off, and if the subject had possessed for me the same touching fascination which it held for him, doubtless, we would have done so, but—

"And how is it now, mon ami? Are you living in the same place? running your little ménage as before, my poor Cavanelle?"

"Oh, yes, madame, except that my Aunt Félicie is making her home with me now. You have heard me speak of my aunt—No? You never have heard me speak of my Aunt Félicie Cavanelle of Terrebonne! That, madame, is a noble woman who has suffer' the mos' cruel affliction, and deprivation, since the war.—No, madame, not in good health, unfortunately, by any means. It is why I esteem that a blessed privilege to give her declining years those little comforts, ces petits soins, that is a woman's right to expec' from men. ''

I knew what "des petits soins" meant with Cavanelle; doctors' visits, little jaunts across the lake, friandises of every description showered upon "Aunt Félicie," and he himself relegated to the soup and bouillie which typified his prosaic existence.

I was unreasonably exasperated with the man for awhile, and would not even permit myself to notice the beauty in texture and design of the mousseline de laine which he had spread across the counter in tempting folds. I was forced to restrain a brutal desire to say something stinging and cruel to him for his fatuity.

However, before I had regained the street, the conviction that Cavanelle was a hopeless fool seemed to reconcile me to the situation and also afforded me some diversion.

But even this estimate of my poor Cavanelle was destined not to last. By the time I had seated myself in the Prytania street car and passed up my nickel, I was convinced that Cavanelle was an angel.

Tante Cat'rinette

Tante Cat'rinette

❦

IT happened just as every one had predicted. Tante Cat'rinette was beside
herself with rage and indignation when
she learned that the town authorities had for
some reason condemned her house and intended to demolish it.

"Dat house w'at Vieumaite gi' me his own
se'f, out his own mout', w'en he gi' me my
freedom! All wrote down en règle befo' de
cote! Bon dieu Seigneur, w'at dey talkin'
'bout!"

Tante Cat'rinette stood in the doorway of
her home, resting a gaunt black hand against
the jamb. In the other hand she held her corn-
cob pipe. She was a tall, large-boned woman
of a pronounced Congo type. The house in
question had been substantial enough in its
time. It contained four rooms: the lower two
of brick, the upper ones of adobe. A dilapi-

dated gallery projected from the upper story
and slanted over the narrow banquette, to the
peril of passers-by.

"I don't think I ever heard why the property was given to you in the first place, Tante
Cat'rinette," observed Lawyer Paxton, who
had stopped in passing, as so many others did,
to talk the matter over with the old negress.
The affair was attracting some attention in
town, and its development was being watched
with a good deal of interest. Tante Cat'rinette
asked nothing better than to satisfy the lawyer's curiosity.

"Vieumaite all time say Cat'rinette wort'
gole to 'im; de way I make dem nigga' walk
chalk. But," she continued, with recovered
seriousness, "w'en I nuss 'is li'le gal w'at all
de doctor' 'low it 's goin' die, an' I make it
well, me, den Vieumaite, he can't do 'nough,
him. He name' dat li'le gal Cat'rine fo' me.
Das Miss Kitty w'at marry Miché Raymond
yon' by Gran' Eco'. Den he gi' me my freedom; he got plenty slave', him; one don'
count in his pocket. An' he gi' me dat house
w'at I'm stan'in' in de do'; he got plenty
house' an' lan', him. Now dey want pay me

t'ousan' dolla', w'at I don' axen' fo', an' tu'n
me out dat house! I waitin' fo' 'em, Miché
Paxtone," and a wicked gleam shot into the
woman's small, dusky eyes.   " I got my axe
grine fine.   Fus' man w'at touch Cat'rinette
fo' tu'n her out dat house, he git 'is head bus'
like I bus' a gode."

"Dat's nice day, ainty, Miché Paxtone?
Fine wedda fo' dry my close."   Upon the gallery above hung an array of shirts, which
gleamed white in the sunshine, and flapped in
the rippling breeze.

The spectacle of Tante Cat'rinette defying
the authorities was one which offered much
diversion to the children of the neighborhood.
They played numberless pranks at her expense; daily serving upon her fictitious notices
purporting to be to the last degree official.
One youngster, in a moment of inspiration,
composed a couplet, which they recited, sang,
shouted at all hours, beneath her windows.

" Tante Cat'rinette, she go in town;
    W'en she come back, her house pull' down. "

So ran the production.   She heard it many
times during the day, but, far from offending
her, she accepted it as a warning,—a predic-

tion, as it were,—and she took heed not to offer to fate the conditions for its fulfillment. She no longer quitted her house even for a moment, so great was her fear and so firm her belief that the town authorities were lying in wait to possess themselves of it. She would not cross the street to visit a neighbor. She waylaid passers-by and pressed them into service to do her errands and small shopping. She grew distrustful and suspicious, ever on the alert to scent a plot in the most innocent endeavor to induce her to leave the house.

One morning, as Tante Cat'rinette was hanging out her latest batch of washing, Eusèbe, a "free mulatto" from Red River, stopped his pony beneath her gallery.

"Hé, Tante Cat'rinette!" he called up to her.

She turned to the railing just as she was, in her bare arms and neck that gleamed ebony-like against the unbleached cotton of her chemise. A coarse skirt was fastened about her waist, and a string of many-colored beads knotted around her throat. She held her smoking pipe between her yellow teeth.

"How you all come on, Miché Eusèbe?" she questioned, pleasantly.

"We all middlin', Tante Cat'rinette. But Miss Kitty, she putty bad off out yon'a. I see Mista Raymond dis mo'nin' w'en I pass by his house; he say look like de feva don' wan' to quit 'er. She been axen' fo' you all t'rough de night. He 'low he reckon I betta tell you. Nice wedda we got fo' plantin', Tante Cat'rinette."

"Nice wedda fo' lies, Miché Eusèbe," and she spat contemptuously down upon the banquette. She turned away without noticing the man further, and proceeded to hang one of Lawyer Paxton's fine linen shirts upon the line.

"She been axen' fo' you all t'rough de night."

Somehow Tante Cat'rinette could not get that refrain out of her head. She would not willingly believe that Eusèbe had spoken the truth, but— "She been axen fo' you all t'rough de night—all t'rough de night." The words kept ringing in her ears, as she came and went about her daily tasks. But by degrees she dismissed Eusèbe and his message from her mind. It was Miss Kitty's voice that she could hear in fancy following her, calling out through the night, "W'ere Tante Cat'rinette? W'y Tante Cat'rinette don' come? W'y she don' come—w'y she don' come?"

All day the woman muttered and mumbled to herself in her Creole patois; invoking council of "Vieumaite," as she always did in her troubles. Tante Cat'rinette's religion was peculiarly her own; she turned to heaven with her grievances, it is true, but she felt that there was no one in Paradise with whom she was quite so well acquainted as with "Vieumaite."

Late in the afternoon she went and stood on her doorstep, and looked uneasily and anxiously out upon the almost deserted street. When a little girl came walking by,—a sweet child with a frank and innocent face, upon whose word she knew she could rely,—Tante Cat'rinette invited her to enter.

"Come yere see Tante Cat'rinette, Lolo. It's long time you en't come see Tante Cat'rine; you gittin' proud." She made the little one sit down, and offered her a couple of cookies, which the child accepted with pretty avidity.

"You putty good li'le gal, you, Lolo. You keep on go confession all de time?"

"Oh, yes. I'm goin' make my firs' communion firs' of May, Tante Cat'rinette." A dog-eared catechism was sticking out of Lolo's apron pocket.

"Das right; be good li'le gal. Mine yo' maman ev't'ing she say; an' neva tell no story. It's nuttin' bad in dis worl' like tellin' lies. You know Eusèbe?"

"Eusèbe?"

"Yas; dat li'le ole Red River free m'latto. Uh, uh! dat one man w'at kin tell lies, yas! He come tell me Miss Kitty down sick yon'a. You ev yeard such big story like dat, Lolo?"

The child looked a little bewildered, but she answered promptly, "'Tain't no story, Tante Cat'rinette. I yeard papa sayin', dinner time, Mr. Raymond sen' fo' Dr. Chalon. An' Dr. Chalon says he ain't got time to go yonda. An' papa says it's because Dr. Chalon on'y want to go w'ere it's rich people; an' he's 'fraid Mista Raymond ain' goin' pay 'im."

Tante Cat'rinette admired the little girl's pretty gingham dress, and asked her who had ironed it. She stroked her brown curls, and talked of all manner of things quite foreign to the subject of Eusèbe and his wicked propensity for telling lies.

She was not restless as she had been during the early part of the day, and she no longer mumbled and muttered as she had been doing over her work.

At night she lighted her coal-oil lamp, and placed it near a window where its light could be seen from the street through the half-closed shutters. Then she sat herself down, erect and motionless, in a chair.

When it was near upon midnight, Tante Cat'rinette arose, and looked cautiously, very cautiously, out of the door. Her house lay in the line of deep shadow that extended along the street. The other side was bathed in the pale light of the declining moon. The night was agreeably mild, profoundly still, but pregnant with the subtle quivering life of early spring. The earth seemed asleep and breathing,—a scent-laden breath that blew in soft puffs against Tante Cat'rinette's face as she emerged from the house. She closed and locked her door noiselessly; then she crept slowly away, treading softly, stealthily as a cat, in the deep shadow.

There were but few people abroad at that hour. Once she ran upon a gay party of ladies and gentlemen who had been spending the evening over cards and anisette. They did not notice Tante Cat'rinette almost effacing herself against the black wall of the cathedral. She breathed freely and ventured from her retreat only when they had disappeared from view. Once a man saw her quite plainly, as she darted across a narrow strip of moonlight. But Tante Cat'rinette need not have gasped with fright as she did. He was too drunk to know if she were a thing of flesh, or only one of the fantastic, maddening shadows that the moon was casting across his path to bewilder him. When she reached the outskirts of the town, and had to cross the broad piece of open country which stretched out toward the pine wood, an almost paralyzing terror came over her. But she crouched low, and hurried through the marsh and weeds, avoiding the open road. She could have been mistaken for one of the beasts browsing there where she passed.

But once in the Grand Ecore road that lay through the pine wood, she felt secure and free to move as she pleased. Tante Cat'rinette straightened herself, stiffened herself in fact, and unconsciously assuming the attitude of the professional sprinter, she sped rapidly beneath the Gothic interlacing branches of the pines. She talked constantly to herself as she went, and to the animate and inanimate objects around her. But her speech, far from intelligent, was hardly intelligible.

She addressed herself to the moon, which she apostrophized as an impertinent busybody spying upon her actions. She pictured all manner of troublesome animals, snakes, rabbits, frogs, pursuing her, but she defied them to catch Cat'rinette, who was hurrying toward Miss Kitty. "Pa capab trapé Cat'rinette, vou-zot; mo pé couri vite cotĕ Miss Kitty." She called up to a mocking-bird warbling upon a lofty limb of a pine tree, asking why it cried out so, and threatening to secure it and put it into a cage. "Ca to pé crié comme ça, ti céléra? Arete,   mo trapé zozos la, mo

mété li dan ain bon lacage." Indeed,
Tante Cat'rinette seemed on very familiar
terms with the night, with the forest, and with
all the flying, creeping, crawling things that
inhabit it. At the speed with which she traveled she soon had covered the few miles of
wooded road, and before long had reached her
destination.

The sleeping-room of Miss Kitty opened
upon the long outside gallery, as did all the
rooms of the unpretentious frame house which
was her home. The place could hardly be
called a plantation; it was too small for that.
Nevertheless Raymond was trying to plant;
trying to teach school between times, in the
end room; and sometimes, when he found
himself in a tight place, trying to clerk for
Mr. Jacobs over in Campte, across Red River.

Tante Cat'rinette mounted the creaking
steps, crossed the gallery, and entered Miss
Kitty's room as though she were returning to
it after a few moments' absence. There was
a lamp burning dimly upon the high mantel-
piece. Raymond had evidently not been to
bed; he was in shirt sleeves, rocking the baby's cradle. It was the same mahogany cra-

dle which had held Miss Kitty thirty-five years before, when Tante Cat'rinette had rocked it. The cradle had been bought then to match the bed,—that big, beautiful bed on which Miss Kitty lay now in a restless half slumber. There was a fine French clock on the mantel, still telling the hours as it had told them years ago. But there were no carpets or rugs on the floors. There was no servant in the house.

Raymond uttered an exclamation of amazement when he saw Tante Cat'rinette enter.

"How you do, Miché Raymond?" she said, quietly. "I yeard Miss Kitty been sick; Eusèbe tell me dat dis mo'nin'."

She moved toward the bed as lightly as though shod with velvet, and seated herself there. Miss Kitty's hand lay outside the coverlid; a shapely hand, which her few days of illness and rest had not yet softened. The negress laid her own black hand upon it. At the touch Miss Kitty instinctively turned her palm upward.

"It's Tante Cat'rinette!" she exclaimed, with a note of satisfaction in her feeble voice.

"W'en did you come, Tante Cat'rinette? They all said you wouldn' come."

"I'm goin' come ev'y night, cher coeur, ev'y night tell you be well. Tante Cat'rinette can't come daytime no mo'."

"Raymond tole me about it. They doin' you mighty mean in town, Tante Cat'rinette."

"Nev' mine, ti chou. I know how take care dat w'at Vieumaite gi' me. You go sleep now. Cat'rinette goin' set yere an' mine you. She goin' make you well like she all time do. We don' wan' no céléra doctor. We drive 'em out wid a stick, dey come roun' yere."

Miss Kitty was soon sleeping more restfully than she had done since her illness began. Raymond had finally succeeded in quieting the baby, and he tiptoed into the adjoining room, where the other children lay, to snatch a few hours of much-needed rest for himself. Cat'rinette sat faithfully beside her charge, administering at intervals to the sick woman's wants.

But the thought of regaining her home before daybreak, and of the urgent necessity for doing so, did not leave Tante Cat'rinette's mind for an instant.

In the profound darkness, the deep stillness
of the night that comes before dawn, she was
walking again through the woods, on her way
back to town.

The mocking-birds were asleep, and so
were the frogs and the snakes; and the moon
was gone, and so was the breeze. She walked
now in utter silence but for the heavy guttural
breathing that accompanied her rapid footsteps. She walked with a desperate determination along the road, every foot of which
was familiar to her.

When she at last emerged from the woods,
the earth about her was faintly, very faintly,
beinning to reveal itself in the tremulous,
gray, uncertain light of approaching day. She
staggered and plunged onward with beating
pulses quickened by fear.

A sudden turn, and Tante Cat'rinette stood
facing the river. She stopped abruptly, as if
at command of some unseen power that forced
her. For an instant she pressed a black hand
against her tired, burning eyes, and stared
fixedly ahead of her.

Tante Cat'rinette had always believed that
Paradise was up there overhead where the sun

and stars and moon are, and that "Vieumaite" inhabited that region of splendor. She never for a moment doubted this. It would be difficult, perhaps unsatisfying, to explain why Tante Cat'rinette, on that particular morning, when a vision of the rising day broke suddenly upon her, should have believed that she stood in face of a heavenly revelation. But why not, after all? Since she talked so familiarly herself to the unseen, why should it not respond to her when the time came?

Across the narrow, quivering line of water, the delicate budding branches of young trees were limned black against the gold, orange, —what word is there to tell the color of that morning sky! And steeped in the splendor of it hung one pale star; there was not another in the whole heaven.

Tante Cat'rinette stood with her eyes fixed intently upon that star, which held her like a hypnotic spell. She stammered breathlessly:

"Mo pé couté, Vieumaite. Cat'rinette pé couté." (I am listening, Vieumaite. Cat'rinette hears you.)

She stayed there motionless upon the brink of the river till the star melted into the brightness of the day and became part of it.

When Tante Cat'rinette entered Miss Kitty's room for the second time, the aspect of things had changed somewhat. Miss Kitty was with much difficulty holding the baby while Raymond mixed a saucer of food for the little one. Their oldest daughter, a child of twelve, had come into the room with an apronful of chips from the woodpile, and was striving to start a fire on the hearth, to make the morning coffee. The room seemed bare and almost squalid in the daylight.

"Well, yere Tante Cat'rinette come back," she said, quietly announcing herself.

They could not well understand why she was back; but it was good to have her there, and they did not question.

She took the baby from its mother, and, seating herself, began to feed it from the saucer which Raymond placed beside her on a chair.

"Yas," she said, "Cat'rinette goin' stay; dis time she en't nev' goin' 'way no mo'."

Husband and wife looked at each other with surprised, questioning eyes.

"Miché Raymond," remarked the woman, turning her head up to him with a certain

comical shrewdness in her glance, "if somebody want len' you t'ousan' dolla', w'at you
goin' say? Even if it's ole nigga 'oman?"

The man's face flushed with sudden emo-
tion. "I would say that person was our bes'
frien', Tante Cat'rinette. An'," he added, with
a smile, "I would give her a mortgage on the
place, of co'se, to secu' her f'om loss."

"Das right," agreed the woman practically.
"Den Cat'rinette goin' len' you t'ousan'
dolla'. Dat w'at Vieumaite give her, dat
b'long to her; don' b'long to nobody else. An'
we go yon'a to town, Miché Raymond, you
an' me. You care me befo' Miché Paxtone.
I want 'im fo' put down in writin' befo' de
cote dat w'at Cat'rinette got, it fo' Miss Kitty
w'en I be dead."

Miss Kitty was crying softly in the depths of
her pillow.

"I en't got no head fo' all dat, me," laughed
Tante Cat'rinette, good humoredly, as she
held a spoonful of pap up to the baby's eager
lips. "It's Vieumaite tell me all dat clair an'
plain dis mo'nin', w'en I comin' 'long de Gran'
Eco' road."

A Respectable Woman

A Respectable Woman

🎋

MRS. BARODA was a little provoked to learn that her husband expected his friend, Gouvernail, up to spend a week or two on the plantation.

They had entertained a good deal during the winter; much of the time had also been passed in New Orleans in various forms of mild dissipation. She was looking forward to a period of unbroken rest, now, and undisturbed tête-a-tête with her husband, when he informed her that Gouvernail was coming up to stay a week or two.

This was a man she had heard much of but never seen. He had been her husband's college friend; was now a journalist, and in no sense a society man or "a man about town," which were, perhaps, some of the reasons she had never met him. But she had unconsciously formed an image of him in her mind.

She pictured him tall, slim, cynical; with eye-glasses, and his hands in his pockets; and she did not like him. Gouvernail was slim enough, but he wasn't very tall nor very cynical; neither did he wear eye-glasses nor carry his hands in his pockets. And she rather liked him when he first presented himself.

But why she liked him she could not explain satisfactorily to herself when she partly attempted to do so. She could discover in him none of those brilliant and promising traits which Gaston, her husband, had often assured her that he possessed. On the contrary, he sat rather mute and receptive before her chatty eagerness to make him feel at home and in face of Gaston's frank and wordy hospitality. His manner was as courteous toward her as the most exacting woman could require; but he made no direct appeal to her approval or even esteem.

Once settled at the plantation he seemed to like to sit upon the wide portico in the shade of one of the big Corinthian pillars, smoking his cigar lazily and listening attentively to Gaston's experience as a sugar planter.

"This is what I call living," he would utter

with deep satisfaction, as the air that swept across the sugar field caressed him with its warm and scented velvety touch. It pleased him also to get on familiar terms with the big dogs that came about him, rubbing themselves sociably against his legs. He did not care to fish, and displayed no eagerness to go out and kill grosbecs when Gaston proposed doing so.

Gouvernail's personality puzzled Mrs. Baroda, but she liked him. Indeed, he was a lovable, inoffensive fellow. After a few days, when she could understand him no better than at first, she gave over being puzzled and remained piqued. In this mood she left her husband and her guest, for the most part, alone together. Then finding that Gouvernail took no manner of exception to her action, she imposed her society upon him, accompanying him in his idle strolls to the mill and walks along the batture. She persistently sought to penetrate the reserve in which he had unconsciously enveloped himself.

"When is he going—your friend?" she one day asked her husband. "For my part, he tires me frightfully."

"Not for a week yet, dear. I can't understand; he gives you no trouble."

"No. I should like him better if he did; if he were more like others, and I had to plan somewhat for his comfort and enjoyment."

Gaston took his wife's pretty face between his hands and looked tenderly and laughingly into her troubled eyes. They were making a bit of toilet sociably together in Mrs. Baroda's dressing-room.

"You are full of surprises, ma belle," he said to her. "Even I can never count upon how you are going to act under given conditions." He kissed her and turned to fasten his cravat before the mirror.

"Here you are," he went on, "taking poor Gouvernail seriously and making a commotion over him, the last thing he would desire or expect."

"Commotion!" she hotly resented. "Nonsense! How can you say such a thing? Commotion, indeed! But, you know, you said he was clever."

"So he is. But the poor fellow is run down by overwork now. That's why I asked him here to take a rest."

"You used to say he was a man of ideas," she retorted, unconciliated. "I expected him to be interesting, at least. I'm going to the city in the morning to have my spring gowns fitted. Let me know when Mr. Gouvernail is gone; I shall be at my Aunt Octavie's."

That night she went and sat alone upon a bench that stood beneath a live oak tree at the edge of the gravel walk.

She had never known her thoughts or her intentions to be so confused. She could gather nothing from them but the feeling of a distinct necessity to quit her home in the morning.

Mrs. Baroda heard footsteps crunching the gravel; but could discern in the darkness only the approaching red point of a lighted cigar. She knew it was Gouvernail, for her husband did not smoke. She hoped to remain unnoticed, but her white gown revealed her to him. He threw away his cigar and seated himself upon the bench beside her; without a suspicion that she might object to his presence.

"Your husband told me to bring this to you, Mrs. Baroda," he said, handing her a filmy, white scarf with which she sometimes enveloped her head and shoulders. She accepted the scarf from him with a murmur of thanks, and let it lie in her lap.

He made some commonplace observation upon the baneful effect of the night air at that season. Then as his gaze reached out into the darkness, he murmured, half to himself:

"'Night of south winds—night of the large few stars!
Still nodding night——'"

She made no reply to this apostrophe to the night, which indeed, was not addressed to her.

Gouvernail was in no sense a diffident man, for he was not a self-conscious one. His periods of reserve were not constitutional, but the result of moods. Sitting there beside Mrs. Baroda, his silence melted for the time.

He talked freely and intimately in a low, hesitating drawl that was not unpleasant to hear. He talked of the old college days when he and Gaston had been a good deal to each other; of the days of keen and blind ambitions and large intentions. Now there was left with him, at least, a philosophic acquiescence to the existing order—only a desire to be permitted to exist, with now and then a little whiff of genuine life, such as he was breathing now.

Her mind only vaguely grasped what he was saying. Her physical being was for the moment predominant. She was not thinking of his words, only drinking in the tones of his voice. She wanted to reach out her hand in the darkness and touch him with the sensitive tips of her fingers upon the face or the lips. She wanted to draw close to him and whisper against his cheek—she did not care what—as she might have done if she had not been a respectable woman.

The stronger the impulse grew to bring herself near him, the further, in fact, did she draw away from him. As soon as she could do so without an appearance of too great rudeness, she rose and left him there alone.

Before she reached the house, Gouvernail had lighted a fresh cigar and ended his apostrophe to the night.

Mrs. Baroda was greatly tempted that night to tell her husband—who was also her friend —of this folly that had seized her. But she did not yield to the temptation. Beside being a respectable woman she was a very sensible one; and she knew there are some battles in life which a human being must fight alone.

When Gaston arose in the morning, his wife had already departed. She had taken an early morning train to the city. She did not return till Gouvernail was gone from under her roof.

There was some talk of having him back during the summer that followed. That is, Gaston greatly desired it; but this desire yielded to his wife's strenuous opposition.

However, before the year ended, she proposed, wholly from herself, to have Gouvernail visit them again. Her husband was surprised and delighted with the suggestion coming from her.

"I am glad, chère amie, to know that you have finally overcome your dislike for him; truly he did not deserve it."

"Oh," she told him, laughingly, after pressing a long, tender kiss upon his lips, "I have overcome everything! you will see. This time I shall be very nice to him."

Ripe Figs

Ripe Figs

MAMAN-NAINAINE said that when the figs were ripe Babette might go to visit her cousins down on the Bayou-Lafourche where the sugar cane grows. Not that the ripening of figs had the least thing to do with it, but that is the way Maman-Nainaine was.

It seemed to Babette a very long time to wait; for the leaves upon the trees were tender yet, and the figs were like little hard, green marbles.

But warm rains came along and plenty of strong sunshine, and though Maman-Nainaine was as patient as the statue of la Madone, and Babette as restless as a humming-bird, the first thing they both knew it was hot summer-time. Every day Babette danced out to where the fig-trees were in a long line against the fence. She walked slowly beneath them, carefully peering between the gnarled, spreading branches. But each time she came disconsolate away again. What she saw there finally was something that made her sing and dance the whole long day.

When Maman-Nainaine sat down in her stately way to breakfast, the following morning, her muslin cap standing like an aureole about her white, placid face, Babette approached. She bore a dainty porcelain platter, which she set down before her godmother. It contained a dozen purple figs, fringed around with their rich, green leaves.

"Ah," said Maman-Nainaine, arching her eyebrows, "how early the figs have ripened this year!"

"Oh," said Babette, "I think they have ripened very late."

"Babette," continued Maman-Nainaine, as she peeled the very plumpest figs with her pointed silver fruit-knife, "you will carry my love to them all down on Bayou-Lafourche. And tell your Tante Frosine I shall look for her at Toussaint—when the chrysanthemums are in bloom."

Ozème's Holiday

Ozème's Holiday

🐚

OZÈME often wondered why there was
not a special dispensation of providence
to do away with the necessity for work.
There seemed to him so much created for
man's enjoyment in this world, and so little
time and opportunity to profit by it. To sit
and do nothing but breathe was a
pleasure to Ozème; but to sit in the company
of a few choice companions, including a
sprinkling of ladies, was even a greater delight; and the joy which a day's hunting or
fishing or picnicking afforded him is hardly to
be described. Yet he was by no means indo-
lent. He worked faithfully on the plantation
the whole year long, in a sort of methodical
way; but when the time came around for his
annual week's holiday, there was no holding
him back. It was often decidedly inconveni-
ent for the planter that Ozème usually chose

to take his holiday during some very busy season of the year.

He started out one morning in the beginning of October. He had borrowed Mr. Laballière's buckboard and Padue's old gray mare, and a harness from the negro Séverin. He wore a light blue suit which had been sent all the way from St. Louis, and which had cost him ten dollars; he had paid almost as much again for his boots; and his hat was a broad-rimmed gray felt which he had no cause to be ashamed of. When Ozème went "broading," he dressed—well, regardless of cost. His eyes were blue and mild; his hair was light, and he wore it rather long; he was clean shaven, and really did not look his thirty-five years.

Ozème had laid his plans weeks beforehand. He was going visiting along Cane River; the mere contemplation filled him with pleasure. He counted upon reaching Fédeaus' about noon, and he would stop and dine there. Perhaps they would ask him to stay all night. He really did not hold to staying all night, and was not decided to accept if they did ask him. There were only the two old people, and he rather fancied the notion of pushing on to Beltrans', where he would stay a night, or even two, if urged. He was quite sure that there would be something agreeable going on at Beltrans', with all those young people—perhaps a fish-fry, or possibly a ball!

Of course he would have to give a day to Tante Sophie and another to Cousine Victoire; but none to the St. Annes unless entreated—after St. Anne reproaching him last year with being a fainéant for broading at such a season! At Cloutierville, where he would linger as long as possible, he meant to turn and retrace his course, zigzagging back and forth across Cane River so as to take in the Duplans, the Velcours, and others that he could not at the moment recall. A week seemed to Ozème a very, very little while in which to crowd so much pleasure.

There were steam-gins at work; he could hear them whistling far and near. On both sides of the river the fields were white with cotton, and everybody in the world seemed busy but Ozème. This reflection did not distress or disturb him in the least; he pursued his way at peace with himself and his surroundings.

At Lamérie's cross-roads store, where he stopped to buy a cigar, he learned that there was no use heading for Fédeaus', as the two old people had gone to town for a lengthy visit, and the house was locked up. It was at Fédeaus' that Ozème had intended to dine.

He sat in the buckboard, given up to a moment or two of reflection. The result was that he turned away from the river, and entered the road that led between two fields back to the woods and into the heart of the country. He had determined upon taking a short cut to the Beltrans' plantation, and on the way he meant to keep an eye open for old Aunt Tildy's cabin, which he knew lay in some remote part of this cut-off. He remembered that Aunt Tildy could cook an excellent meal if she had the material at hand. He would induce her to fry him a chicken, drip a cup of coffee, and turn him out a pone of corn-bread, which he thought would be sumptuous enough fare for the occasion.

Aunt Tildy dwelt in the not unusual log cabin, of one room, with its chimney of mud and stone, and its shallow gallery formed by the jutting of the roof. In close proximity to the cabin was a small cotton-field, which from a long distance looked like a field of snow. The cotton was bursting and overflowing foam-like from bolls on the drying stalk. On the lower branches it was hanging ragged and tattered, and much of it had already fallen to the ground. There were a few chinaberry-trees in the yard before the hut, and under one of them an ancient and rusty-looking mule was eating corn from a wood trough. Some common little Creole chickens were scratching about the mule's feet and snatching at the grains of corn that occasionally fell from the trough.

Aunt Tildy was hobbling across the yard when Ozème drew up before the gate. One hand was confined in a sling; in the other she carried a tin pan, which she let fall noisily to the ground when she recognized him. She was broad, black, and misshapen, with her body bent forward almost at an acute angle. She wore a blue cottonade of large plaids, and a bandana awkwardly twisted around her head.

"Good God A'mighty, man! Whar you come from?" was her startled exclamation at beholding him.

"F'om home, Aunt Tildy; w'ere else do you expec'?" replied Ozème, dismounting composedly.

He had not seen the old woman for several years—since she was cooking in town for the family with which he boarded at the time She had washed and ironed for him, atrociously, it is true, but her intentions were beyond reproach if her washing was not. She had also been clumsily attentive to him during a spell of illness. He had paid her with an occasional bandana, a calico dress, or a checked apron, and they had always considered the account between themselves square, with no sentimental feeling of gratitude remaining on either side.

"I like to know," remarked Ozème, as he took the gray mare from the shafts, and led her up to the trough where the mule was— "I like to know w'at you mean by makin' a crop like that an' then lettin' it go to was'e? Who you reckon's goin' to pick that cotton? You think maybe the angels goin' to come down an' pick it fo' you, an' gin it an' press it, an' then give you ten cents a poun' fo' it, hein?"

"Ef de Lord don' pick it, I don' know who gwine pick it, Mista Ozème.   I tell you, me an' Sandy we wuk dat crap day in an' day out; it's him done de mos' of it."

"Sandy?   That little—"

"He ain' dat li'le Sandy no mo' w'at you rec'lec's; he 'mos' a man, an' he wuk like a man now.   He wuk mo' 'an fittin' fo' his strenk, an' now he layin' in dah sick—God A'mighty knows how sick.   An' me wid a risin' twell I bleeged to walk de flo' o' nights. an' don' know ef I ain' gwine to lose de han' atter all."

"W'y, in the name o' conscience, you don hire somebody to pick?"

"Whar I got money to hire?   An' you knows well as me ev'y chick an' chile is pickin' roun' on de plantations an' gittin' good pay."

The whole outlook appeared to Ozème very depressing, and even menacing, to his personal comfort and peace of mind.   He foresaw no prospect of dinner unless he should cook it himself.   And there was that Sandy —he remembered well the little scamp of eight, always at his grandmother's heels when she was cooking or washing. Of course he would have to go in and look at the boy, and no doubt dive into his traveling-bag for quinine, without which he never traveled.

Sandy was indeed very ill, consumed with fever. He lay on a cot covered up with a faded patchwork quilt. His eyes were half closed, and he was muttering and rambling on about hoeing and bedding and cleaning and thinning out the cotton; he was hauling it to the gin, wrangling about weight and bagging and ties and the price offered per pound. That bale or two of cotton had not only sent Sandy to bed, but had pursued him there, holding him through his fevered dreams, and threatening to end him. Ozème would never have known the black boy, he was so tall, so thin, and seemingly so wasted, lying there in bed.

"See yere, Aunt Tildy," said Ozème, after he had, as was usual with him when in doubt, abandoned himself to a little reflection; "between us—you an' me—we got to manage to kill an' cook one o' those chickens I see scratchin' out yonda, fo' I'm jus' about starved. I reckon you ain't got any quinine

in the house? No; I didn't suppose an instant
you had. Well, I'm goin' to give Sandy a
good dose o' quinine to-night, an' I'm goin'
stay an' see how that'll work on 'im. But
sun-up, min' you, I mus' get out o' yere."

Ozème had spent more comfortable nights
than the one passed in Aunt Tildy's bed,
which she considerately abandoned to him.

In the morning Sandy's fever was somewhat
abated, but had not taken a decided enough
turn to justify Ozème in quitting him before
noon, unless he was willing "to feel like a
dog," as he told himself. He appeared before Aunt Tildy stripped to the undershirt,
and wearing his second-best pair of trousers.

"That's a nice pickle o' fish you got me in,
ol' woman. I guarantee, nex' time I go
abroad, 'tain't me that'll take any cut-off.
W'ere's that cotton-basket an' cotton-sack o'
yo's?"

"I knowed it!" chanted Aunt Tildy—"I
knowed de Lord war gwine sen' somebody to
holp me out. He war n' gwine let de crap
was'e atter he give Sandy an' me de strenk
to make hit. De Lord gwine shove you 'long
de row, Mista Ozème. De Lord gwine give

you plenty mo' fingers an' han's to pick dat cotton nimble an' clean."

"Neva you min' w'at the Lord's goin' to do; go get me that cotton-sack. An' you put that poultice like I tol' you on yo' han', an' set down there an' watch Sandy. It looks like you are 'bout as helpless as a' ol' cow tangled up in a potato-vine."

Ozème had not picked cotton for many years, and he took to it a little awkwardly at first; but by the time he had reached the end of the first row the old dexterity of youth had come back to his hands, which flew rapidly back and forth with the motion of a weaver's shuttle; and his ten fingers became really nimble in clutching the cotton from its dry shell. By noon he had gathered about fifty pounds. Sandy was not then quite so well as he had promised to be, and Ozème concluded to stay that day and one more night. If the boy were no better in the morning, he would go off in search of a doctor for him, and he himself would continue on down to Tante Sophie's; the Beltrans' was out of the question now.

Sandy hardly needed a doctor in the morning. Ozème's doctoring was beginning to tell favorably; but he would have considered it criminal indifference and negligence to go away and leave the boy to Aunt Tildy's awkward ministrations just at the critical moment when there was a turn for the better; so he stayed that day out, and picked his hundred and fifty pounds.

On the third day it looked like rain, and a heavy rain just then would mean a heavy loss to Aunt Tildy and Sandy, and Ozème again went to the field, this time urging Aunt Tildy with him to do what she might with her one good hand.

"Aunt Tildy," called out Ozème to the bent old woman moving ahead of him between the white rows of cotton, "if the Lord gets me safe out o' this ditch, 't ain't to-morro' I'll fall in anotha with my eyes open, I bet you."

"Keep along, Mista Ozème; don' grumble, don' stumble; de Lord's a-watchin' you. Look at yo' Aunt Tildy; she doin' mo' wid her one han' 'an you doin' wid yo' two, man. Keep right along, honey. Watch dat cotton how it fallin' in yo' Aunt Tildy's bag."

"I am watchin' you, ol' woman; you don' fool me. You got to work that han' o' yo's spryer than you doin', or I'll take the rawhide. You done fo'got w'at the rawhide tas'e like, I reckon"—a reminder which amused Aunt Tildy so powerfully that her big negrolaugh resounded over the whole cotton-patch, and even caused Sandy, who heard it, to turn in his bed.

The weather was still threatening on the succeeding day, and a sort of dogged determination or characteristic desire to see his undertakings carried to a satisfactory completion urged Ozème to continue his efforts to drag Aunt Tildy out of the mire into which circumstances seemed to have thrust her.

One night the rain did come, and began to beat softly on the roof of the old cabin. Sandy opened his eyes, which were no longer brilliant with the fever flame. "Granny," he whispered, "de rain! Des listen, granny; de rain a-comin', an' I ain' pick dat cotton yit. W'at time it is? Gi' me my pants—I got to go—"

"You lay whar you is, chile alive. Dat cotton put aside clean and dry. Me an' de Lord an' Mista Ozème done pick dat cotton."

Ozème drove away in the morning looking quite as spick and span as the day he left home in his blue suit and his light felt drawn a little over his eyes.

"You want to take care o' that boy," he instructed Aunt Tildy at parting, "an' get 'im on his feet. An', let me tell you, the nex' time I start out to broad, if you see me passin' in this yere cut-off, put on yo' specs an' look at me good, because it won't be me; it'll be my ghos', ol' woman."

Indeed, Ozème, for some reason or other, felt quite shamefaced as he drove back to the plantation. When he emerged from the lane which he had entered the week before, and turned into the river road, Lamérie, standing in the store door, shouted out:

"Hé, Ozème! you had good times yonda? I bet you danced holes in the sole of them new boots."

"Don't talk, Lamérie!" was Ozème's rather ambiguous reply, as he flourished the remainder of a whip over the old gray mare's sway-back, urging her to a gentle trot.

When he reached home, Bodé, one of Padue's boys, who was assisting him to unhitch, remarked:

"How come you didn' go yonda down de coas' like you said, Mista Ozème? Nobody didn' see you in Cloutierville, an' Mailitte say you neva cross' de twenty-fo'-mile ferry, an' nobody didn' see you no place."

Ozème returned, after his customary moment of reflection:

"You see, it's 'mos' always the same thing on Cane riva, my boy; a man gets tired o' that à la fin. This time I went back in the woods, 'way yonda in the Fédeau cut-off; kin' o' campin' an' roughin' like, you might say. I tell you, it was sport, Bodé."